THE
FALL
OF THE
LOOM

A Novel

M. E. Auman

For Mom.
And for every artist who inspires me.

Chapter 1

Honyeoke Falls

Three more days. Sophie wandered aimlessly between buildings on the edge of the plaza. The countdown to college was torture, and the unexpected heat wave wasn't helping her mood. Even in the shade, the concrete radiated heat and sweat glistened down her legs, soaking the loose strings of her cut-off shorts.

She'd passed most of the summer helping at her parent's tapestry repair shop, but her mother had given her the last week off to get ready for school. She missed the smell of the wool and the tautness of thread beneath her fingers, but at least it got her away from her mother's recent horrible mood.

Sophie rounded a corner, thinking vaguely of visiting the museum, but she'd already been a million times and she wasn't in the mood to pay the entry fee — she'd need all the money she had once she got to school. Plus, there might be a few commuters there, late on their way to work, and she didn't want to answer any more questions about her plans. People's curiosity seemed to dampen her enthusiasm. She'd spent the summer enduring questions about how she would handle the gray English weather — as if western New York was some sort of tropical paradise she would regret leaving.

There was a flurry of footsteps behind her, and a familiar voice reached her ear. "Hey, Slim." She turned around to see her best friend giving her a wide grin. He held out a paper bag from the bakery.

"Brownies?" Sophie asked hopefully. Annemarie's were the best in town, and that was before she added the pot.

"Nope," Rush replied with a shrug. "Sold out already. But I got you the next best thing." He thrust the bag towards Sophie, who opened it and breathed in the scent of freshly baked croissants. She went to sit on a nearby bench, but Rush grabbed her by the wrist and pulled her along. "Come on," he said, "I've got something to show you."

He was about to pull her arm from the socket. "Rush, slow down," she panted. That was Rush, in a hurry all the time. Rush's boundless energy meant he was always up for an adventure. This was usually fine, especially since Sophie was bored, but she would have appreciated a minute to eat her croissant.

He stopped short in the center of town. Sophie eyed the heavy oak doors surrounded by carved sandstone columns. She gave the museum a dirty look before turning to Rush. "Can we *please* do something else? I really don't want to run into anyone today."

"Trust me," Rush replied, pulling her around to the side door, "You're going to want to see this."

They entered through the employee door, pausing briefly at the sight of Rush's mom, seated in her office in an elegant white suit, her dark hair skimming her shoulders. People in town criticized her for dressing up to work at a small town museum, but Sophie appreciated it. It showed she thought this museum was as important as some fancy, big-city one.

Mrs. Rigo hummed softly along with "Rhiannon," which played from the radio perched on a pile of books in the corner of the office. More books were shoved into the shelves lining the walls and a stack teetered precariously on the edge of the desk. It was cooler in here than outside, though not by much.

"Hey, Ma." shouted Rush, while Sophie chimed, "Hi, Mrs. Rigo."

Rush's mom looked up from her papers. "Sophie, dear, how many times have I told you to call me Carla?" Sophie nodded, but it just didn't feel right. Like the suits, it seemed a show of respect. Before Sophie could answer, Carla addressed her son with a twinkle. "I knew you wouldn't be able to resist showing it to her before you both left." Then growing stern, she added, "Just be careful, it hasn't been tested yet."

Her curiosity firmly piqued, Sophie let Rush lead her into the storage room. It was mostly dark, a jumble of shelves and boxes, a few rolled tapestries stacked on a shelf against the wall. Thin shafts of light came in from a small bank of windows so high they almost touched the ceiling. Taking up most of the back wall, which was usually empty, was the largest tapestry Sophie had ever seen at the museum. Even in the dim light, it was magnificent.

A dark, swirling sky filled with towering clouds loomed above a tiny village, nestled in a valley in the distance. Patches of lavender dotted the hills closest to them, while a smattering of ponies grazed among the landscape. It was a masterclass in color gradation. Blues shifted into purples then into grays and greens and back again.

"Where... how..." Sophie stammered.

"Where did she get it?" Rush laughed, delighted by Sophie's awe. "An old woman had it in her collection. Rarely even went through it, or so she claimed. Somehow Ma found out and convinced her to sell before it ended up at an auction."

Impressive, but not surprising. This was something Mrs. Rigo and her mother had in common: always on the hunt for hidden gems. But while her mother had to settle for the damaged or passed over — either to repair, usually for resale, or if they were too damaged, to pull apart for the precious wool — Mrs. Rigo had the budget to buy something this incredible, in this condition, even if it had taken some clever negotiations.

"But, does that mean..." Sophie said, comprehension dawning.

"Yep, this one belongs to the museum. It's staying here." And then he added, "Unlike you."

"Don't give me that shit," she chided him, still not taking her eyes off the tapestry. She inched closer, torn between her desire to take in the full picture and an urge to examine every inch in painstaking detail. "You're leaving too."

"Ok, but I'm just going to another state. You're going to a whole other country."

Sophie ignored this, though she did feel a little pang of annoyance. Of course the town would get something this good when she was about to leave.

After several long minutes, she became acutely aware that Rush was staring, not at the tapestry, but at her.

"What?" Sophie blushed.

"The way you look at tapestries. Most people glance at them quickly. They only care about where they'll take them. But not you. You look at them..." He trailed off, trying to find the right word. "...like they're special."

"Because they are."

"I'm going to miss that when you're gone." He was so earnest, all his attention turned toward Sophie.

"No attachment, remember."

As she said it, Sophie remembered the first time she said those words. They had been standing in this same room. Okay, not *standing* at that point.

It was another summer day, last summer, or, if she was being honest, maybe the summer before. Sophie's mom had asked her to take a tapestry back to the museum. With

Frances's well-earned reputation, her's was the only repair shop Mrs. Rigo trusted with the museum's work.

The day was hot, like this one. Sophie, panting heavily, drenched with sweat, trudged to the museum, the roll of heavy tapestry across her shoulder, when the sky opened with a sudden summer thunderstorm. The tapestry, as always, was well protected, wrapped in so much canvas it was impervious to the rain. Sophie was not. By the time she got to the museum, water pooled in her shoes and her sopping clothes clung to her.

"Where's your mom?" she grunted at Rush, who was sitting in the storage room reading a book. Reading was the only time Rush sat still.

"She's at a meeting in Rochester." The thud of the tapestry onto the floor made him look up. "Holy shit, Slim. Did you swim here?"

In the cool air of the storeroom, Sophie started to shiver.

"We need to get you out of those wet clothes," he said, grabbing a handful of questionably clean towels.

He hadn't meant it like that, but damn, it came out so smooth. By the time he helped her struggle out of her damp shirt and draped a towel around her shoulders, she was kissing him fiercely. Her hands grasped his dark curls while his found the small of her back. And they fell, a jumble of arms and legs, into a pile of boxes. She had expected it to be awkward, but somehow with Rush it just fit. The feel of his hands as he lifted her onto him. The way her lips found the curve of his neck, half kissing and half biting to stop herself from yelling out.

Afterward, Sophie gave Rush a stern look. "No attachment, okay." She wanted to be clear, this changed nothing between them. They were not a couple. They were best friends who just happened to help each other scratch a very particular itch. Which they did again, from time to time.

"Hello, Slim, are you there?" She heard Rush's voice calling, and she realized he'd been going on about how his mom acquired the tapestry while she was lost in thought.

"It really is incredible," Sophie murmured, clicking back into the conversation, "that it ended up here."

She stepped closer and the threads seemed to sparkle with anticipation. This wasn't some chunky affair, crudely done to move people quickly from place to place. These were fine threads, woven with precision. The kind of weaving Sophie hoped to do one day.

Without thinking, Sophie reached up to touch the tapestry, but Rush quickly grabbed her wrist. "Don't," he cautioned. "Ma says it hasn't been tested yet!"

Her initial instinct was to feel the surface, nothing more, but Rush's unusual air of caution made her suddenly reckless. Besides, this was certainly her only chance before she left town.

"Since when are you so careful?" She laughed, shoving him playfully towards the tapestry. It was enough to throw him off balance. As he toppled backward, he kept his hand tightly on her wrist, pulling her along with him.

As they fell through the tapestry, there was the familiar feeling of dissolving through mesh and being squeezed back out the other side. They tumbled onto the grass, the dark sky thundering above. Taking in the stunning scene, Sophie was acutely aware of Rush still grasping her wrist. She turned towards him, sliding her fingers into his, when a man's sharp voice broke the moment.

"Oi! Where'd you come from?"

There was no way to know, in an untested tapestry, whether they were welcome or not, so they ran for it. Not back through the tapestry, as would have been logical, but toward the rolling hills, kicking up lavender in their wake.

They stopped, hands on their knees, and when they finally caught their breath, it was Rush's turn to stare in awe. Down in the valley, a neatly trimmed garden led into a charming old village. It didn't look like any place Sophie had seen before.

"I wonder where we are," Rush asked, surveying the landscape.

"Aren't you supposed to know everything?" Sophie teased him.

"Ma's still researching the provenance. Another reason she didn't want us to go through."

She watched him now, the way he had watched her looking at the tapestry. It was so unusual to see him standing still.

"I'm going to miss you too," she said sincerely.

"I thought you said no attachment," he chided her. But even as he said it, he grabbed her by the waist and pulled her quickly towards him. Suddenly, the sky opened into a deluge of rain. Sophie couldn't help herself. She kissed him, tugging alternately at her sopping clothes and his. They tumbled into the tall grass, hoping the man, or the ponies, didn't turn up.

Laying in the grass, watching the sky clear above the little valley, Sophie listened to Rush's breathing slow as he drifted off to sleep. To her surprise, the prospect of saying goodbye to Rush suddenly brought up all kinds of feelings that ran counter to Sophie's "no attachment" policy. Before she could do something she might regret, she got up, tugged on the rest of her damp clothes, and headed back in the direction they'd come from. She found the spot, moving her hands through the air until she caught the reassuring feel of fabric that would take her back home, being careful not to let Mrs. Rigo see her on the way out of the museum.

—#—

Two days to go. It had already been a rough morning.

Sophie went to see Rush, to apologize for leaving so abruptly yesterday. She caught Mrs. Rigo, dressed in a pale yellow suit, just as she was heading out the door. Like everyone else who lived and worked in the same town, Mrs. Rigo walked to work. Tapestries were meant to take you to another town, another place, not down the block. Unlike everyone else, Mrs. Rigo managed to walk to work every day in heels, in any weather, while keeping her stunning suits impeccable and her hair perfectly in place.

Sophie tried to tame her own flyaway hair and plucked an errant string from her cut-off shorts, the same ones, she realized with a flush of shame at her pathetically small wardrobe, she was wearing the day before.

"Rush isn't here, dear," Mrs. Rigo announced, the moment she spotted Sophie. "He left for school this morning. I figured you knew that."

Mrs. Rigo had adopted her son's nickname along with everyone else.

"I do hope," Mrs. Rigo continued, "that the two of you will stay in touch while you're at school." There was a knowing tone in Mrs. Rigo's voice as if she suspected there was something more to their friendship.

"Obviously," Sophie replied, a little annoyed. Rush was her best friend. The distance wouldn't change that. But, her moment of weakness the day before notwithstanding, she meant it when she said "no attachment." And she certainly wasn't planning on taking a vow of celibacy at college.

Sophie said goodbye to Mrs. Rigo, feeling dejected. She had intended to apologize to Rush for leaving him alone in the tapestry, and of course, say a proper goodbye. But now she wasn't sure if he was mad at her for ditching him, or if, in true Rush fashion, he was just in a hurry to move on to the next thing.

Her next stop was the repair studio, to see what tapestry her mother was working on today. Sophie's banishment from the studio had made this past week even more unbearable, and with Rush gone, she couldn't think of anywhere else to kill time. But this too turned out to be a mistake.

The repair studio sat next to the O'Toole's home, connected by a breezeway. As kids, Sophie and her siblings would play there, bundled from the cold or shielded from the rain, out from underfoot in the repair shop, but still close enough to keep an eye on. The front of the house had a series of small, rectangular windows, stacked vertically in some places and horizontally in others. "To give the family privacy," Sophie's dad explained once. But the front of the repair shop had a massive plate glass window, and passersby would often stop and observe Frances at work.

Today it was Sophie's turn to watch. Her mother was alone, her eyes fixed on a tapestry stretched across a wooden frame, her dark hair, laced with gray, as full of flyaways as Sophie's. As a young girl, Sophie would steal away from games with her siblings to stare through this window, fascinated by the workings inside, until her father started giving her little jobs to do around the shop. By the time she was ten, she was allowed to work on simple repairs by herself.

Frances struggled with a difficult repair, trying to recreate a patch the size of her hand that had worn through. A few other tapestries were spread out across the room, also in need of work.

Sophie stepped through the door, reaching up instinctively to stop the bells from tinkling. Her father insisted they put them in, otherwise a customer was apt to stand there for an hour before Frances felt their presence. But all the bells did was jar her mother's already frazzled nerves. Sophie stepped into the light streaming from the window, taking in the familiar, comforting smell of wool. It was only when Sophie's shadow fell across her work that her mother looked up.

"Can I help?" Sophie offered, glancing around at the other tapestries lying in wait.

Frances was in no mood. "You should be home packing," her mother admonished, fumbling with a loose thread.

Immediately defensive, Sophie snapped. "I hardly have anything to pack. I've still got plenty of time." Why was her mother so worried about her packing? It's like she wanted to shove her out the door.

"That's because you haven't done any shopping," her mother spat back. "I gave you money. You better not be saving it to blow in pubs. It's for *clothes.*" She put a little too much emphasis on the last word, stabbing at the tapestry as she did.

"I know that," Sophie stammered, storming out of the repair shop before the argument could get worse. Why didn't her mother trust her? She fully intended to spend the money on clothes, just not here. She had no idea what people would be wearing in England, and she didn't want to stick out before she even opened her mouth. She planned to wait and scour thrift shops once she got there. Besides, it was much easier to cart around a pocket full of cash than a bag full of clothes.

Most of all, it was her mother's assumption that she was going to school in another country to fritter her time away in pubs. Her mother should know she was serious. It was Sophie, after all, who had done all the research, who had put together countless letters and essays and portfolios, all to ensure she had gotten a scholarship to one of the finest weaving colleges in the world.

Sophie stomped back into the house, not even bothering to say hello to her dad and the twins in the kitchen. Instead, she headed straight for her room, slamming the door behind her.

Her little sister Delilah was on Sophie's bed. She jumped when Sophie entered, hastily jamming something under the covers.

"What are you doing?" Sophie bellowed.

"Nothing," Delilah sputtered, obviously lying.

"Let me see!"

"I know I'm not supposed to…" Delilah trailed off, on the verge of tears. "But I just wanted to look at it one more time before you left."

From under the covers, she proffered a well-worn book. The dust jacket was long gone, but the words *Great Tapestries* were etched in faded gold across the red cloth. It was a hulking volume, featuring illustrations of the finest tapestries from around the world. Though of course, no book could really do a tapestry justice. Sophie found it in a secondhand bookshop years ago and convinced the owner to hold it for her while she saved enough money working in the repair shop to buy it. It was her prized possession, and her younger siblings knew it was off-limits.

Seeing the fear on her sister's face, Sophie's frustration melted. "You know what, De. You keep it."

"Really?" Her sister's dark saucer eyes grew even wider. "Are you serious?"

"Yeah. It's pretty heavy to cart with me. And besides," she said, flopping onto the bed and giving her sister a playful squeeze, "I'll be seeing lots of amazing tapestries in person when I'm away at school. Way better than some dusty old book."

"Oh, that reminds me," her sister said hesitantly, moving towards her dresser. "This came for you." Delilah handed Sophie an official-looking envelope and she breathed a sigh of relief. Her passport.

The college had sent a letter to all students, reminding them they would need passports for study trips abroad. Of course, as an international student, Sophie needed her passport just to get to school. She'd applied for it months ago, as soon as she'd gotten the acceptance letter from East Lawn. But as weeks ticked by and it hadn't arrived, she'd gotten more and more worried, even making trips to the passport office in Rochester. They insisted it was en route and they didn't know what the hold-up was. She'd stopped just short of ordering a new one. Passports were expensive, one of the reasons none of the O'Toole children had one. But now it had finally arrived.

Sophie's relief turned towards suspicion as she gave her sister a sharp look. "When did this get here?" she asked slowly. The postmark on the envelope was dated a month earlier.

Delilah's eyes grew wide again, but this time she burst into tears and, to Sophie's surprise, threw her arms around Sophie's waist. "I don't want you to leave," Delilah wailed.

This sudden outpouring of emotion caught Sophie completely off-guard. She and Delilah may have shared a room, but their four-year age gap meant they shared little else, save for the occasional fight. And now here was Delilah, clinging to Sophie like they were the best of friends.

She looked up at Sophie. "I'm sorry, I know I should have told you earlier, but..." Her voice trailed off into big, hiccuping sobs.

Sophie patted her sister's hair. She wanted to be angry, to yell at Delilah for wasted trips to Rochester, for making her stress. But it was impossible to berate someone who was clearly in so much distress.

"I'll be back before you know it," Sophie said. "And you'll have Penny for company while I'm gone."

At this, Delilah stopped crying and gave her sister a withering stare. "What am I supposed to do with a six-year-old?"

"The twins then." Their brothers, Sandro and Dante, were only two years younger than Delilah. But even as Sophie suggested it, she knew it was pointless. The twins were an impenetrable pair, unlikely to let anyone in, least of all one of their sisters.

Her sister gave her a look of distress, then added, through tears, "And don't even bother suggesting Collin." Sandwiched between the two older girls, their brother had never managed to get along with either one of them.

"Ok, fine," Sophie conceded. "But look on the bright side." She gestured around. "You'll finally have a room to yourself."

Delilah seemed to compose herself. "Not if you don't start packing."

Sophie gave her an exasperated sigh. "Who are you, Mom?"

But Delilah had a point. Sophie pulled out her duffle and started piling in clothes.

Chapter 2
Honyeoke Falls

One day to go. Breakfast that morning was a miserable affair. Since she was leaving early the next morning, her father made all of her favorites, a table piled high with breads and pastries and French toast, and her mother insisted that all her siblings join them before running off for the day.

"How long is this going to take?" Collin whined, grabbing a croissant and heading towards the door. "We're moving Mrs. Fisher's piano today and I've got to be in Mendon by ten to install the receiving tapestry at her daughter's house." Collin had found a summer job working for a moving company, and while he liked to pretend he was important, Sophie knew he was mostly there as muscle — carrying heavy things through the temporary tapestries that were hung in either location when someone needed to transport stuff from one place to another.

Mrs. O'Toole shot her son a stern look and he reluctantly squeezed into a space at the crowded table. Unfortunately, this was not her mother's only insistence. Sophie thought she would be off the hook now that she had packed, but her mother found other things to pick at. Maybe she should get a haircut. Maybe she needed new shoes. Was her bag big enough? It was when her mother suggested that she get her nails done, something they never did, that Sophie finally had enough.

"What does it matter what I look like?" she shouted, shoving back her chair. "You're not going to see me anymore anyway!"

The sound of her youngest sister Penelope bursting into tears followed her as she stormed from the kitchen.

"I thought I might find you here." Her father's deep voice penetrated her frustration.

Sophie sat on the bench in the center of her family's gallery, staring, not at the tapestries, but at a patch of scuffed wood underneath her feet. Normally, Sophie was grateful for the gallery. Families like hers, families with more kids than money, were lucky if they owned one tapestry, let alone the six — "one tapestry for each of you kids," her father liked to joke — that were currently hanging there. It pained her to admit it in this moment, but Sophie had her mother, and her ability to find and repair a diamond in the rough, to thank for this.

"Let's take a walk," her father suggested, heading towards the tapestry at the far end. The trees teemed with fiery tones, the oranges and reds that drew visitors to the woods every October.   But when they emerged, it was into the tangled greens and crunchy browns of late summer. Dappled light filtered onto the path, which wound its way down towards a creek, its shallow water sparkling in the morning sun. Small swarms of bugs drifted through the humid air. Sophie swatted at a few as if they were the source of her frustration.

"Don't be too hard on your mom, Fi." As was often the case, Peter was the one to step in to try and mend the fences between his wife and daughter.

"Why not," Sophie stopped short, swatting at a few more bugs. "She's being hard on me."

"She's having a tough time."

"What, because her little girl is leaving? You're going to miss me, and you aren't acting like a jerk." She said it as a joke, but was surprised to see the corners of her dad's eyes were wet.

"Eh," he said, recovering quickly and giving her a wink. "I've still got your sisters at home."

Sophie took a step towards him, knocking her arm into his. "Good luck with those two without me around to keep them in line."

He smiled, then went on, as if she hadn't interrupted. "Don't you get it? She's jealous."

"Jealous," Sophie laughed incredulously. "Of what? Of me?"

"Yes. You're getting to do what she never had a chance." He continued as if he'd been wanting to tell someone this for years. "Your mother loves the repair shop, and she's damn good at it," he added, "but do you honestly think that was her dream in life?"

Sophie stopped walking for a moment. It never occurred to her that her mother had dreams of her own.

"She wanted to go to school to become a weaver," her father confessed.

This was the first time Sophie had heard any of this. "What happened? She could have—"

Peter cut her off. "No, she couldn't."

"Why not?" She wasn't yet at a point where she felt sympathy for her mother, just frustration that she was taking her life regrets out on Sophie.

"Your Aunt Sofia."

Sophie had never met or even heard much about her mother's older sister, other than to know that she was sort of named after her. But she was used to the gaping hole that was her mother's side of the family. Sophie had never even met her grandparents.

"Everyone thought Sofia was going places. She had a gift for weaving, just like you."

"So what happened?" Sophie's annoyance began to drift into intrigue.

"She got a scholarship to study at RIT." The Rochester Institute of Technology was one of the most revered weaving programs in the US. If Sophie hadn't gotten a scholarship to study in England, that's where she would have ended up. "But then," her father continued, "in her third year, she just vanished."

"What? What do you mean, vanished?"

"No one knows. She was supposed to come home for spring break, but she didn't. Her roommates didn't know where she went either. Your grandparents were frantic. They poured all their time and money and resources into trying to track Sofia down, but she was just…" His voice trailed off. "… gone."

Sophie stared, unable to process what she was hearing. Why had no one told her she was named after an aunt who had disappeared?

Her father went on. "It practically killed your mother, too. This was her big sister, her everything. But it didn't stop her from wanting to study weaving. It became her dream, the way it had been Sofia's. But your grandparents said no. They'd already lost one daughter. They were afraid of losing another. They wanted to keep her at home forever. But that just made your mother miserable. Eventually, they agreed to let her go to repair school, so she could come back and work in the family shop."

"And that's where she met you," Sophie finished. She knew this part of the story. How her parents had met in their first week of school, how her dad was immediately smitten with the pretty, dark-haired girl who could weave circles around him.

"Your grandparents were pissed when your mother decided to spend the summer galavanting around Europe with me," he said with a grin. "But she was done living under their thumb."

Suddenly, it made sense, why Sophie and her siblings had their father's last name, O'Toole, though it was customary to take your mother's. Why her mother had changed her last name to that of her husband's, a true rarity. She wanted a clean break. Her only nod to her family had been naming Sophie, in part, after her vanished sister.

"Your mother's happy for you—"

"She has a funny way of showing it," Sophie interjected, but she stopped when her father gave her a look.

"She really is, but it also reminds her of the chance she didn't get. She just needs a little more time to come around." He kissed her on the cheek. "I should go. The twins offered to clean up after breakfast, which means there's a good chance they've already eaten everything I had planned for dinner tonight." She gave a weak chuckle and watched him walk down the path and disappear back into the gallery.

Sophie wandered in and out of tapestries, trying to muster some empathy for her mother, but finding it a bit thin. If her mom was acting out of fear, worried that Sophie might meet the same fate, well, maybe that she could understand. But jealousy? That was bullshit. Mothers are supposed to support their children's dreams, not be jealous of them.

It made her uneasy, leaving for school with things so rocky between her and her mother, especially after the way she left things with Rush, but she couldn't bring herself to be the bigger person.

Her mother was wrong, not her, and if she wasn't willing to mend the fracture before Sophie left, well then, Sophie wasn't either.

Chapter 3
Honyeoke Falls

It took Sophie five tapestries to get from Honyeoke Falls to East Lawn College.

The sandstone building in the center of town was as regional a museum as you could get. It featured just three commuter tapestries — to Rochester, Buffalo, and Syracuse, — practically indistinguishable if it weren't for the labels flanking them; each reflecting the vertical tans of the cities' buildings, the green foliage of trees, and the dull gray skies that blanketed upstate New York for much of the year, as well as a few local tourist destinations; a beach on Lake Ontario, the Finger Lakes, the Adirondacks, and the American side of Niagara Falls. That last one was one of Mrs. Rigo's surprise finds, the jewel of the museum. At least until the new tapestry went on display.

Sophie didn't linger here. These tapestries had long since lost their luster, and she wasn't keen to have another awkward conversation with Mrs. Rigo, or anyone else in town for that matter.

Nor did she linger at the museum in Rochester. The Memorial Art Gallery looked as though someone had taken the facade of the small museum in Honyeoke Falls and stretched it to three times its original width. And like her hometown museum, the tapestries here were largely familiar to Sophie.

Though not all the tapestries. A security guard stood at the entrance to the east wing of the museum, checking passports, and for a moment, Sophie was tempted to enter this portion of the museum that had, until now, been off-limits to her. She could hop a tapestry to Toronto or Montreal, just for the thrill of it. But there would be plenty of time to use her passport, she reminded herself, as she dragged her duffel along the polished floor, past tapestries heading to Cleveland and Pittsburgh, the latter a fascinating tangle of arches and vertical lines hovering over three horizontal bands, representing the city's rivers and bridges.

From Rochester to the Breuer, the imposing brutalist structure in New York City. If Rochester's museum was Honyeoke's Fall's stretched to its limit, the Breuer was several Memorial Art Galleries, with all their ornamentation stripped, stacked on top of each other. Here, Sophie could catch a tapestry to every major city in the US, and she lingered for a moment in front of the cool forest greens and watery blues of a tapestry heading to Seattle, then the bright, almost blinding light of one destined for Los Angeles. It seemed to glow even more against the dark concrete walls.

The Breuer didn't do international tapestries, so Sophie had to hop one uptown to the Guggenheim. It was here where Sophie's trip practically ground to a halt. She'd been to the Breuer before on trips to New York, but without a passport, she'd never been able to enter a museum built only for international travel.

With its tapestries arranged along a corkscrew that moved upwards around a central atrium, the Guggenheim didn't have the efficiency Sophie expected from a place designed for international travel. Instead, it made her want to linger even more. The tapestry to London was on an upper level, and Sophie took her time as the walkway spiraled upwards. More than once, she infuriated a traveler who hadn't expected someone to be stopped directly in front of a tapestry, staring, with a massive duffel bag at their feet.

A shimmering tapestry caught her eye. Light emanated from within, evoking clear skies and tall trees waving softly in the breeze, though none of that was explicitly pictured. Sophie stood there for ages, basking in the brilliance until a disgruntled commuter knocked her out of the way.

"Idiot," they grumbled under their breath. "This is why they should just make the transport tapestries all one color."

But it was that commuter, Sophie thought, rubbing her hip where they had collided with her, who was the idiot. It was the design, or, more specifically, the vibration of different colors within the design, that made the tapestries work at all. A tapestry with only one color would do as much good as hanging a wet blanket on a wall.

From the Guggenheim, it was on to the British Museum in London. Sophie couldn't bring herself to stay long. The tapestries here were like a litany of Britain's devastating colonial history, a record of all the places the empire had done damage. As beautiful as the tapestries were, it was hard not to imagine the devastation that had occurred on the other end or who had been hurt in the making of those tapestries. Fortunately, Sophie could make her escape quickly. East Lawn was so important as a center of tapestry history and repair that there was a tapestry she could take straight to the center of campus.

Holding her breath, Sophie stepped through the final tapestry and into whatever East Lawn had in store for her.

Chapter 4
East Lawn

F or such a prestigious school, East Lawn was a surprisingly small campus. Even still, by the time Sophie exited the castle-like central building — ivy trailing up its walls as if it was some kind of law — and made her way across the sweeping expanse of grass to her dorm, her back ached so badly she could barely lift her duffle. And her mother wanted her to bring *more* clothes?

It was a relief to finally open the door to her room and heave her bag inside. Sophie had expected her dorm to be a big blocky affair, like the kind she'd seen visiting RIT, but Pepper Hall was an old stone building that looked like it had stood for centuries — though not always as a dorm. It had the air of a barn or some sort of outbuilding. But for all the charm of the exterior, Sophie's room was surprisingly spare. Three beds jutted out into the room at various angles, each accompanied by a desk. A large row of doors, painted white to match the walls, hid what Sophie assumed were their closets.

Someone had already hung a tapestry on the wall directly across from the door. An imposing manor house rose stoically from a misty English moor, clouds swirling above. There was something vaguely familiar about those clouds.

"Beautiful, isn't it?" A blonde girl flounced into the room, ponytail bouncing behind her, wearing a lacy white blouse under a chic burgundy jumper. Or whatever they called it, Sophie corrected herself, remembering that here, sweaters, not dresses, were called jumpers. Whatever it was called,

Sophie couldn't fathom why someone would wear something that nice for move-in day. Sophie only had on her best cords because she didn't want the weight in her bag. "I'm Vivienne," the girl said, coming over to give Sophie a hug. Even in heels, she was shorter than Sophie.

"Sophie." She turned towards the tapestry. "Your home?"

"Of course," Vivienne replied. "Weddlesmoore. Daddy bought it for Mum as a wedding present."

Vivienne looked at Sophie's bag, lying on the floor looking pathetically small for something that had caused so much pain, then up at the wall. "Where's yours?"

"I don't have one," Sophie replied.

"But," Vivienne seemed confused, "how will you get home?"

Sophie shrugged. "Through the museums."

"Public transport?" A mix of incredulity and disgust crossed Vivienne's face. "Does your family not own any tapestries?"

Of course they had tapestries, more than most families she knew, but their collection was for escape, not transportation. Besides, she didn't know anyone who had personal tapestries for international travel, what with the additional costs of getting them permitted.

But rather than explain any of this, she decided to bait Vivienne instead.

"If you can't handle public tapestries, how will you ever deal with shared bathrooms?"

Oblivious, Vivienne took Sophie's teasing for concern. "Ugh, I know right? Daddy tried to get me an ensuite, he even offered a donation, but they aren't allowed for first years." Who talked like this? Was Sophie really going to have to put up with this rich brat all year?

There was an awkward pause, as Sophie couldn't think of a good rebuttal. Vivienne looked up at the tapestry again, now frowning slightly. "Daddy insisted I hang it up, but I'll probably take it down. Can't have him dropping by at all hours. What if I'm otherwise engaged? A girl's got needs, after all."

"What about us?" A tall girl with olive skin and high cheekbones stood in the doorway, wearing a fitted denim jumpsuit that accentuated her long legs. Her wild, curly hair made Sophie's usual flyaways look tame in comparison.

Sophie thought she heard Vivienne inhale sharply, but her face was passive as she replied, "Well, I assume you have needs too. We'll have to come up with a system."

"What, like a sock on the door?" The girl replied, rolling her eyes at Sophie.

"Oh, I'm sure we can come up with something better than that," Vivienne said, with a wave of her hand. "I'm Vivienne. Vivienne Maxwell."

"I'm Eryka." She looked incredibly uncomfortable, as Vivienne bounded forward to give her a hug. "Adnan-Phillips," she added.

"I'm Sophie. And…" Sophie's voice got quiet. "Should we be talking about…" She had just noticed two women her mother's age standing in the doorway behind Eryka.

"Oh," Eryka laughed, gesturing towards them. "They don't care. Though they are a little disappointed I turned out straight."

Now Sophie was sure she saw a flash of disappointment on Vivienne's face.

"Her brother, too. I don't know where we went wrong." The taller woman laughed, gesturing towards the young man who had just appeared behind her. He had the same long legs and wild, curly hair as his sister, though his was cropped shorter. His shoulders were broader, and swirls of dark hair peeked out from the unbuttoned collar of his shirt. It was Sophie's turn to inhale sharply, but she kept her face passive when Vivienne glanced in her direction.

"Don't look at me," the shorter woman replied. "They were your eggs."

"Yeah, but you birthed them." Her accent sounded vaguely French.

"Something she never lets me forget," Eryka added, kissing the shorter woman on the cheek and grabbing one of the suitcases. Each woman was carrying one, and the young man behind them had two. "This is Simone," she gestured to the taller woman, "and Claire," Eryka continued, "and my brother Jazz, um, I mean Jasper."

There was a round of "nice to meet yous" as Jasper took the suitcases from the hall, grabbed the other from Claire's hand, and heaved them into the room.

"I've got to get to my own dorm," he said, giving his sister a kiss on the cheek and then turning to Sophie and Vivienne. "I'm sure I'll be seeing you around," he said, flashing them a wide smile. Sophie's legs gave a little wobble. He gave each of his mothers a kiss on the cheek, then stepped through the door, grabbed his own suitcase and disappeared down the hall.

"We should go too," Simone added, sending a couple of air kisses in Eryka's direction. "Your mother insists on giving me a tour of the campus as if she hasn't done that every year since Jazz started."

"It's my only chance to relive my glory days," Claire laughed, hugging Eryka before leading Simone from the room.

"My mom went here," Erika explained, as the two women left the room.

"Both?" Sophie asked. She couldn't imagine going to school someplace where other people in her family had a history. Part of the appeal of going to school in another country was the complete anonymity it granted her.

"Just Claire. Simone studied in France." Eryka flung the first suitcase on the bed, then added, by way of apology after seeing the look on Sophie's face, "I'm a bit of a clotheshorse."

That was an understatement. It was the correct call, Sophie decided, not to do any shopping before she left. Hopefully, the other girls could steer her in the right direction. She only worried that direction might be on the costlier side.

"Are you really going to unpack all of that now?" Vivienne asked, stamping her foot and moving closer to Eryka's bed. "Let's go do something fun instead."

"Like what?" Eryka asked.

"I don't know. We should at least explore campus while it's still daylight." Vivienne suggested.

There were plenty of hours left in the day. Then again, it might take Eryka that long to put away all her clothes.

"I'd like to see more of campus," Sophie agreed. "Eryka, maybe you could show us around." Vivienne had the air of wanting to play cruise director, but Sophie wasn't sure how much more of her manic rich girl energy she could take.

Fortunately, Eryka seemed willing to take charge. "Do you want the official, mom-approved tour, or the secret spots Jazz told me about?"

The other two looked at her like that wasn't even a question.

The last traces of summer were hanging on at East Lawn. Flowers bloomed in the campus garden and the sun glinted off the buildings, making the stones sparkle. Sophie guessed it wouldn't last. In a couple of weeks, she'd be trading her t-shirt for a sweater. Maybe by then, she'd be calling it a jumper too. But she could appreciate it now, especially because summer here seemed to be at least fifteen degrees cooler than what she'd left at home.

They followed the sweeping lawn back towards the main building, a hulking castle that Eryka informed them had in fact been a home until it was bequeathed to the trustees who created the college. The building stretched out in front of them, a haphazard collection of walls and turrets on either side of a not-quite central tower with an arched entryway. Inside were lecture halls, offices, and not one, but two galleries. There was the gallery Sophie had arrived through from London, filled with transport tapestries to hubs across England, from nearby Brighton all the way up to Manchester and Liverpool. The other gallery was ostensibly for study, featuring some of the finest tapestries Sophie had ever seen. Most looked like they had been woven centuries ago.

"According to Jazz," Eryka continued, "this is where students go when they need a little, um, privacy." She shot Vivienne a look when she said this. For a moment, Sophie imagined sneaking in here with Jasper, but then turned her attention back to her roommates.

Vivienne eyed the tapestries, and Eryka, with a look of longing, before turning on her heel. "Let's get out of here," she said. "I'm sure we'll be spending too much time here as it is."

"We'll really only be here for history of tapestry classes," Eryka informed her. "Our practical classes are in the weaving studios on the other side of campus."

"Fine," Vivienne conceded with a little pout. "But there's got to be other places around campus where a girl can go to have some fun."

They continued their exploration of the grounds, Eryka taking care to show Vivienne other places where she might find a little privacy. It seemed clear to Sophie that if Vivienne did have as many needs as she claimed, Eryka was hoping she'd satisfy them in places other than their room. Partly to bring the discussion away from Vivienne's sex life, but mostly to satiate her curiosity about Jasper, Sophie steered the conversation around to their families.

Eryka's parents, it turned out, ran a tapestry gallery in Brussels, specializing in international locations — a fitting occupation given their backgrounds. Simone spent her childhood shuffling between France and Lebanon, and Claire had grown up in England. The two women met in Amsterdam before settling in Brussels and having children.

"What about your parents?" Sophie asked Vivienne.

"Oh, well, Daddy runs a tapestry manufacturing firm. And mum was a designer."

"Wait," Eryka said, comprehension dawning on her face. "Was your mother Sabrina Maxwell?"

Something about that name sounded familiar to Sophie, but she couldn't recall where she'd heard it. Vivienne nodded but didn't say anything.

"But then she's—" Eryka stopped herself mid-sentence, her hand to her mouth, her eyes on Vivienne.

"What?" Sophie demanded, clearly missing something.

Eryka gave Sophie a warning look that implied she would explain everything later, but Vivienne chimed in. "She's dead." And then she added with a shrug, "She was murdered."

"What?!?." Sophie's head spun. How could Vivienne seem so nonchalant about this? But Eryka interjected.

"It was a long time ago, wasn't it?"

Vivienne nodded again. This was the most subdued Sophie had seen her since they met. But she didn't seem sad, just kind of flat. "I was two when it happened. I don't even remember her."

A million questions exploded in Sophie's brain, but between Eryka's warning looks and Vivienne's closed expression, she knew better than to continue.

As the conversation petered out, Sophie found herself more intrigued by her pretty, perky roommate than she would have believed possible a few hours ago.

Chapter 5
East Lawn

"Let's go shopping," Vivienne announced the next morning, returning from the bathroom fully dressed. Her dull mood had blown out completely. "We've got an entire day before orientation, I want to do something fun."

"I'm down," Eryka replied. "I've got a list of stores to check out in London."

They turned to Sophie, still in bed. Her body couldn't register what time it was. She had never experienced tapestry lag this bad before. She should probably go shopping with them, if only for Eryka's style advice. But she had a hunch they would be shopping in places she couldn't afford. Sophie had danced around the topic of money the previous night, not wanting to reveal how precarious her financial situation was compared to the other two, that she was only at East Lawn thanks to a generous scholarship.

Plus, she had something more important she wanted to do today.

Sophie responded slowly. "Actually, I was thinking of going to the V&A."

"A museum?" Vivienne snorted. "Seriously? We've got all semester to study, why would you want to start before we have to?"

Sophie had dreamed of seeing the tapestries at the Victoria & Albert since she was a little girl, and that longing had only intensified when she'd bought her copy of *Great*

Tapestries. But after Vivienne's question, her reasons sounded unconvincing in her head. Thankfully, Eryka saved her.

"You've never been? You should absolutely do that. You're going to love it." Eryka continued, as Sophie gave her a look of thanks, "Why don't we all go into London together, and then you can meet up with us for a pint when you're done?"

Vivienne seemed fine with this compromise since it gave her Eryka to herself for most of the day, so the three of them set off for London.

They didn't take the tapestry to the British Museum that Sophie had taken on her way to school, but one that spit them out at the Museum of London. Sophie hesitated for a moment, wanting to see what other tapestries this museum held, but was grateful when Vivienne and Eryka rushed her out the door. The Museum of London was mostly a transport hub. There would be even more incredible things to see at the V&A.

As they stepped out of the museum, Vivienne and Eryka arguing about where they wanted to go first, a man's voice hissed from the side of the building.

"Oi, ladies," he called. "You weaving students? Need some extra cash—"

Before he could finish, Eryka was dragging them off in the opposite direction.

"What was that about?" Sophie asked.

"Trafficker," Eryka replied, scowling. "Looking to lure young weavers into sweatshops," she went on. "It's so gross. Literal slave labor."

"What?" Vivienne was wide-eyed, and in that moment Sophie recognized just how sheltered she was.

Before Eryka could reply, Sophie turned to Vivienne. "You don't seriously think all those cheap tapestries come out of amazing working conditions, do you?"

"Cheap tapestries?" Vivienne looked confused, as if she couldn't imagine a world where someone would want a cheap tapestry, let alone a world where someone would need one.

Sophie felt her blood start to boil. "Not everyone can afford new, well-made tapestries. And some people would rather buy cheap crap than something used."

"Used tapestries?" Vivienne said it with the same level of disgust she had used when she found out Sophie traveled by public tapestry.

"Used is a hundred times better than the cheap shit that's been flooding the market." Sophie was getting worked up now. She'd heard her mother's rants on this topic a thousand times but had experienced it firsthand when she started working in the repair shop. People brought in cheap tapestries, worn to shreds after only a few years of use — the threads prone to breaking as the quicker, looser weave caught on fingers and clothes as people passed through. Sophie's mother flat-out refused to work on them, saying it wasn't worth her time. "Try one of the repair shops in Victor," she would tell them, shaking her head. Then, as they stomped out, she looked at Sophie. "Those cheap asses. They wouldn't pay what I would charge anyway."

Sophie felt a little more sympathy than her mother. These people were just trying to get by, to make it to work, or school, or to visit family, or maybe just get away for a while. And if they didn't have the knowledge or experience to seek out used tapestries, to give them a little TLC, she could see how it was easy to get sucked into buying a shiny new tapestry for a steal, even if it would be useless in a few years.

No, Sophie didn't blame the people who bought the cheap tapestries. She blamed the sweatshop owners for forcing people to work in such horrible conditions and governments for failing to put a stop to it. Her anger with Vivienne's naïveté spilling over, she had half a mind to go back and tell off that trafficker.

But Eryka intervened. "The V&A is that way," she said, pointing in the opposite direction. "You better get going if you want to see everything today."

The Victoria & Albert Museum was a sprawling mishmash of architectural elements and materials. Long brick expanses, punctuated by triangular windows and domed roofs flanked a central facade, dripping with decoration like some kind of stone wedding cake. As she stepped through the imposing museum doors and into the vast entryway, Sophie took a deep breath, letting the cool stillness of the museum wash over her. She was finally here, in the presence of some of the most incredible tapestries in the world.

There were few visitors; most families were done with their vacations for the season but it was too early for school trips, and the people that were there hurried towards their favorite tapestries, bursting through them in eager anticipation of where they might end up.   Unlike museums made for transport, the V&A was intended for pleasure. Every tapestry led to a place people would go in their time off. Sophie strolled past gardens and forests, mountains and beaches. She took her time, lingering in front of each tapestry, taking in the skillfulness of construction, the way colors blended seamlessly into each other, or else jumped abruptly from one shape to the next, carving a myriad of surfaces out of nothing more than colored thread.

She stood so long in front of one tapestry, stepping forward and back to take in the full effect before scrutinizing every detail, that a security guard approached her.

"You know you're meant to go through them, right?"

Sophie stammered, unaware that anyone else was even in the room. "Well of course I know that, I just…" Her voice trailed off. Maybe this security guard was numb to the beauty all around him, having spent so much of his time here. Or maybe, he was like most people, who viewed tapestries for where they took them, not what they actually were. Wanting to avoid an awkward conversation, Sophie turned away from the guard and stepped through the tapestry.

She walked out into a lush garden, under a canopy of trees. Looking at the tapestry, Sophie had spotted blooming tulips and daffodils, in an homage to spring. But now, in the waning days of summer, the beds held the last remnants of coneflowers alongside mums waiting to burst forth. Of course, someone who spent their time in a bustling city would be in need of respite in a place like this. But Sophie wasn't interested in escape, at least not today. She wanted to see the magic of the tapestries themselves. She lingered in the garden just long enough to ensure the guard had moved on, then headed back into the museum, eager for what she might find next.

Not every tapestry was intended for leisure, as Sophie discovered several hours into her visit. In the back of the museum, tucked away from the merry-makers, was a room marked with a simple sign: "The History of Transport Tapestries in Britain." The tapestries in this room were smaller — some mere fragments — and much older than anything else in the museum. And they were all cordoned off so that no one could attempt to enter them. Perhaps it was because there weren't any tapestries in the Northeast US as old as these, but Sophie had never experienced tapestries that were displayed but no longer in use. At least at the museums Sophie was familiar with, if a tapestry was too worn or damaged, it was decommissioned, its valuable threads pulled apart for use in repairing other tapestries.

At first, Sophie reveled in a space where no guard would come and chastise her for simply looking. But she had to suppress a snort when she read the wall caption next to the oldest-looking fragment:

> *Transportation tapestries were first invented in Britain over 600 years ago, when wealthy nobles commissioned tapestries of their homes and surrounding property. As these nobles took the tapestries along on their journeys, they discovered they served as portals to return home in a more expedient fashion than traveling by horse or foot.*

Not for the first time that day, Sophie's cheeks burned with anger. What revisionist nonsense was this? She half-wished a guard would show up, just so she could vent her frustrations. The British didn't invent anything. It was common knowledge, at least to Sophie, that the Vikings had been using tapestries to travel for several hundred years before introducing the technology to England and Scotland. That in the process of making sails for their ships, they'd unlocked the secret of traveling directly through the weavings. And that was nothing compared to people in South America, who had woven tapestries to help traverse the mountainous terrain thousands of years before that. Or that weavers in Egypt and the Middle East were believed to also have developed tapestries around that time, and that they eventually shared their secrets across the Mediterranean. But the caption shared none of that.

Sophie's frustration shattered some of the reverence she'd felt as she wandered the museum, enough to make her realize that if she didn't leave soon, she'd be late to meet Vivienne and Eryka. On the way out, she stopped in the gift shop to pick out a postcard of one of the museum's tapestries to send to Rush. She quickly scrawled "I wish you were here" on the back and dropped it in a post box. It was the best Sophie could muster by way of an apology.

The next morning, Sophie returned from breakfast to find a mound of Eryka's clothes on her bed. Several pairs of jeans balanced precariously on a pile of patterned dresses in a riot of greens and yellows, next to half a dozen tops, a coat, and what appeared to be an embroidered vest — loops of thick pink thread popped against the rusty orange fabric.

"I shouldn't have bought so much yesterday," Eryka explained when Sophie gave her a quizzical look. "It won't all fit in my closet. These are yours if you want them." She gestured to the mountain of clothes.

Sophie hesitated. She wasn't sure if Eryka was aware of her financial situation or had surveyed Sophie's meager closet and couldn't stand the thought of palling around with someone so unstylish, but either way, shame rose in her chest.

"I don't need—" Sophie started, grabbing a handful of clothes and shoving them back towards Eryka, but Eryka cut her off.

"If you don't keep them, I'll have to take them to a charity shop."

Sophie flushed. "I'm not a charity case."

"I never said you were," Eryka responded, nonplussed. "Now your wardrobe, on the other hand," she said, gesturing towards Sophie's nearly empty closet.

"I don't want—" Sophie started again.

"Take them or leave them. I really don't care. But I'm not having an argument about it."

Sophie looked at her empty closet and then over at Eryka's, which was full to bursting, with all her new purchases still spread on the bed.

"Thanks," Sophie said lamely, before trying to mimic Eryka's friendly gesture. "You know, you can keep clothes in my closet if you need to."

"First you don't want any of my clothes, and now you want more."

Sophie opened her mouth to argue, then realized Eryka was joking. "At this point, I guess I'll take what I can get," Sophie replied with a smile, turning to survey the pile of clothes on her bed. Eryka was a good few inches taller than her, but Sophie had spent so much time with a needle and thread in her hands that she had everything hemmed by the start of classes a few days later.

Chapter 6
East Lawn

All first-year tapestry students had to take the same classes, regardless of what their focus would eventually be, an expectation that Vivienne in particular seemed most frustrated about.

"Why do I have to take design *and* weaving?" she whined as they made their way to the weaving studio for their first day of class. "I'm going for *business.*"

"Shouldn't you be good at design?" Eryka questioned her. "Genetics and all that."

They had reached a tacit agreement about Vivienne's mother. She could be a topic of conversation, as long as they steered clear of the murder bit.

"I don't think it works that way," was Vivienne's retort. "Besides, you should be just as worried as I am. Can you even draw? Or do you just write things down?"

Eryka planned to study the history of tapestry. Sophie assumed this was to follow in the footsteps of her mothers' gallery, but Eryka corrected her. She was more interested in traveling and research than she was in managing a gallery.

"Don't you worry about me, Princess." Eryka could somehow needle Vivienne back while simultaneously remaining cool, a skill Sophie had yet to develop. "Besides, I have a feeling it's Sophie we have to worry about. All that repair experience, I bet she'll weave circles around us."

Sophie didn't answer. She had been confident of her skills when applying, but now, so far from everything she knew, she worried she was out of her league. Surely there were other students whose talent and experience far surpassed hers.

The weaving studio was on the opposite side of campus from their dorm, and Sophie spent the rest of the walk in nervous silence while the other two continued their discussion about the classes they were taking. But as they stepped into the weaving studio, Sophie let out an audible gasp.

In the center of the room stood a dozen or so looms, all waiting to be warped. Weaving samples were tacked along one wall, while on another, shelves jam-packed with cones of thread stretched to the ceiling. There was even a rolling ladder to reach the upper shelves. Some of their classmates were already seated at benches in front of the looms, whispering to themselves or looking around nervously. Sophie, Eryka, and Vivienne took seats in front of a large, vertical loom.

A petite woman wearing an oversized cardigan and soft wool shoes, her gray hair pulled back into a loose bun, stood at the front of the room. Once everyone was seated, she wasted no time getting started.

"Who can tell me the difference," Professor Rygge asked in a warm Swedish accent, "between tapestry weaving and other forms of weaving?"

The class glanced around at each other, no one willing to speak up. Finally, Vivienne knocked Sophie's elbow, forcing her hand into the air.

Professor Rygge gave her a sharp stare. "Yes, Miss…"

"O'Toole," Sophie said. She took a deep breath. "In most weaving, the weft threads are wound onto a shuttle which travels through the entire width of the warp every pass. In tapestry, threads are wound on bobbins, which are only passed through small sections of warp at a time, to build up discreet areas of color and pattern."

Everyone stared at Sophie, who flushed, but Professor Rygge gave her a small smile. "Precisely. It's the placement of individual colors that creates the vibrations necessary for travel. It's why tapestry is the only form of weaving that lets you move from one place to another.

"Of course," Professor Rygge continued, "it's not just the placement of the colors that makes transportation possible. There's the wool itself. Who can tell me— ah, yes, Miss O'Toole?"

Sophie glared at Vivienne, who had once again knocked her arm into the air, before coughing slightly and turning her attention back to Professor Rygge. "Um, transportation tapestries require wool from certain breeds of sheep. Wandering wool," she added, "which can be very expensive, since the sheep are prone to vanishing from time to time and turning up somewhere completely unexpected." Sophie was even more uncomfortable now that everyone was looking at her. She'd grown up believing the wool was precious, something not to be wasted, but maybe that was more down to her family's finances than the actual cost of the wool.

But it seemed Professor Rygge at least agreed. "Too right," she beamed at Sophie. "Wandering wool is a valuable commodity, one I don't want to see anyone in this class wasting." She fixed them all with a stern gaze, but once she was sure they understood her, it morphed into a look of excitement.

"And finally," she went on with a flourish, spreading her arms wide. "You must weave with intent. Believe that you're creating a portal from one place to another. You must approach your weaving with the destination in mind."

She stared pointedly at the class. "But all of that comes later. You won't achieve transportive results from the outset, especially because you won't be working with wandering wool to start. It's too expensive. You've got to get a hang of the mechanics of weaving first. Get comfortable with the tension and the placement of color. It doesn't matter how much you think about the end goal as you're working. If your weft threads are a wobbly mess, you'll never get the desired results."

Professor Rygge chuckled. "But I'm getting ahead of myself. Before we can think about where the weft threads go, you must warp the loom."

She led them to the back of the classroom where rectangular wooden frames studded with dowels hung across the wall. Professor Rygge pulled a cone of thread from a shelf and demonstrated how to use the frame to measure out sections of the warp. Then she turned to the class.

"Miss O'Toole, perhaps you'd like to help me put this warp on the loom."

Sophie had never warped anything larger than a child's play loom, but her years in the repair shop gave her an instinctive feel for the tension of the thread. She and Professor Rygge worked well together, and soon the warp threads stretched across the loom like guitar strings waiting to be plucked.

Professor Rygge beamed at Sophie, then turned towards three other looms that stood waiting. "Let's divide into groups and get these warped."

There was a clammer as everyone raced to partner with Sophie, but Vivienne and Eryka got there first. "She's our roommate," Vivienne said, pouting at the others in the class until they moved away.

But Sophie wasn't so quick to forgive Vivienne for forcing her to answer Professor Rygge's question at the start of class. She wanted to excel in her weaving class more than any other, but she hadn't planned on being marked as the teacher's pet from day one.

"Actually," Sophie said, turning from Vivienne and walking towards another group. "It would be good if we got to know some of our other classmates."

Eryka grinned behind Vivienne's shoulder, and Sophie was sure seeing Vivienne put in her place was enough for Eryka to forgive her for ditching them.

Vivienne expressed her annoyance again when their first tapestry design class started, not with them making cartoons, the full-scale designs that weavers used when making a tapestry, but with observational drawing on the East Lawn grounds.

"Did you honestly think," Professor Berger replied to Vivienne's indignant huff in her sharp German accent as she ushered them out into the landscape, "that you'd be jumping straight into cartoons?"

It was clear by Vivienne's look that she did. Professor Berger ignored her and went on, gesturing towards the surrounding hills. "Before you can design, you've got to learn to look. You can't draft a tapestry for someplace you've never seen before. Even abstract tapestries must carry the essence of the place they want you to go."

Sophie settled into a quiet spot with her sketchpad, as far away from Vivienne as she could manage. She knew this well. They'd learned as much in her history classes in school. It's what had kept Europeans out of the Americas for so long. It was only after they landed with their boats that the artists they had brought along were able to design tapestries to make the journey easier.

But she was surprised Vivienne didn't realize this. It was the reason why the best tapestry designers were so well-traveled. And why so few tapestry designers wove their own work. Traveling and designing left little time for actually executing a weaving. Surely, Vivienne must have known this about her mother. After the conversation on their first day at East Lawn, Sophie had looked up Sabrina at the library — not that she'd shared this with Vivienne. Her initial curiosity about the murder turned into a fascination with Sabrina's studio. At the height of her success, she'd had a team of nearly a dozen weavers and other technicians — including color theorists, dyers, and seamstresses — working for her. It was exactly the sort of studio Sophie hoped to be a weaver in one day.

Sophie turned back to her sketchbook and began scratching out the landscape. Her dream was to be a weaver, but that didn't mean she wasn't determined to show Vivienne up in their design class as well.

As the weeks wore on, Eryka's prediction that Sophie would top their weaving class held true. Once they'd mastered warping the loom — a few warps had to be cut off and redone because the tension was wrong, though that never happened to Sophie — they moved on to their first weaving samples.

Professor Rygge presented them each with a cartoon. The shapes were basic, but if Sophie squinted hard enough, she could just about imagine a scene.

Vivienne thrust her arm into the air and barely waited for Professor Rygge to acknowledge her before blurting out. "Is this supposed to be a sunset at the beach?"

Professor Rygge eyed her sharply. "The scene doesn't matter, Miss Maxwell. This design is meant to help you practice the basics of forming curves, along with some simple color gradation." Sophie could have sworn Professor Rygge gave her a swift smile before sighing and turning back to Vivienne. "But if you insist, you may think of it as a beach scene." Now she really did turn to Sophie with the hint of a wink. "Though if I'm being honest, I prefer to think of it as a sunrise."

The class gathered their supplies from the wall clearly marked "Practice Wool" but before Sophie had a chance to select the colors that most spoke to her, Professor Rygge called her over and handed her a basket of wool. "I'd like you to use these please, Miss O'Toole."

Sophie hesitated. She'd been looking forward to showing off her prowess when it came to choosing colors — glancing around at her classmates, some of them had chosen some truly horrid combinations — but now she was stuck with the colors Professor Rygge had chosen for it.

Something of her displeasure must have shown on her face, because Professor Rygge urged the basket into her hands, saying "Trust me." Then this time, she really did give Sophie a small wink.

The samples they were producing were only a foot in either direction, which meant several students were working on the same loom. "Even though you are weaving these samples independently," Professor Rygge told them, "weavers work in teams to complete a full-size tapestry. You must get comfortable working next to others on your loom."

To her frustration, Sophie was next to Vivienne, who bashed on the treadles with so much energy that it practically pulled the weft from Sophie's hands. "You're supposed to warn us before you switch," Sophie told her for what felt like the umpteenth time.

Even with Vivienne complicating things, Sophie finished her sample much faster than any of her classmates. Once Sophie had tacked it to the wall, Professor Rygge confidently jammed her hand straight through and withdrew it with a smile on her face, shaking sand onto the floor.

Sophie stared at the ground, trying not to look too pleased with herself.

Next to her, Vivienne was indignant. "I thought you said we wouldn't be able to do that right away. We weren't even working with wandering wool."

Professor Rygge gave her a stern stare, before turning back to Sophie with a smile. "It does happen from time to time, and I had a hunch that might be the case with Miss O'Toole. That's why I gave you a beach scene to start with. And why I may have," she gave them a mischievous grin, "swapped Miss O'Toole's wool out. To see if she had the skills and the mindset straight off the bat. And as I suspected, Miss O'Toole does."

Despite the glares and grumbles of a few of her classmates, Vivienne included, Sophie couldn't help but grin. Her dream of becoming a skilled weaver wasn't misguided or far-fetched. Behind her, she heard Eryka whisper to Vivienne, "Told you so." Sophie couldn't help smiling even wider at that.

It wasn't just the weaving class where Sophie excelled, though it was clear she had chosen the right concentration. Growing up in the repair shop left her with a host of skills, and she found herself breezing through the basics of color theory and bookkeeping with ease.

It was their history of tapestry course where she felt frustrated, but she wasn't alone. Eryka and Sophie had both gotten into an argument with their professor on day one.

"Why are we only focusing on the history of European tapestries?" Eryka complained loudly, after commenting under her breath to Sophie that the syllabus was devoid of any African or Asian subjects.

"Because this is Europe," Professor Ackerman replied dryly as if that put an end to the discussion.

Sophie begged to differ. "What about tapestries from the Americas?" she chimed in.

"Miss O'Toole," their professor interrupted her. "Just because you come from America doesn't mean we need to give it an outsized importance in the history of tapestry. It's a footnote at best."

Sophie wanted to keep arguing, to remind her that tapestries were woven in the Americas centuries before Europeans got their shit together. But Professor Ackerman's tone made it clear there was no room for further discussion. Instead, Sophie crossed her arms and joined Eryka in glowering at the front of the room.

Professor Ackerman seemed to delight in Sophie and Eryka's frustration. "Besides, who cares about tapestries from abroad when we have the daughter of a celebrity in our midst."

All eyes turned to Vivienne, who blushed.

"Of course, we won't get to modern tapestries until next semester, but we'll be looking forward to Miss Maxwell's insider insights when we get there."

Now it was Vivienne's turn to glower. Despite trying to distance herself by not majoring in design, it was clear that Sabrina's ghost would follow Vivienne around campus.

The only other class where Sophie struggled was French. France was such a key country in the production of tapestry that all students were required to be fluent. Vivienne had a French tutor when she was younger, and Eryka grew up speaking French and Arabic at home with her mother Simone, so both had passed the fluency test that let them opt out of classes. But in her small town, it hadn't occurred to Sophie, or any of her school counselors, that French would be a useful thing to learn. She took Spanish for a bit, but mostly what stuck were the curse words Rush used when his mother wasn't around.

—#—

Rush responded to Sophie's postcard with a long letter detailing everything that had happened in his first weeks at school, which Sophie knew meant he had forgiven her for ditching him in the tapestry.

Sophie had just settled onto her bed to read the letter in full when Vivienne snatched it out of her hands. "Who's this from?" she teased. "Your boyfriend?"

"No," Sophie replied. "He's just my friend."

Eryka looked over from above her library book, a deep dive into ancient Middle Eastern tapestry. She had declared that if their history class wasn't covering the topics she wanted, she would do it herself, even though Vivienne pointed out that she'd have plenty of time to study those subjects later.

"It's her fuck buddy," Eryka said slyly, giving Sophie a wink.

Sophie's face flashed. She had told Eryka that in confidence.

"Oh really?" Vivienne replied. "Tell us more."

"There's nothing to tell," Sophie said, glaring at Eryka while she snatched the letter back from Vivienne. Then flashing Vivienne her biggest smile, she continued, "Like you said, a girl's got needs."

—#—

Despite her remonstrations to her mother, Sophie did find herself at the pub quite frequently. The Sheep's Head was quintessentially English, all textured paneling and dark wood, from the booths to the stools to the gleaming central bar, which stretched around the room and seemed to accommodate all of campus. Eryka and Vivienne, wanting to be at the center of campus life, were always eager to go. Sophie tagged along but was on a much tighter budget than the other two. While she refused to let her roommates pay for her drinks, she wasn't opposed to letting the occasional guy buy her one. So far, none of those guys had been interesting enough for Sophie to contemplate going on a date with, let alone going home with, but the free beers helped keep her budget in check.

One Saturday night a few weeks into the semester, they stood around a tiny table, debating whether they should get another round or pack it in in favor of an early night. They had a mountain of work they needed to finish the next day.

"Jazz is here," Eryka exclaimed, spotting her older brother and hurrying off to say hello.

"You have got to stop drooling over her," Sophie whispered, in response to Vivienne's look of longing as Eryka walked away. "She's straight, remember." As much as Vivienne could annoy her, she didn't want to see her wasting her time or getting her heart broken. Especially not by someone who lived in the same room as them.

"You should talk," Vivienne replied. Her eyes darted between Sophie and Jasper.

"What?" Sophie said incredulously, trying in vain to hide the fact that she found Jasper attractive. "At least he's interested in women," she argued.

"Yeah, but he's way out of your league." Though it had the tone of a joke, Sophie didn't take it that way.

"We can't all be as lucky as you," Sophie hissed. "I'm sure there are plenty of girls here on campus that would love to get into the pants of a rich, pretty princess."

Vivienne pouted momentarily before flashing into her usual perky smile as Eryka and Jasper made their way over to them.

"Jazz was just telling me about an Arch party across campus. Want to go? Way more guys than we usually see wandering the weaving halls."

"Who wants that?" Vivienne replied, glancing towards a group of older tapestry students, all of whom were women, who had just entered the pub.

"I guess you're out." Eryka shrugged and turned to Sophie. "You in?"

"I don't know," Sophie hesitated. She was desperate to go to a party with Jasper, but she didn't want to seem too eager. "What if Vivienne needs a wingwoman?"

"I don't need your help to get a girl," Vivienne retorted. In what felt like one sweeping motion, she shook her blonde hair out of its ponytail, reapplied her lipgloss, and flounced over to where the women were settling into a booth. She slid effortlessly into the group, throwing her arm around one of the women and letting out a laugh.

"Guess you're stuck with us then." Jasper broke into a wide smile as he said it, and Sophie had to place a hand on her knee to stop it from shaking.

"I guess so," she murmured in reply. Why had her brain suddenly turned to mush?

They left the pub and walked through campus, past buildings with the occasional light on. Students, their heads bent at work, were silhouetted in the windows. Eryka and Jasper were in furious conversation, catching each other up on their classes and the various tidbits of gossip from back home their moms had let slip in letters.

Sophie loped along behind them, unable to think of a single thing to add to the conversation.

"And then there's Intro to Weaving," Eryka continued, clearly exasperated. "Almost makes me want to give up fibers and switch to stacking blocks." She gave her brother a teasing look. "It's so fucking hard. Unless you're Sophie," she added.

"Oh really," Jasper turned towards her with interest. "That good, huh?"

Sophie felt her stomach drop. "I'm not bad," she stammered.

"Oh please," Eryka interjected. "You should have seen Professor Rygge when we handed in our first weaving samples. I think she was ready to give Sophie her diploma on the spot."

"Well," Sophie said by way of apology, "I've had more experience than most people, working in the repair shop." She didn't know why she was trying to downplay her achievements, other than that she'd never expected to be so vastly better at something than everyone else in her class. But part of her brain was screaming at her, telling her she should brag a little more, let Jasper see how fabulous she was.

It was as if Jasper could read her mind. "If you're half as good as Ryka says you are, I'd love to see some of your samples."

Before Sophie could reply, Eryka laughed. "Samples! It won't be long before we're selling Sophie's finished work in the gallery!"

"That's at least a few years off," Sophie replied. Then, deciding to own her talent, she added. "If you can afford me." Sophie's joke broke the ice, and suddenly she found herself fully immersed in conversation with the pair. Jasper, it turned out, was incredibly easy to talk to, especially once she got him talking about architecture.

"I know, I know," he admitted, "It doesn't have the prestige of weaving. But I love the idea of creating sacred spaces for the world's most incredible tapestries. Maybe if I'm lucky," he continued with a grin, "you'd be willing to grace one of my buildings with something of yours one day."

Chapter 7
East Lawn

As the semester wore on, Sophie found herself looking for opportunities to see Jasper. He had been attentive at the party, stepping away from his friends to check that Sophie was having a good time, and even offered to walk her back to her dorm when Eryka mysteriously melted away with one of Jasper's classmates.

But when Jasper failed to attempt even the slightest hint of a goodnight kiss, Sophie worried that she had mistaken his interest for an older brotherly concern that simply extended to his sister's roommate. They bumped into each other from time to time, but to Sophie's frustration, he remained polite, yet seemingly uninterested, in each interaction.

Eryka hadn't speculated on whether or not her brother had any interest in Sophie. Not that Sophie had asked. She assumed that Eryka wanted to avoid any awkwardness that might come from a relationship between her brother and her roommate. And Vivienne was no help. After Sophie chided her for pining over Eryka, Vivienne made it clear that she would not be discussing any relationships with Sophie.

The three of them settled into an easy tension as roommates. They went to classes, meals, and the pub together, arguing over their classes and helping each other with homework, but personal lives, including families and relationships, were off-limits.

Sophie never had close female friends her age before. At home, she mostly hung around with Rush, and there was a fairly large age gap between her and her sisters, so she wasn't sure if this was standard in the way girls interacted, or the product of her crush on Jasper and Vivienne's obvious and unreciprocated feelings for Eryka.

This made it all the more surprising when Vivienne invited — or rather insisted — that Sophie come home with her for winter break. Sophie had hoped for an invitation from Eryka, but whether she didn't want to run afoul of Vivienne, who could be unbearable when she didn't get her way, or if she was keen to keep Sophie away from her brother, the invitation didn't come.

And there was no way Sophie was going home over break. Rush wrote that he would be traveling with his new college buddies, and Sophie couldn't stomach an icy couple of weeks with her mother, with no one but her siblings for company. While Sophie had received long missives from her father and sisters, her mother hadn't written at all. Her father insisted she was busy in the repair shop, but it felt like she was wallowing in jealousy for her daughter. With the alternative being a boring and possibly tense trip home, Sophie accepted Vivienne's invitation with a mixture of trepidation and curiosity.

On the first morning of winter break, Eryka helped Vivienne rehang the tapestry of her family's estate. True to her word, Vivienne had taken it down the moment they'd all settled into the room.

"How are you and Jasper getting home?" Sophie asked Eryka, trying to keep her voice light, but hoping Jasper would stop by to pick Eryka up. She was still angling for any excuse to see him, to make conversation that would help him see how dazzling she was.

"Through the museums," Eryka replied, a hint of knowing in her voice. "Jasper is meeting me there."

"Oh," said Sophie, trying and failing to hide her obvious disappointment. "Well, have a good break."

"You too," Eryka smiled, giving her a hug and whispering in her ear, "Have fun with Princess."

Before Sophie could reply that she was sure it would be fine, Vivienne stamped her foot, pouted, and insisted they get going. The moment Sophie grabbed her bag, Vivienne shoved her through the tapestry.

Sophie blinked into the cold grey air as she stepped out from the tapestry, Vivienne at her heel.

If Sophie had been awed by the building in the tapestry, it was nothing to what loomed before her now. A perfectly symmetrical building rose from a sweeping lawn and hedges that, even devoid of leaves for the winter, were perfectly manicured. The manor was made of stone, but not the rough-hewn stone of the buildings at East Lawn. Instead, these blocks were so straight and even they looked like they'd been carved with a ruler, their faces ground so smooth they were practically polished. Windows paraded across the front in two rows, though the house seemed tall enough to contain four or five stories. A massive triangular portico topped the center of the building, and behind it were at least six chimneys, also lined up in two neat rows.

The full extent of Vivienne's wealth hit Sophie with the force of one of those massive stone blocks. Forget Sophie's house, the whole of Honyeoke Falls, including the museum, would fit inside. What had she gotten herself into?

"Why are you being so slow?" Vivienne huffed, grabbing Sophie by the wrist and dragging her towards the manor. They crunched up the gravel walkway towards an imposing wooden door. Vivienne pushed it open and they emerged in a grand entryway with a sweeping staircase framing either side, heading to an upper balcony, most of which was obscured by a massive chandelier made from crystal and wrought iron. Every place where wall met ceiling was trimmed with elaborate molding. Before Sophie could express her amazement, a stern woman appeared, dressed in an impeccable uniform with her hair pulled back into a severe bun.

"Your father is in his study," she informed Vivienne, giving no inclination that Sophie was even there.

"Thanks, Mrs. Winthrop," Vivienne replied, surprising Sophie by giving the woman a quick peck on the cheek. "Tell Daddy I'll see him in a bit." She dropped her bag onto the carpet and gestured for Sophie to do the same, before grabbing her wrist and dragging her through the entryway. She pulled Sophie past the stairway and pushed open another set of heavy doors.

As the doors swung open, Sophie gasped. Instead of a hallway, they were standing in a massive gallery, one befitting a museum rather than a house. On the warm white walls, which stretched upwards towards an ornamented ceiling dotted with frosted skylights, hung the largest collection of tapestries Sophie had ever seen outside a major museum — even the one in Honyeoke Falls didn't have this many — their colors reflected on the gleaming parquet floor below.

"Wow," Sophie murmured in awe. "Are these your mother's?"

Vivienne was already halfway across the room and didn't realize Sophie hadn't been following her until she heard the question. She turned impatiently, her hands on her hips. "These?" she gestured around with her head. "No, they're all older. Daddy was a collector before he met Mum."

"But where are your mother's?" It was a little strange that none of Sabrina's tapestries had been given pride of place, unless the house was hiding some other, even larger gallery. Given the size of the manor, that wouldn't have been out of the question.

Vivienne shrugged. "Daddy put them in storage after she died. It was too painful. Now, come on!" She turned again, then disappeared into a tapestry at the far end of the room.

It featured a lush jungle, teeming with every shade of green, framing a bright blue sea and clear sky. Sophie hesitated, taking in the wildlife hiding inside the foliage — she thought she spotted a bright macaw and a family of monkeys — but Vivienne's voice called again, impatient and muffled from beyond the tapestry, and Sophie resigned herself and stepped through.

"I've missed this," Vivienne shouted, laughing and shedding clothes as she ran down the beach. Her naked frame splashed into the waves before she dove effortlessly below the water. After a few moments, her head popped back up and she beckoned for Sophie to join her.

Sophie hesitated again.

"Come on," Vivienne insisted. "There's nobody here to see you. It's a private island."

Of course it was. But it wasn't that. She cast around for a good reason. Finally, she shouted back at Vivienne with a rush of shame and embarrassment, "I can't swim."

"What?" Vivienne splashed towards her, looking shocked. "Don't you ever go to the beach?"

Sophie shook her head. Swimming had never been a priority. There were plenty of lakes near where she grew up, but they were freezing most of the time. Sophie vaguely remembered visiting one through a tapestry her mother had found. When she dipped her toes in the water, the cold was such a shock she flat-out refused to go in any further. Even at a young age, Sophie was stubborn, and her parents, no doubt busy with the other children, hadn't bothered to push her. The tapestry hadn't stayed long. Her mother flipped it, and after that, the family gallery was filled with scenes of woods and mountains and gardens, but no water, save the occasional shallow stream.

"Do you want to learn?" It was obvious Vivienne was trying to be polite, but Sophie could see her longing to escape back into the water.

"No thanks," Sophie responded, watching the look of relief cross Vivienne's face. "You go, I'll just explore around the shore."

Vivienne flung her wet hair behind her, giving Sophie a playful spray, and dove back into the clear blue water. Sophie kicked off her shoes, rolled up her pant legs, and stepped to the edge of the water. It was surprisingly warm. They must be somewhere much further south. Maybe she would let Vivienne teach her how to swim. Not today, but perhaps at some point over break. She had a feeling Vivienne would be returning to this tapestry a lot.

Sophie walked along the water's edge but quickly grew bored. She abandoned the beach in favor of the lush vegetation, intrigued by the foliage, and amused, if not slightly startled, every time a monkey skittered across her path. But even that wore thin. With a backward glance at Vivienne, bobbing in the ocean and seemingly in no hurry to get out, Sophie stepped back into the gallery. She'd rather investigate the other tapestries on display than wander the beach.

The hall was dim after the bright light of the beach, and Sophie sat on a bench to brush the sand from her feet while her eyes adjusted. Another reason her family didn't have any beach tapestries. She could only imagine her father's frustration at six kids constantly dragging in sand.

As she stood to make her way around the room, she realized she wasn't alone. Someone was standing at the far end of the room, watching her.

"You must be Sophie." His voice was warm, and with his blonde hair and pale skin, he could only be Vivienne's brother. But while Vivienne came across as bright and perky, his look was more reserved. But somehow that only served to make him more attractive, standing there in slacks and a heathered sweater, the sleeves pushed up slightly to reveal the cuffs of his button-down shirt — and a hint of his forearms — underneath.

Sophie stood there, mouth slightly open, unsure of what to say. Vivienne never said anything about a brother.

"I'm Holden," he said, striding forward to shake her hand. "I take it Vivienne never mentioned I existed." Sophie felt a wash of relief that he was taking her unawareness of his existence in good stride. "Where is my sister, anyway?"

Sophie, still in shock, nodded towards the tapestry at the far wall.

Holden laughed. "Of course. She loves that place. She might be in there for hours."

Finally finding her voice, Sophie replied, "I had a feeling. I was bored. I can't sw..." She trailed off, not sure why she didn't want to admit to Holden that she couldn't swim. "I wanted to see what other tapestries were here."

"Vivienne mentioned you were a boffin."

The term caught Sophie off guard. "A what?"

"A boffin." He repeated. "Sorry, I believe you Americans call it a nerd. Vivienne said you were tapestry mad, even for someone in school studying tapestry."

Sophie flushed. How did he know so much about her when Vivienne hadn't even mentioned he existed? She hated being on such unequal footing. "Would you like company?" Holden continued, "Or would you rather be alone?"

Sophie wasn't sure which she wanted. Her curiosity pulled her in two directions. She wanted to explore the tapestries, but she was intrigued by Holden. There was a twinge of longing behind the proper English breeding as if he carried some kind of secret waiting to be unlocked. And while he wasn't her usual type, there was no denying he was extremely handsome.

Holden took her silence for polite refusal. "Of course," he responded, taking her hand and kissing it lightly. "I'll see you at dinner, Sophie O'Toole." He winked and strode from the gallery. It took several minutes before Sophie finally turned her attention back to the tapestries.

Sophie had time to study every tapestry in the hall, noting the use of color and construction, before Vivienne emerged from the tapestry, glistening wet and only half-dressed.

"Feel better," Sophie asked, as Vivienne shook out her hair, dripping saltwater over the wood floor.

"Much," Vivienne replied. "I needed that."

"You could've come home at any point during the semester." Sophie reminded her.

At first, Vivienne didn't respond. "We've got to get cleaned up before dinner," she said finally, changing the subject. "Come on, I'll show you to your room."

When the two of them arrived for dinner, Holden was already seated at the head of the long table, which could have easily sat twenty on its heavy upholstered chairs. With dark wood wainscoting and tapestries suspended over the papered upper walls, the dining room wouldn't have looked out of place a hundred years ago. Sophie had just registered three place settings, chargers topped with lacy napkins and surrounded by glass goblets and heavy gilt silverware, when Vivienne spoke up.

"Isn't Daddy joining us?" she asked Mrs. Winthrop, who walked in carrying three bowls of soup on an ornate silver tray.

Holden answered. "You honestly thought he would join us?" His tone was harsh, but he smiled at Sophie as he stood and pulled out a chair for her.

"Your father is in his study," Mrs. Winthrop replied, placing Sophie's soup in front of her without acknowledging her presence. Something about Sophie seemed to offend her sensibilities. "He requested that you see him before you turn in for the night."

Vivienne gave a small pout but turned to Sophie with a smile. "Daddy's very busy. Running a tapestry manufactory is no easy task."

Holden responded with a sour expression. "Exactly. It takes a lot of work to drive your wife's reputation into the ground."

"Stop that," Vivienne hissed, her cheeks getting red. "You know he's doing his best."

"His best," Holden sneered. "Pumping out piss-poor versions of her work. It's a joke."

"He respects her legacy," Vivienne was practically shouting now. Sophie had never seen her like this. "That's why he wants to make her work available to more people."

"Respects her legacy?" Holden's voice rose to match Vivienne's. "If he respects her so much, why doesn't he have her tapestries on display in the house? Why did he immediately change the name of the company to H. J. Morris and Co.?"

"You know it was too painful for him!"

"Bollocks," Holden responded.

"Wait," Sophie interjected, putting together the pieces. "Morris... Does that mean your father is related to..."

Holden gave a harsh laugh. "He wishes. There's never been any proof that he's related, but he throws the name around as if he is. Just another convenient way to distance himself from Mum's legacy." He glared at Vivienne as he continued, "The only difference is, he doesn't have the rights to make terrible knock-offs of dear old William's designs."

Vivienne opened her mouth to argue again, her cheeks still bright pink, then shrugged and turned to her soup. "I'm starving after such a long swim."

The rest of dinner continued in awkward silence. Sophie ate slowly, watching Holden and Vivienne, who refused to look at one another. The difference in opinion they held of their father was startling. Perhaps Holden, being a few years older than Vivienne, was more aware of the relationship between his parents before their mother died. Or maybe Vivienne was just a quintessential daddy's girl.

But that didn't make sense either. Vivienne acted as if her father hung the moon, but she hadn't made a single visit home during the semester, and she opted to jump through a tapestry before bothering to say hello. Perhaps this was just normal, upper-class British family dynamics, but hopefully, Sophie thought, tucking into the chicken Mrs. Winthrop had wordlessly placed before her, it wouldn't be the tone for the entirety of her stay.

Hours later, Sophie lay awake, enveloped in a strange silence. The only noise was the wind whipping across the outer walls of the manor. She had never slept in a room by herself. Perhaps when she was little, but her memories only stretched as far back as Delilah's crib on the opposite wall from her bed.

Growing up in cramped quarters had made the transition to dormitory life, and two talkative roommates, much easier. Many nights, Sophie drifted off while Vivienne and Eryka were still trading playful barbs.

But now she was alone, in the largest bedroom she'd ever encountered. Even the heavily embroidered curtains of the four-poster bed couldn't fool her into thinking the space was cozy. She got out of bed, pacing the room. On one wall hung a tapestry, a dark and moody composition showing a forest. It would have been creepy even in the daylight, but Sophie knew better than to go wandering the woods at night. To add insult to injury, it was poorly made, with clunky threads and lazy color transitions. Clearly, Mr. Morris relegated his lesser tapestries to the guest rooms. The details of its construction hardly held her attention. She slipped on a dressing gown — something she would never have felt compelled to don anywhere else, but its presence at the end of the bed made it seem almost mandatory — and padded from the room.

Sophie wished for something to light the way in the dark hallway. A flashlight, or perhaps a candle. That seemed the sort of thing she should have to wander the halls of an old manor. She thought vaguely of heading back to the main hall to spend more time with the tapestries when she noticed light creeping out from underneath another door. Without thinking, she headed in that direction but was startled all the same when the door opened and Holden stepped out.

His face broke into a grin. "A fellow insomniac, I see."

Sophie hesitated. She usually didn't have trouble sleeping. It was just this strange, quiet castle that was keeping her awake. "No," she started. "I just, um, thought I'd go back to the tapestry gallery."

Holden eyed her empty hands with a slight smile. "In the dark?"

"Well, I figured I'd find a light switch when I got down there."

"And I don't suppose you want company this time either?"

She tried and failed to suppress a small grin. "You can come. I was hoping you'd be able to answer some of my questions."

"Of course," he said, smiling back at her. Then he hesitated for a moment, staring at Sophie as if weighing a very important decision. "Actually, I have a better idea," he said finally, giving a small nod. "Come on, there's something I want to show you."

"What is it?" Sophie asked. "I really was hoping to spend more time in the gallery."

"Trust me," Holden grinned. "This is better."

Sophie couldn't imagine anything better than a private tapestry gallery, but she followed him down the stairs, through the entryway, down a few hallways, and another flight of stairs, before he finally paused beside a small wooden door.

As he pulled an old key out of his pocket and fitted it into an iron lock, he turned to Sophie conspiratorially, "Don't tell Vivienne about this. Or my father, for that matter. Not that you're likely to see him while you're here."

Sophie nodded, hardly able to contain her curiosity. What could be hiding in here that required a lock, a key, and such secrecy?

As the door swung open, the enormity of the space shocked her. She had expected a much smaller room. Instead, it was almost the size of the gallery upstairs, but with lower ceilings and rough-hewn walls, as if it had been carved out of the bedrock. On every one of those walls, lit by a series of sconces, were the most exquisite tapestries Sophie had ever seen.

"Your mother's?" she asked, in barely a whisper, her face filled with awe.

Holden smiled at her obvious delight, clearly relishing his decision to bring her into this secret gallery. "Yes," he replied. "Father put them all in storage after she died. It was like watching her die all over again."

Sophie tore her gaze from the tapestries to study the sadness in Holden's face as he went on. "I asked so many questions about them that eventually he forbade me from talking about them. But a few years later, Mrs. Winthrop showed me where they were. Well, she accidentally let it slip one day. And then I found this hall no one was using — the key was just stuck in the lock — and knew I had to put them back on display."

This was a side of Mrs. Winthrop Sophie had yet to see. It seemed an unlikely coincidence that she would just "leave" the key in the door.

Holden continued. "I've never shown these to anyone. But I knew you would appreciate them."

Sophie felt a sudden flush, a mix of embarrassment and gratitude, and turned back towards the tapestries. "They're stunning. I've never seen anything like them..." Even as she said it, a tapestry hanging in the far corner caught her eye. Fluffy clouds swirled above a tiny village, surrounded by fields of lavender. The angle and time of day were different, but there was no mistaking it. This was the same scene as the tapestry Mrs. Rigo had secured for the museum back home. Did this mean that tapestry was also designed by...

Sophie let out an audible gasp, and Holden followed her gaze towards the tapestry. "Incredible, isn't it?" He walked towards it, while Sophie followed, trying to keep her breath steady. "This is the village Mum grew up in. It was one of her favorite motifs."

As she got closer, it was unmistakable how similar it was to the tapestry at the museum in Honyeoke Falls. The shifts in color, the swirling sky, the attention to detail. How could she not have realized the tapestry Rush showed her was also a Sabrina Maxwell? Had Rush mentioned that and she just didn't register? Did Mrs. Rigo not know? Rush said she was still researching provenance. Surely, she must have suspected. Otherwise, why would she have worked so hard to secure it?

Sophie was suddenly aware that Holden was watching her taking in the tapestry, the same way Rush had done that day. She stepped closer, trying to move from his direct line of sight, but he followed suit. His voice was still soft as he asked, "Would you like to go in?"

"No." Sophie's reply came out much stronger than she intended. She tried to cover up her awkwardness as Holden gave her a questioning look. Something told her it wasn't a good idea to walk through a tapestry that was potentially connected to one in her hometown. She might bump into someone she knew wandering the village. And was it even legal for a small public museum in the US to own a tapestry that transported you to a village in England? After all, they had no passport control. She didn't want to get Mrs. Rigo in trouble.

Holden was still staring at her, looking confused by her outburst.

"It's just that... I want..." she stammered, "... to take them all in before I go through any of them."

Holden accepted her explanation without further question. "Spoken like a true boffin." He gestured towards the rest of the room, sweeping his hand and giving a low bow. Sophie couldn't help but chuckle.

She moved from tapestry to tapestry, stepping back to take in the full composition before moving forward to grasp the details of its construction. She ran her fingers gently along the surface, feeling the texture of the weave, and a few times she peered so close her nose broke the plane. Holden, for the most part kept quiet, only responding when Sophie asked a question, but it was clear from his responses that he was bursting with pride for his mother and a font of knowledge about her working process.

Sophie could have stayed for hours, absorbing every detail of the tapestries, but the more she looked, the heavier her eyes grew. Despite her best attempts to stifle it, a yawn slipped out.

"Well I know you're not bored by the tapestries," Holden teased. "I guess you're not as much of a night owl as I thought."

Sophie started to apologize, but Holden just smiled and gestured for them to leave. He walked her to her door, then, to Sophie's surprise, leaned in and kissed her on the cheek. "Good night, Sophie O'Toole," he whispered in her ear. He was halfway down the hall to his room before she could even think to respond.

Chapter 8
Weddlesmoore

All too soon, Vivienne banged on Sophie's door, shouting that breakfast was ready. As they made their way into the dining room, Sophie was disappointed to see only two place settings.

"No Holden?" she asked, trying to keep her voice casual, and looking across the room to avoid Vivienne's prying gaze on her tired face.

"You look exhausted. Rough night?" Suspicion dripped from Vivienne's voice.

Sophie tried to stifle a yawn and shrugged. She couldn't share anything about bumping into Holden last night that wouldn't risk giving away the secret room full of Sabrina's tapestries. "Couldn't sleep. Strange house," she explained, making a beeline for the table and the pot of tea.

Mrs. Winthrop chose that moment to decide that Sophie did in fact exist, and as she entered the room, she answered her question. "Holden is never up this early, bloody night owl." Her eyes twinkled in Sophie's direction, and she wondered if Mrs. Winthrop suspected something about her late-night wanderings. "And even when he's awake, he takes breakfast in his room these days." Then she added, almost as an afterthought, "Can you blame him? Who'd want to eat alone in this blasted dining room every day?"

"Your dad doesn't join him?" Sophie asked Vivienne.

But again, it was Mrs. Winthrop who responded. "Like two ships passing. You'd hardly even guess those two were related."

"What does Holden do?" Sophie asked, her curiosity getting the better of her. She knew he was older than Vivienne, but she wasn't sure if he was still in school. Mrs. Winthrop's comment made it sound like he lived in the manor full-time.

Vivienne snorted into her toast. "Fuck all." This caused Mrs. Winthrop to give a quick, scolding "Vivienne!"

"Sorry," Vivienne replied, "But you know as well as I do, he doesn't do anything. He should be helping Daddy with the business, but he just stays in his room, brooding over Mum's murder."

"What?" This didn't sound like the Holden Sophie had met. True, there was a lingering sadness in him that Vivienne didn't seem to have, but he had been so animated when showing Sophie his mother's tapestries.

Vivienne rolled her eyes. "Oh, you have no idea. He graduated last spring with a pointless degree in forensic science. Like that was going to make it easier to solve a sixteen-year-old murder. I don't even know why Daddy allowed it. What a waste. He never intended to get a job. He just sits in his room, looking over the old case files."

Sophie stared at Vivienne, her jaw practically on the floor. Vivienne had never gone into any details about her mother's murder.

"It's not like there's even anything to solve," Vivienne continued. "Kidnapping gone wrong. They arrested some guy. But Holden still seems to think there was some sort of cover-up." Vivienne shrugged and turned back to her breakfast, and Sophie decided not to push the issue any further.

"So," she said to Vivienne, careful to keep her voice light, "What are we going to do today?"

As she suspected, Vivienne wanted to go back to the beach tapestry. Sophie reluctantly agreed, but only because she knew better than to argue with Vivienne. Even when they weren't at her house, Vivienne usually got her way.

"Let me go grab my bag," Sophie told her. If she was going to be stuck on the beach all day, she was at least bringing some entertainment. A book, her sketchbook perhaps. She still wasn't ready to let Vivienne teach her how to swim.

"Fine, but hurry." Vivienne stamped her foot impatiently.

By returning upstairs, Sophie hoped she might bump into Holden. She couldn't quite figure out what her fascination was, but she had to admit that she enjoyed his company far more than Vivienne's. There was no sliver of light under his door, so she hastily slammed a few items in her bag and went back downstairs, where Vivienne dragged her back through the tapestry.

Sophie couldn't fathom how anyone could spend as much time in the water as Vivienne. As the morning wore on, Vivienne played and splashed in the ocean, looking more like a delighted little girl than the impatient young woman she usually was. Sophie tried to read, but her eyes kept sliding out of focus, and eventually, she gave up and took a nap on the sand. She didn't know how much time passed, but when she woke up, Vivienne was still in the water.

A sharp voice from behind Sophie caused her to jump. "Ladies, afternoon tea is served." Mrs. Winthrop looked out of place, standing on a tropical beach in her crisp uniform.

Sophie called for Vivienne, and the two of them headed back into the hall after Mrs. Winthrop, who shot Vivienne dirty looks as she dripped saltwater in her wake.

They took tea not in the dining room, but in a study lined with books. Sophie wondered if it belonged to Mr. Morris, and whether or not he might be joining them when

Holden strode into the room. Sophie was surprised by how excited she was to see him.

"Showing Sophie Mother's study, are you?" He questioned his sister, grabbing a cup and settling into a chair opposite Sophie.

Sophie flushed with private embarrassment, taking in the titles of the books. Of course this was Sabrina's study. She didn't know much about Mr. Morris, but after seeing her tapestries, it seemed obvious now that all the life and energy on the shelves had belonged to Sabrina.

Holden continued, looking at Vivienne, "I didn't realize that you even bothered to come in here?"

"You aren't the only one who still thinks about Mum," Vivienne retorted, flushing with anger once again.

"Could've fooled me."

Sophie was taken aback by how cruel Holden was to his sister. This seemed beyond the kind of playful banter she was used to with her brothers. There was real malice in the way Holden spoke those words.

"I don't have to take this," Vivienne huffed, and she turned on her heel, grabbed a handful of sandwiches, and stormed from the room.

Sophie was surprised to see Holden break into a grin. He turned to Sophie. "Well now that she's gone…"

"You didn't have to be mean to her just to get me alone." Sophie shot back, and Holden's face fell. Before he had a chance to utter an apology, Sophie stormed from the room.

She found Vivienne sitting on a bench in the gallery. She hastily wiped her eyes when she saw Sophie enter the room. Sophie sat down beside her and put an arm around her shoulder. "He's a jerk," Sophie said, even though she didn't fully believe it. Her feelings about Holden were even more confusing than she'd thought possible an hour ago. But he'd certainly been a jerk to Vivienne.

"He doesn't get it," Vivienne looked at Sophie through watery eyes. "How am I supposed to think about someone I barely remember? The study is all of hers I have." With a pang of guilt, Sophie thought of the room full of Sabrina's tapestries. What right did Holden have to hide them from his sister? But what right did Sophie have to spill Holden's secret? So she said nothing, and let Vivienne continue. "Just because I don't go in it when he's in there doesn't mean I never go in it. And, shit," Vivienne stood up suddenly, flinging Sophie's arm off of her, her sadness transforming to anger once again. "He has no idea what it's like to be at a school where all anyone cares about is that you're Sabrina Maxwell's daughter. I have to think about her all the time. I can't escape it."

She stopped pacing and sat back down, her head in her hands. "Sometimes I wish I'd taken the easy route like him. I never should have bothered with tapestry school."

"Yeah, but then you'd never have met me." Sophie joked, and Vivienne returned a weak smile. "Or Eryka," Sophie added, giving Vivienne a wink and bumped her shoulder.

Vivienne managed a weak chuckle. "Fat lot of good that got me." Then she turned to Sophie, with an attempt to get her usually bubbly composure back, but not totally succeeding. "Sorry," she apologized before bursting out again. "This place makes me mental." It made sense now, why Vivienne hadn't returned home all semester, and why she immediately set off for the beach.

Vivienne turned towards the tapestry at the end of the hall. "Want to get out of here?"

"Please no, not the beach again." Sophie couldn't help herself but was relieved when Vivienne laughed. "The pub. Shopping. Anything but the beach!"

"I never thought I'd see the day when you wanted to go shopping," Vivienne laughed.

"Turns out all you had to do was make me sit on a beach all day."

"I won't torture you anymore," Vivienne replied. "Come on, I know the perfect pub." And she led Sophie towards a tapestry on the other side of the room, a bustling street scene filled with shops and, by the looks of it, several pubs.

It was late when they got back from the pub, and Sophie was willing to admit she'd had a good time. It felt like they were back at school, albeit without Eryka, as she and Vivienne shared a few pints and teased each other about who was checking them out. Vivienne kept eyeing a pretty young woman at the end of the bar, but politely declined when she offered to buy her a drink.

"I thought you had needs," Sophie joked as the girl walked away, obviously disappointed.

"You're my guest," Vivienne retorted. Sophie was glad to see her usual perky energy had returned. "I'm not going to ditch you for the first piece of ass I find at the pub."

"Ah, I see," Sophie joked back. "Holding out for someone better. Just remember," Sophie said, downing the rest of her pint, "I won't put out no matter how many drinks you buy me."

"You're not my type," Vivienne flashed back, signaling the bartender for another round.

Now that they were back at the manor, Sophie practically had to carry Vivienne up the stairs. She flopped around, moaning dramatically about how much she missed Eryka, if she could only make Eryka see.

"Shush," Sophie hissed. "You'll wake the whole house."

"It's fine," Vivienne shouted, flinging her arm into Sophie's face. "Daddy sleeps on the other side of the manor and Holden never goes to bed this early." It was well past midnight, not what most people would call early.

"What about Mrs. Winthrop?"

"The old bat has her own cottage on the other side of the property. And the rest of the staff don't live here." Of course there was more staff, Sophie should have realized it took more than Mrs. Winthrop to maintain a property of this size, "Most tapestry in from town every morning."

Sophie helped Vivienne to her room and was disappointed to see that, despite what Vivienne said, there was no light shining under Holden's door. He must have gone to bed early. Or perhaps he had gone out, Sophie thought, with another wave of disappointment.

But she had barely started to undress when there was a knock at her door. She opened it a crack to see Holden's smiling face.

"I'm still mad at you," she muttered, attempting to shut the door, but Holden jammed his foot into the opening.

"I know," he said, turning serious. "And I'm sorry. I wasn't trying to be mean. Fighting is the only way that Vivienne and I know how to get along. It's nothing personal."

Sophie raised her eyebrow. "Well, she certainly took it personally."

"I see that now. And I am sorry. I'll apologize to Vivienne in the morning too."

Sophie's expression softened a little, and he gave a slight smile. "But I thought you wouldn't be able to resist spending a little more time with Mum's tapestries." He held up the old key.

"Does that mean you're going to let me go without you?"

"Not a chance," he replied, and she was happy to see a trace of disappointment on his face at the thought that she was more interested in the tapestries than him. "Besides, how would you find the room again without me?"

"I have an excellent sense of direction," Sophie retorted. "But I supposed I'll let you escort me, Mr. Maxwell." Then, she added, "on one condition."

"Name it," he said, his face hopeful.

"No more fighting with Vivienne, at least not while I'm here."

"Done," he agreed, reaching out to shake her hand. When she grabbed his in return, he pulled her out the door and down towards the tapestries.

The next morning, Sophie was surprised to see Holden, not Vivienne, seated at the breakfast table. "I thought you didn't get up this early," Sophie teased, settling into the seat across from him.

"By the way Vivienne sounded when the two of you got back from the pub last night, I doubt she'll be up anytime soon. And I couldn't let our guest breakfast alone."

"How chivalrous of you," Sophie replied with a dry smile. Holden made no mention of their late-night trip to see Sabrina's tapestries, which once again ended with a polite kiss on the cheek as he deposited her at her bedroom door several hours later. She flushed lightly thinking about the feel of his lips on her skin. But at that moment, Vivienne entered the room, looking more than a little worse for wear.

"How are you feeling?" Sophie asked, as Vivienne winced, her hand shielding her face as she slid into the seat next to Holden.

"I think she looks lovely," Holden responded, turning and kissing his sister on the cheek. For some reason, Sophie felt let down by this show of brotherly affection.

"What's the catch?" Vivienne eyed him. "I know I look awful."

"I can't lie," Holden replied. "You look bloody terrible. But I was trying to make up for yesterday."

It wasn't quite the apology Sophie had in mind, but Vivienne leaned over and gave him a quick squeeze. "Forgiven," she mumbled, surveying breakfast through bloodshot eyes.

Holden handed her a plate of toast. "You'll feel better once you eat something."

"I seriously doubt that," Vivienne replied.

"What are you ladies up to today?" he asked.

"Please," Sophie begged, "not the beach again."

"Fine," Vivienne replied. "But only because the light hurts my eyes." Then she added, "But we're not going to the pub either."

Sophie turned to Holden. "Any ideas?"

"Why don't we take Sophie on a tour of the grounds?"

"We?" Vivienne asked him.

"Well you don't seem fit to give her a proper tour."

"We'll see about that," Vivienne said, regaining a bit of her usual spunk. "Just give me at least an hour to rejoin the land of the living."

While she waited for Vivienne to freshen up, Sophie wandered back into Sabrina's study. She thought Holden might join, but when he didn't, she was happy to spend time in the space alone. It was like stepping inside the mind of a master. There were books full of botanical illustrations, books on color theory, and books on weaving techniques. Sophie pulled as many as she could carry off the wall and settled into a chair.

In the corner of the study, an array of notebooks had been haphazardly jammed into a shelf. Unable to ignore them, Sophie got up to examine them and discovered they were Sabrina's diaries and journals. Sketches for tapestry ideas mingled with dye recipes and notes on the progress of specific tapestries, including the weavers who worked on them. Sophie read the women's names eagerly, imagining herself working in a place like that someday. But she also found herself flipping through the pages at a quickening pace, looking for any mention of the tapestry now hanging in her town, and its companion piece in Holden's secret gallery. What a coup it would be for Mrs. Rigo's research if Sophie could share more details.

As she flipped through Sabrina's later notebooks, pages seemed to be missing. Sabrina had meticulously dated each entry, but days or weeks would go by without anything, and occasionally a fragment of page lingered in the spine. Sophie turned to the date of the last entry, and after doing some quick math, determined it was almost a year before Sabrina died. She couldn't find a single notebook, or even a single entry, from the last few months of her life.

"Ready to go?" Vivienne burst into the room, remarkably perky compared to her state an hour ago, and Sophie startled, hastily jamming the notebooks back into the shelf.

Holden entered the room behind Vivienne, giving a quick glance at where Sophie was standing. "Find anything good?" he asked.

"I was just—" Sophie stammered, wondering if she'd intruded where she shouldn't have, but then realized Holden was smiling. "Your mother's books are incredible."

"Quite the collection, right?" Holden acknowledged, while Vivienne just rolled her eyes, turning to Holden.

"I told you she was a boffin."

—#—

Despite having to bundle up against the cold, the three of them had a lovely day wandering the grounds. Sophie had no idea the estate was so large, though she shouldn't have been that surprised based on the size of the house. There were manicured gardens, wooded areas, and wide moors. It didn't get any more British than this. Vivienne and Holden pointed out Mrs. Winthrop's cabin and a little playhouse from when they were kids.

"You actually went outside?" Sophie teased Vivienne. "I figured you just flitted from tapestry to tapestry your entire childhood."

"That," Vivienne said, with a pointed look at her brother, "was Holden. I found them all pretty boring until Mrs. Winthrop showed me the beach and taught me how to swim."

"And then she never went out to the grounds again," Holden finished.

"Can you blame me? Who'd want to spend time in the grey English mist when you can swim in a tropical sea?"

Holden opened his mouth, presumably to needle his sister, then closed it again. True to his promise to Sophie, he refrained from picking another fight.

—#—

After a hardy dinner, where again Mr. Morris did not join them, Vivienne, her hangover seemingly forgotten, convinced them to return to the pub. "You don't have a choice," she said to Holden. "You've got to stop spending all your time cooped up in this place. You'll go mad. You're practically there already."

Holden didn't argue, and Sophie was glad. Now that the pair of them had stopped fighting, she was happy to have another companion besides Vivienne. Holden's calm balanced out some of Vivienne's perkiness in much the same way Eryka did when the three of them were at school.

They were partway through their second round of pints when Sophie saw Vivienne's eyes dart towards the pretty young woman from the day before. The girl glanced at them quickly and then looked away, slightly embarrassed.

"Just go," Sophie told her. "It's fine."

"But—" Vivienne started to protest.

"Go," Holden added. "I'll make sure *your* guest makes it home safely."

"What a hardship for you," Sophie teased. "Having to entertain some random American."

Vivienne gave a questioning look between the pair of them, before throwing a longing look at the girl. "Fine," she replied. "I've had enough of you two anyway."

They watched her bounce off towards the girl, who seemed only too happy to let Vivienne buy her a drink.

"What should we do now?" Holden asked as Sophie drained her pint. "Another round?" Vivienne and the girl had absconded to a more private booth at the back of the pub.

"I was actually thinking…" Sophie started slowly.

"You want to go back to my mother's tapestries?" Holden laughed, before tacking on, "You really are a boffin."

Sophie nodded, pleased he had read her mind. She wanted to look at them again, now that she had insight into Sabrina's process.

"Should we tell Vivienne we're leaving?" Sophie asked, hesitating for a moment, unsure if Vivienne might feel obligated to leave with them, ruining her chance of going back to the tapestries, at least until Vivienne went to bed.

Holden glanced over towards a booth, where Vivienne and the woman were now sitting so close they practically blended into one person. "I think she'll figure it out." Then he added, "Eventually."

Once they were back in the tapestry gallery, Sophie did a few laps around the room, noticing areas she had seen in Sabrina's sketches, or trying to remember notes about colors or weaving patterns. Like the previous two nights, Holden hung back, watching her take it all in.

There was a long bench in the center of the room, and Sophie sat, gesturing for Holden to join her.

"Will you tell me about her?" she asked.

Holden's face lit up, and he looked even more like Vivienne. "She was beautiful." He started. "And so happy, always laughing. Always excited about everything. Except when she—" he shook his head, as if trying to expel a painful memory, then regained his smile and went on. "She used to take me to her workshop—"

"Vivienne too?" Sophie interjected.

"No, she was too little. She stayed behind with Mrs. Winthrop." It was obvious now that Vivienne had spent much of her childhood under the care of Mrs. Winthrop. No wonder she showed Vivienne the tropical tapestry and taught her how to swim. She probably got sick of spending her days out in some drafty old playhouse, while Vivienne bossed her through endless tea parties.

Sophie realized Holden was waiting for her to prompt him. "What was the workshop like?"

"It was incredible," he said, all too happy to continue. Sophie wondered if he had shared these memories with anyone else. "All these looms, shelves and shelves of yarn, organized by color. I remember the women there always seemed so carefree, like it was hardly a job. Listening to music as they worked, singing along. They would show me what they were doing, give me little treats."

Sophie could picture the weavers fawning over a little blonde Holden.

"Then Mum would bring me into her studio. It was filled with paints and paper, and there was this whole wall covered with inspiration and ideas and designs in progress. I would just stare at it for ages."

Sophie found herself suddenly jealous of Holden's childhood, to be immersed in such a world. It made her mother's repair shop pale in comparison. Then she remembered he was only eight when his mother died, and her jealousy faded. "Is it still there? I would love to see it."

"I don't know. After she died, Father never mentioned it. I asked him once if we could go, and he just told me no, that it was closed. But whether that means he sold it or just locked it up and threw away the key, I don't know."

"I'm sorry." Now she understood why this room full of tapestries meant so much to him and why he never shared it with Vivienne. It was a connection to the mother and the childhood he had lost, a childhood his sister had never experienced. "I'm surprised he kept her study," she added, even more grateful for the hour she'd spent there this morning.

"He wasn't going to. He ordered Mrs. Winthrop to box everything up and put it in storage. But I cried so much that Mrs. Winthrop talked him out of it."

Underneath her stern exterior, it seemed Mrs. Winthrop was a real softie. At the very least, she had Vivienne's and Holden's best interests at heart.

"Tell me about some of her designs." Sophie gestured around the room. "I want to know everything."

"Boffin," Holden teased her, but he sprang from the bench and pointed at one of the tapestries, sharing everything he remembered. Now, it was Sophie's turn to watch him. She had never seen a guy talk about tapestries with such passion. But it was also clear that Holden's enthusiasm was as much for his mother, her seeming perfection frozen forever in his young mind, as it was for the tapestries themselves.

They stayed for several more hours. Sophie wished she had a notebook to jot down the words spilling from Holden's mouth, but she was held in too rapt attention to write anyway. Eventually, he seemed to talk out all he had to say, memories of his mother and her work that he had been holding inside for the past sixteen years, and they decided to call it a night.

He walked her to her room, as he had done the previous two nights, and when they reached her door, he leaned over to kiss her on the cheek. Sophie couldn't help herself. She turned her head at the last moment so that his lips grazed hers instead. She felt his mouth stiffen, worried that she had misread his feelings for her, when suddenly he leaned in, grabbing her by the waist and kissing her harder.

With her foot, Sophie pushed open the door behind her and pulled him into her room. There was something tender about him. He didn't rush to extricate her from her clothes, but moved slowly, undressing her softly, kissing her as he went, a form of pleasurable torture Sophie was more than willing to bear.

This was uncharted territory for Sophie. With Rush, it had always felt like a race, not to see who could finish first, but more so to check a box, scratch that itch, so they could move back to the friendship part of their relationship. But with Holden, it was more like a leisurely stroll, one that attuned Sophie to places she hadn't noticed before.

"Should I go?" Holden asked afterward, kissing her arm gently.

"No, stay," she replied. The room, the manor, it all felt less strange with someone else in her bed. Lying next to Holden's warm body, Sophie drifted off into an easy sleep for the first time since she arrived and slept so soundly that it was morning before she realized Holden was no longer in her bed.

Chapter 9
Weddlesmoore

"How was your night last night," Sophie asked Vivienne with a grin as they settled in for breakfast the next morning.

"A little awkward," Vivienne responded with her usual perkiness. Before Sophie could ask why, Vivienne went on. "I didn't want to bring her back here because Daddy always says not to flaunt our wealth," Sophie had to stifle an eye roll at this. Even without seeing the manor, it was obvious Vivienne had money. But Vivienne didn't seem to notice and continued on. "So we went back to her place. This tiny little studio apartment."

"How terrible for you," Sophie said, trying hard not to laugh.

"That wasn't the awkward part," Vivienne stamped. "This guy showed up claiming to be her boyfriend. I guess he's not. Just some guy that's obsessed with her, who refuses to believe her when she tells him she's gay, but still, she couldn't get him to leave."

"That must have been disappointing," Sophie deadpanned.

"She got him to leave eventually," Vivienne said with her usual air of impatience. "By telling him that she'd tell him all about our night later."

Sophie couldn't hold her laugh in any longer. "I don't think offering to recount her sexual exploits with another woman is the way to end his obsession."

Vivienne shrugged. "Probably not, but it got him out of our hair and I got what I needed, so..." Then she looked at Sophie, a note of seriousness in her voice. "Thanks for that, by the way. I mean, for taking care of Holden. I hope he wasn't too much of a bore after I left."

As she said it, Sophie pictured Holden's broad, bare shoulders, and the way he brushed his hair from his face while he talked excitedly about his mother's tapestries. Sophie blushed a little. "No, he was fine. Actually, we, um—"

But Vivienne cut her off. "You don't have to lie," she said. "I know he's not the easiest person to be around."

Sophie had been about to admit to Vivienne what she and Holden had done last night. Not the part about visiting Sabrina's tapestries. That still didn't feel like Sophie's secret to tell. But the part after. But before she could say anything, Vivienne chimed in again.

"Still. We should probably ask Holden if he wants to come to the beach today." She paused at the questioning look on Sophie's face, which had more to do with the fact that she was once again being dragged to the beach and not the idea that Holden join them. "I think he's lonely," she went on. "He was never great at making friends. And this house is so empty. It's nice for him to have company."

Before Sophie could say anything, Vivienne set off to find Holden but returned a few minutes later alone. "Weird. He hardly ever leaves his room. I wonder where he went." Then she shrugged. "Oh well, guess it's just you and I."

Sophie wasn't sure what to make of Holden's sudden absence. On one hand, she would be lying if she said she hadn't been thinking of him all morning. On the other, she wasn't sure how she would react if he joined them. A sun-kissed Holden on a tropical beach was a little much. She was relieved to get a break and clear her head. She certainly hadn't planned on this when she agreed to come home with Vivienne for break. She didn't even know Vivienne had a brother. And she wasn't looking for anything serious. She had meant to give Holden the same "no attachment" speech she'd delivered so many times to Rush, but had fallen into a comfortable sleep before she could get to it. Not that she'd tried hard to bring it up.

All and all, it was a conflicted and pensive Sophie who followed Vivienne through the tapestry and onto the shimmering sand. Vivienne immediately dove for the water, and Sophie settled on a blanket on the beach with her sketchbook. She distracted herself by sketching and writing down everything she could remember from Holden's walkthrough of the tapestries last night.

She was so engrossed in getting it all down that she didn't realize someone else was on the beach until a shadow fell across the page.

"I see you were paying attention last night."

Sophie couldn't hide her delight at Holden's arrival. "I thought maybe you were avoiding me," she joked.

"I would never," he gasped in mock outrage. "I just had some things to take care of this morning." Looking out across the water, he added "I see my sister has ditched you once again."

"I'm used to it," Sophie replied.

He sat down beside her and started playing with the ends of her hair. This is the moment, Sophie thought, trying to buck herself up. Time for the "no attachment" speech.

But she couldn't do it. It felt so nice, sitting on the sand, his hand now caressing the back of her neck. She didn't want it to stop, and she was worried that he was more sensitive than Rush. What if he took "no attachment" personally, and didn't want to see her for the rest of her visit? If she upset him, she'd loose access to Sabrina's tapestries, along with some other newly discovered perks, a thought that was confirmed as his other hand slid slowly up her thigh. She didn't even worry about Vivienne noticing, she was so far out in the water, not paying attention at all.

Sophie was torn between trying to de-escalate the situation and pulling Holden into a spot in the lush vegetation where she was sure Vivienne couldn't see them when he moved his hand to her sketchbook.

"You really did get a lot out of last night," he said in amazement.

"Well," she replied, regaining a little of her composure. "I had a good teacher." Then she whispered in his ear, "Can I have another lesson tonight?"

"There you are!" Vivienne's voice was loud as she made her way from the water. "I looked for you this morning." She grabbed a towel and gave Holden her typical pout. "And what were you two looking at?"

"Sophie was just showing me her sketchbook." It was clear from Holden's tone that he had no intention of telling Vivienne about last night. "She made a few sketches based on things she saw in Mum's study."

"Oh," Vivienne replied, making it very clear that she had zero interest in anything Sophie found in Sabrina's study. Then she turned back to Holden. "Come on, you look like you could use a good swim."

He got up, turning back to Sophie. "You joining us?"

Before Sophie could say anything, Vivienne chimed in. "She can't swim." Sophie's face flushed, as Vivienne continued. "And don't bother offering to teach her, she already told me she wasn't interested."

Sophie had no choice but to remain lamely on the beach, watching brother and sister splash through the waves. She would have been much more inclined to let Holden teach her to swim. It seemed like the perfect excuse to be near him, his hands wrapped around her waist, supporting her in the water. Or at least, that's how she imagined the lesson going. But Vivienne had shut the door on that option, and Sophie couldn't think of a logical way to explain that she was more than happy to let Holden teach her.

She wasn't on the beach long before Holden came back out of the water, pushing his slick hair off his face. Seeing him emerge from the sea, glistening in the sun, she had to tell herself to get a grip. What was she doing? *No attachment*, she reminded herself.

"Vivienne swims like a fish," he said, giving a shake of his head and spraying Sophie with water. "I swear, she's never going to leave the water."

"Don't have the stamina to keep up, huh?" Sophie replied.

He grinned at her, and once again she flushed. "That's not what you said last night."

Sophie thought Vivienne might be keen to go to the pub again, but she said she was tired after being in the sun all day and suggested a cozy night in. After supper, the three of them settled in Sabrina's study to play cards. Sophie feigned ignorance while Holden and Vivienne taught her the rules, but it became pretty clear a few hands in that Sophie was hustling them.

"Sorry," she laughed, pulling their chips towards her as Vivienne slammed down her cards. "My brothers and I play this game at home all the time."

Vivienne suddenly announced she was tired, but from the way she stormed from the room, she was upset about losing or being duped, or both.

"You get used to it," Holden said matter-of-factly.

"Do you?" Sophie had only been Vivienne's roommate for a few months, but she wasn't sure she would ever get used to her tantrums.

They sat in awkward silence for a moment before Sophie asked, "Tapestries?" inclining her head towards the secret gallery.

"Can't get enough, can you you?" Holden laughed and started putting away the cards. Before Sophie could answer, he continued, "Fine, but on one condition."

"What's that?" Sophie replied, wondering if it had anything to do with the events of last night.

"We actually go in some of the tapestries tonight."

Sophie didn't answer, just slowly nodded her head. She had been worried about this. She was happy to venture into some of them, though she could be just as happy examining each in more detail, but she didn't want to go into the tapestry of the village. Suppose they bumped into someone from her town? What if they ran into Mrs. Rigo? That could lead to some very awkward questions.

She was silent on the way to the gallery, her brain spinning with a million lame excuses. Should she say she was allergic to lavender? Or horses? Or maybe she could focus their attention on some of the other tapestries. If they spent enough time in those, the village wouldn't even be an issue.

To Sophie's immense relief, Holden didn't seem interested in that tapestry when they entered the gallery.

"Come on," he said, grabbing her hand and making a beeline for a tapestry on the opposite wall. "I want to show you my favorite place."

"Just promise me it's not the beach," Sophie joked.

It wasn't. At least, not technically. A small, clear pool, fed by a series of shallow waterfalls, sat nestled in a rocky valley. They stepped through the tapestry to the water's edge, dark, except for a few highlights where the moon broke through the clouds. Holden stripped off his clothes and eased into the water before Sophie could register what was happening.

"Come on," he called to her, his naked frame barely visible against the rocks.

"You know I can't swim," Sophie shouted, a little annoyed.

"It's not deep," he reassured her. "Now come on."

Sophie reluctantly pulled off her clothes. For a family that lived in a landlocked manor, they certainly spent a lot of time in the water. "You know," she called back to him, "if you wanted to get me naked, there are easier ways to go about it."

"Trust me," he said, a grin in his voice. "Once you hit the water, you'll know this has nothing to do with sex."

He was right. The first tentative step took Sophie's breath away, a cold so painful it felt like being pricked by a thousand needles. Holden waded in up to his waist, seemingly unfazed.

"How are you doing that?" Sophie shrieked.

"It's refreshing," he laughed, splashing towards her. "Just don't judge…"

Too late. Sophie looked down. "Wow," she laughed. "You really weren't kidding that this isn't about sex."

"It's the cold," he said, and before Sophie could reply, he scooped up a handful of water and flung it across her breasts. "Now we're even," he said, pointing towards her nipples.

"You're going to pay for that," Sophie shot back, kicking water in his direction, but he just turned and submerged even more of his body into the pool.

"Doesn't bother me."

"Well, I'm freezing. How long do we have to stay here?" Sophie's teeth chattered as she bobbed up and down, trying to get warm.

"We can call it," Holden said, moving toward her again and wrapping his arms around her. Sophie squealed as his icy skin met hers. "Unless you want me to teach you how to swim?" he asked, squeezing her closer.

"Not in this water," she said. "But you are going to have to think of some way to help me get warm."

"Come on," he said. "I know just the place."

They struggled into their clothes, which stuck to their damp skin, and Holden led them down a path toward the mountain. The brisk pace did nothing to warm Sophie up, as the wind whipped the wet ends of her hair. She was just about to suggest they head back to the gallery when they rounded a corner and a tiny cabin appeared. She was even more shocked when Holden led her up the porch steps, unearthed a key from above the door frame, and led her inside.

The entirety of the cabin consisted of a single room. A large bed stood against one wall, taking up most of the space, opposite a stone fireplace so massive it wouldn't have looked out of place in a cabin three times the size. Tucked into a corner, a few dishes and a battered tea kettle sat on a rough wooden counter. Everything had the air of a place that was rarely used, but surprisingly well cared for.

"Whose is this?" Sophie asked, as Holden arranged a few logs in the fireplace. He lit a match and the first tentative flames took hold.

"It was Mum's," Holden explained, grabbing a blanket from the bed, draping it around Sophie, and directing her to the rug in front of the fire. "Another reason this is my favorite tapestry," he added.

"Did you come here a lot as kids?" Sophie asked. She hastily corrected herself, "I mean, before she…"

Holden gave a small smile. "Actually, no. She brought Vivienne and I here a few times, and I remember Father coming once, but mostly, this was her place. She'd come here when everything — I mean, when the pressure of work — got to be too much."

From everything Holden had told Sophie about Sabrina's work, she couldn't imagine it ever being too much. But she also supposed that, when you became famous as young as Sabrina had, you might sometimes need an escape. Someplace private to get away and just be.

As if he could read her thoughts, Holden continued. "I like to come here sometimes, to get away from Father, from the manor. Sometimes I think about moving here full time, but it's lacking in, let's just say, creature comforts."

Another scan around the cabin revealed a complete lack of running water, but after a week at Weddlesmoore, Sophie appreciated the coziness of it. "We should sleep here tonight," she told Holden, squeezing her body closer to his. The fire was starting to take hold, and the warmth after the frigid pond was making Sophie sleepy.

"Just sleep?" Holden asked her.

"You said this wasn't about sex," Sophie reminded him, but even as she said it, she reached her hand out under the blankets, feeling for the waistband of his pants. "Besides," she said, leaning in towards him, "I doubt your sister will come looking for either of us. As long as we're back early enough—"

But Holden didn't need any more convincing. Before Sophie could say another word, he scooped her up and carried her over to the bed.

—#—

Sophie woke the next morning, well-rested and satisfied. Ironic, that her best night of sleep since arriving at Weddlesmoore didn't take place in the manor. She nuzzled Holden. "We should get going."

"You go," he murmured. "I want to take a quick dip before heading back." He opened his eyes a little wider and grinned at Sophie, "unless you want to join me."

"Not a chance," Sophie replied. She could barely stand the thought of the ocean, let alone the frigid rock pool and she had no intention of spending time in either that day.

Sophie expressed the same sentiment to Vivienne when she suggested the beach later that morning at breakfast.

"Go without me," she told Vivienne. "I'm just going to hang around here."

"What are you going to do? Sit in Mum's study, reading all day?" Vivienne said it like she couldn't imagine a more awful punishment, but to Sophie, it was preferable to a day spent watching Vivienne swim.

"That," Sophie said lightly. "Maybe I'll spend time exploring more of the tapestries in the gallery too."

"Do you want me to go with you?" Vivienne asked, then, comprehension dawning on her face, she added, "Oh wait, or by explore, you mean just look at them, don't you?"

"Well, yeah," Sophie replied, warming to her day of freedom from Vivienne. "A few of them have some really interesting construction, I'd like to look a little more closely."

Vivienne rolled her eyes. "You're on your own."

Sophie did start her morning in the tapestry gallery. Mr. Morris had a wide-ranging collection, and Sophie wasn't kidding about wanting a closer look. She had been fortunate to spend time around a lot of tapestries growing up, even if it was mostly in short spurts while they were in for repair, but this collection was something else. Mr. Morris had a discriminating eye, and she guessed that at least a few of the tapestries were several hundred years old, or older. Here was Vivienne, growing up surrounded by this treasure trove, and all she wanted to do was go to the beach.

If there was one thing that could tear Sophie away, it was Sabrina's study. Yes, Mr. Morris's tapestry collection was amazing, but there were amazing tapestries all over the world. The chance to step inside Sabrina's process, the closest anyone could ever get to stepping inside her mind — that was an opportunity Sophie might never get again.

She grabbed a few books from the shelves and a handful of Sabrina's journals at random and settled into an armchair. As a designer and not a weaver, the number of books on weaving and dyeing techniques in Sabrina's collection was impressive. But that was also, Sophie realized, what made her tapestries so incredible. She didn't simply paint cartoons in the hopes that her weavers would figure out what to do. It was clear from her notes that she thought about weaving at every step of the process and worked intimately with her weavers. This, Sophie was sure, made the weavers' jobs much easier, enabling them to execute such incredible work.

The door opened slowly and Sophie looked up from the pages smiling, expecting it to be Holden. But she nearly jumped out of her skin as a much older man appeared. He was pale and sallow, like Holden, but with lines around his face, and the last traces of color through his graying hair were much darker than either of his children. This had to be Mr. Morris.

"I'm so sorry to startle you," he moved forward, wringing his hands apologetically. "You must be Sophie. It's nice to finally meet you. I apologize for my absence. It's been a busy time at work."

He said all this slowly, but Sophie couldn't get her brain in gear quickly enough to respond. The work comment in particular threw her. That had been Vivienne and Mrs. Winthrop's excuses for his absence so far, but Sophie couldn't understand why. If she had to guess, Mr. Morris was a good twenty years older than her parents, and the family clearly didn't lack for money. Shouldn't he be retired? Or at least slowing down.

Sophie finally found her voice. "Oh, of course. I understand." Then remembering her manners, she added, "Thank you so much for allowing me to visit your lovely home, Mr. Morris."

"Please," he said, "call me Henry. I'm happy to have a friend of Vivienne's here. Holden was never much for inviting guests." His eyes tracked around the books and journals spread out around Sophie's chair. "I see you've been enjoying my wife's study," he said softly.

Sophie paused, then got momentarily angry, remembering what Holden had told her. "I'm just grateful that it's here," she said, not quite able to contain the ire in her voice. "Holden said you wanted it all boxed up and put it away."

"So I did," Mr. Morris said, a trace of sadness in his voice. He sat down in a chair opposite Sophie. "Grief does funny things. But I am glad," he said, gesturing around the room, "that Holden and Mrs. Winthrop talked me out of it."

"Oh," Sophie replied, unsure of how to respond. Vivienne and Holden had painted very different pictures of Mr. Morris, and Sophie had to admit that Vivienne's version, of a grieving man haunted by his dead wife's presence, seemed to be a more accurate reflection of the man sitting across from her.

Mr. Morris continued, "It's nice to have a space to feel her presence." Sophie thought of the tapestries hidden in the basement gallery and Holden's explanation that Mr. Morris had closed Sabrina's tapestry workshop almost immediately.

"It's not just grief," Mr. Morris continued, his eyes on Sophie. She guessed he didn't often have an audience for these thoughts. "I feel some sense of responsibility for her death."

"What?" Sophie sputtered at this revelation.

"The night she died," he continued, hanging his head. "We were supposed to see a play together. But I, uh," he paused, "wasn't feeling well. She offered to stay home too, but I insisted she go. She was leaving the theater when she... when it happened." He trailed off as Sophie sat there, mouth agape.

"I'm so sorry," Mr. Morris continued. "I didn't mean to burden you with all of this. I just— I wasn't expecting anyone else to be here." He looked at Sophie, "And I'm sure you weren't expecting company. I'll leave you be."

Sophie wanted to tell him to stay, it was his house after all, but she was at a loss for words. "Uh, thank you." Then she added quickly, "And thank you again for letting me stay, Mr. Morris."

"My pleasure," he responded, sweeping towards the door. "And as I said, please call me Henry."

Sophie sat in stunned silence for several minutes, trying to steady her breathing. She hadn't expected such an emotional first meeting with her host. Once she'd calmed down, she hastily returned the books and journals to their shelves and left the study, making a beeline for Holden's room.

As she banged heavily on the door, she heard Holden's muffled voice call, "Just a minute," along with the noise of things hastily being put away.

He looked flustered when he opened the door a few moments later, but smiled when he saw Sophie.

"You hiding another girl in there?" she asked, trying to keep her voice casual, but obviously failing.

"Of course no— what's wrong?" Holden asked.

"I met your dad," Sophie said, sitting lightly on the edge of the bed. "It was... weird."

"That's him," Holden replied dryly, but he looked at her with concern. "Do you want to tell me about it?"

As Sophie recalled the story of what happened in the study, and Mr. Morris's show of remorse, she was surprised to see Holden grow angrier and angrier.

"It's bollocks." He blurted out when Sophie had finished.

"He seemed sincere." Sophie felt guilty for sharing with Holden. She hadn't meant to upset him; she was just trying to calm herself. She tried to put her hand on his arm, but he stormed up and began pacing the room.

"He's always been a good actor." Holden spat. "The only remorse he has is that the will wasn't set up better. He thought he'd get sole control of her designs. Instead, they went into a trust."

"Don't you think you're being a little harsh?" Sophie had not expected this angry, brooding Holden. It was almost scary.

"Don't be a fool, Sophie. He was playing you."

The words came out with such force that Sophie stepped back as if he'd slapped her. She turned to make for the door, but Holden softened.

"I'm sorry," he said, grabbing her wrist and pulling her back. She was surprised to see his eyes welling with tears. "You just don't know him like I do."

Almost automatically, he turned towards a messy stack of papers on a big, imposing desk in the corner of the room. Sophie's gaze followed.

"Is that what you've been doing all these years?" she asked. "Trying to find dirt on your father?" Comprehension dawning, she continued, "Do you think he murdered your mother?"

"I don't know." Holden hung his head and sat back on the edge of the bed, swiping at the tears leaking down his cheeks. "It's just never tracked for me, the kidnapping angle. Those are so rare. And it just happened to take place on the night he wasn't there." Sophie could see the sadness turning back into anger. "They went to the theater together all the time, and the one night he wasn't fucking there."

"That's hardly proof of murder," Sophie said. She wasn't sure why she was disagreeing with him, other than nothing about her brief meeting with Mr. Morris made him seem like a murderer. "It's just a really awful coincidence."

"There are other things too." He said, gesturing back towards the desk. "Legal shit. Shady dealings. I don't know." He put his head in his hands and started to cry harder, his whole body shaking. "I've been looking at it for so long."

Sophie put her arm around him and stroked his shoulder.

"It's not your fault." She told him gently. "And you shouldn't put that much pressure on yourself. Nobody asked you to solve her murder. And..." she paused, unsure of whether to continue, but it needed to be said, "It won't bring her back."

Holden looked up at Sophie, taking in great gasps of air. "I know." He shook his head. "But I feel like I owe it to her."

"I didn't know her," Sophie said, reaching up to wipe the tears from his face. "But from everything you've told me, I think the thing she'd want most is for you to be happy. Not locked in your room, torturing yourself over her death."

He nodded, tears still streaming down his face. She reached up and wiped them away.

"Thank you," he said softly, leaning in and kissing her forehead gently. And then she was kissing his tear-stained cheeks, then his lips, and suddenly they were falling back into the bed, all memory of Sophie's meeting with Mr. Morris forgotten.

—#—

"Where were you this afternoon?" Vivienne demanded when Sophie arrived in the dining room that evening. Sophie cringed, unsure how to respond. She had spent all afternoon in bed with Holden, but since she never got around to telling Vivienne about the first time, she felt awkward bringing it up now.

"I looked in the gallery, and Mum's study, and knocked on your door," Vivienne continued huffily. At least she hadn't come knocking on Holden's door. "And I couldn't find you anywhere."

This was the moment, Sophie thought, to come clean about her and Holden. But she thought of the way Holden had evaded the subject on the beach yesterday and lost her nerve. "Oh," said Sophie, thinking fast, "I must have been inside one of the tapestries. I went exploring, and um, lost track of time." This wasn't strictly a lie if you substituted tapestries for the hangings around Holden's four-poster bed. And she had lost track of time exploring every inch of Holden's body.

"Fine," Vivienne stamped her foot again. "I'm starving, let's eat."

"Shouldn't we wait for Holden," Sophie asked cautiously.

"He's a grown man," Vivienne retorted, settling down at the table. "If he can't make it in time for dinner, that's his problem."

"What's my problem," Holden asked, striding in and flashing a smile at his sister, though purposefully avoiding Sophie's eye.

"You're so late to dinner," Sophie replied, "that your sister was going to eat your share too."

"We'll see about that," he responded, moving past Vivienne and swiping a dinner roll off her plate as he did so.

"Hey," Vivienne protested. Turning to Sophie, she added, "Daddy said he finally met you this morning."

"Oh, um, yeah," Sophie went on a little awkwardly. Now she was avoiding Holden's gaze. "He was very nice. I'm glad I got to thank him for letting me stay."

"*I* let you stay," Vivienne insisted, and Holden practically snorted into his plate. "What?" She turned to her brother. "I'm the one who invited her."

Holden kept his face passive, but gave Sophie a quick smile as he replied to his sister, "And we're all very glad you did."

The three of them fell into a routine for the rest of the break. After breakfast, Vivienne headed to the beach, while Sophie wandered the tapestry gallery or settled into Sabrina's study. She was occasionally joined by Holden, and more than a few times she was relieved the study door locked from the inside.

In the evenings, they would venture out to the pub or stay in and play games. Once Vivienne had turned in for the night, Holden would sneak back to Sophie's room and they would head down to visit Sabrina's tapestries — if they didn't get too distracted by other things first.

At breakfast on their last full day of break, Mrs. Winthrop announced that Mr. Morris would be joining them that evening for dinner. Vivienne let out a squeal of delight, but Holden merely scowled.

"Last day," Vivienne said, a mixture of relief and disappointment in her voice. "Either of you want to join me at the beach?"

"I can go to the beach anytime I want," Holden reminded his sister. "I live here."

"Except you never do," Vivienne replied, her voice dripping with derision. "Sophie?"

"I'm good," Sophie replied with a laugh. The pull of one final day in Sabrina's study was too strong. She had no idea when she'd be back.

"You two are so boring," Vivienne whined, turning from the pair of them and practically bouncing out of the room. Sophie expected she would squeeze every last minute of the day on the beach.

Holden waited until he was sure Vivienne was gone before turning to Sophie, his eyes wide with excitement. "I have something I want to show you."

"This better be good," Sophie replied. "I was going to spend the day in your mom's study."

"Trust me," Holden said, standing up and gesturing for her to follow. "This is much better."

Sophie raised an eyebrow but followed him from the room. He led her to Sabrina's tapestry gallery and once they were inside, made a beeline for a tapestry featuring a charming village set beside a small, slow-moving river. A mill sat on its banks. As Sophie followed the line of the river back towards the top of the tapestry, she noticed what looked like a barn set amongst a copse of trees.

This wasn't a tapestry they had gone into on any of their previous outings. It was beautifully made, but, if Sophie was being honest, it was the weakest of Sabrina's tapestries, at least the ones in this room. It seemed more utilitarian than anything else.

"Come on," Holden said, grabbing her hand and pulling her through the tapestry, barely able to contain his excitement. "I hope you don't mind," Holden added, leading her towards a path along the river. "We've got a bit of a walk."

Sophie thought he was overhyping whatever was about to happen, though she did have to admit it was a very pleasant, if chilly day, strolling along the river, her hand in his. She tried to pay attention to the scenery, but she couldn't help but notice his gaze glued firmly on her.

"What?" she said, flushing with a hint of exasperation.

"Just wait," he teased with a wink.

"Ok, seriously." Sophie started to get annoyed. "What's the big deal?"

"Alright, fine. If you can't wait any longer for the surprise. You're worse than Vivienne—"

"I am not!" She cut him off. "No one is that bad."

"So you can wait until we get there?"

"No," she begged, "please, tell me. I need to know if this walk is worth it."

He turned from her towards the barn in the distance, and he started again, slowly, "So you know how you asked about Mum's workshop…"

"What?" Sophie stopped in her tracks and turned to look at him, then the building in the distance, then at him again. "You don't mean— that's not—" She stammered, unable to find her words.

"Look," he said, clearly worried he had oversold it. "I don't know what state it's in, or if there's anything in it, or if we can even get in, but I started thinking about it, and how we used to get there when I was a kid. We didn't use this tapestry, there must have been another — I'm guessing Father destroyed it or hid it away," he added as an aside, more to himself than Sophie, "but I realized last night that the barn in this tapestry looked like her studio."

"And you didn't tell me?" Sophie gave him a slight shove, incensed.

"I can't promise anything is still there," Holden continued, but now it was Sophie who could barely contain her excitement. She grabbed Holden's hand, practically running down the path.

Before long, they were standing in front of an old stone barn, built into the side of a hill. A small door stood at one end, and as they approached, Sophie noted it was padlocked shut. There was also a large "no trespassing" sign posted on the door.

"I don't suppose you have a key for this?" Sophie asked him.

"No," Holden replied, and Sophie could see doubt and disappointment creeping into his face.

"I got it," Sophie replied, pulling a small pick from her hair.

"Got what?" The question dropped from Holden's mouth as Sophie picked the lock. "Where'd you learn that?" he asked.

"A friend," Sophie answered enigmatically. At some point in their childhood, no doubt inspired by a book he was reading, Rush decided they should learn to pick locks. They spent an entire summer practicing until they could make their way into just about any building they wanted. But Sophie hadn't mentioned Rush to Holden and now didn't seem like the time to bring up the other guy she occasionally slept with.

"I'm impressed," Holden replied.

"Do you want to stand there gawking or do you want to go in?" Sophie stepped away from the door and gestured for Holden to open it.

Sophie followed him into a large space, light streaming in from the wall of windows opposite them. Sophie wasn't prepared for how beautiful the light would be. It must have been incredible to weave in this space.

She had just registered that the room was empty, save for a layer of dust, when Holden dropped to his knees next to her. He held his face in his hands, yet big fat tears were already splashing onto the dusty floor.

"It's all gone," he choked.

Sophie knelt beside him, her arms around his shoulders, softly stroking his arm, but said nothing. She had been so excited to see the space that she hadn't even thought of Holden's reaction when they got there.

It seemed Holden, equally excited to show it to Sophie, hadn't thought about it either.

"I'm sorry," he said, turning to face her. "I just didn't expect…"

"Ssshhh," she whispered, pulling him into a hug and stroking his hair. "I know this is hard." They stayed like that for an eternity, until Holden's body relaxed and his tears slowed. "Let's get out of here," she said softly.

"No." He stood up abruptly. "We came because I wanted to show you around. Let me show you around."

"Are you sure?" she asked cautiously.

"Yes," he said. His voice was still shaking, but his jaw was firm. It took him a few more minutes to regain his composure, but soon he took on the same animated air he had the night he talked Sophie through Sabrina's tapestries.

"There was a loom here, and here, and here," he said, walking her across the wide floor. "And over here were the shelves, just rows and rows of yarn. And here were the dye vats. I always hated that as a kid. It stunk like a wet dog."

"I think you mean a wet sheep." Sophie corrected him, laughing.

"Whatever it was, it was disgusting." Now that he had gotten over the shock of the empty space, Sophie could see him brimming with boyhood energy. She imagined a young

Holden, running through the space, charming the weavers and assistants as they worked.

From the workshop, he led her down a flight of stairs to a slightly smaller, but equally light-filled room. A massive oak table, so large you'd practically have to lay on it to reach the middle, stood at the center of the room. Like everything else, it was covered with a layer of dust. An empty pinboard stretched across the largest wall, filled with endless tiny holes and the ghosted outlines of whatever had once hung there.

Holden stiffened as they entered the room, his disappointment palpable, though not as visceral as when they first entered the workshop. What little glimmer of hope he'd had now seemed extinguished.

"Your mother's studio?" Sophie asked.

Holden nodded and began to walk slowly around the table. Sophie followed him to a spot in the corner of the room, where she could see a smaller oak desk, barely knee high, that had previously been blocked by the larger table.

"This was mine," Holden said softly, pointing at the little table. It looked like it was hewn from the same wood as the bigger table, and Sophie pictured a little Holden, cut from the same cloth as his mother, leaning over the desk, furiously scribbling away.

She understood now, Holden's pain compared to Vivienne's detachment. It was Holden whom Sabrina had been grooming to follow in her footsteps. Perhaps she would have done the same with Vivienne, but she was so young when Sabrina died that the opportunity vanished with her. It also explained Holden and Vivienne's different life choices. Sophie could see how studying tapestry, in any form, would be too painful for Holden. A reminder of a life he was supposed to have and lost. Vivienne, without those memories, could approach her studies as a form of family obligation, without the painful history attached.

"Thank you for bringing me here," she whispered to Holden, taking his hand in hers and giving it a squeeze, then kissing him gently on the cheek. She wanted to convey that she understood how hard this must have been for him.

He turned to face her, leaning his forehead against hers. "Thank you for giving me a reason."

Chapter 10
Weddlesmoore

They whiled away the rest of the afternoon in Sabrina's study until Vivienne flounced in, her hair still wet with saltwater, announcing it was time to get dressed for dinner.

"Dressed?" Sophie asked, looking up from her book and raising an eyebrow.

Vivienne eyed her faded jeans with a look of contempt and replied, "You can't wear those. Come on, I'll loan you a dress."

Sophie turned to Holden and gave him a look that plainly said, *help me*, but Holden just shrugged and laughed before turning to put the books back on the shelves.

When they arrived at dinner a little while later, Sophie feeling uncomfortable in some ruffled dress of Vivienne's, Holden was already seated at the table looking handsome in a light grey suit.

"You look nice," she whispered to him, as he pulled back her chair.

"You look…" he started awkwardly, but she cut him off.

"Weird, I know, don't say it."

He leaned in closer to her ear, "My sister's clothes aren't really a turn-on."

"Good thing," Sophie whispered back. She looked around to make sure Vivienne hadn't heard anything, but Mr. Morris had just entered the room, and Vivienne squealed

"Daddy," and dashed across the room to kiss him on the cheek and lead him to his seat.

They sat in silence for a few minutes, until Mrs. Winthrop came in to serve the soup.

"So," said Mr. Morris, just as Sophie brought a spoonful to her lips, "are you girls excited for the start of term?"

Sophie couldn't answer, and Vivienne just shrugged. "It's fine," Vivienne said. "I'll just be happy when this year is over and I don't have to take any more design or weaving classes. When I can just concentrate on business." She flashed her father a smile as she said this, but Holden let out a small snort.

"What?" Vivienne turned to him, flashing with anger.

Holden looked like he wanted to say something, but looked at Sophie and quickly shoveled soup into his mouth. True to his promise, he had avoided fighting with his sister.

"What?" Vivienne demanded again. "Are you judging me for not going into design? Whatever. At least I'm still doing something to help the family business. Unlike you." She let the last words out like a sneer. Still, Holden said nothing.

"Vivienne, dear," Mr. Morris started. It was clear he was accustomed to his children's fights and was trying to avert another one in front of their guest

"Please, Daddy," she turned to him. "You know you could use the help in the business. You shouldn't have to work this hard at your…" her voice trailed off, then she quickly changed tracks, "I mean, anymore."

"It's ok, dear." Mr. Morris said, still keeping his voice calm. "In a few years, I'll have your help."

"See," Holden said finally. "It's fine."

"Fine?" Vivienne spat back. "I don't care what Daddy says. He needs help. But you couldn't even be bothered to think about studying anything related to weaving. No, you had to pursue your stupid passion project, avenging Mother's death. And for what?" Vivienne was standing now. Sophie had never seen her this angry, the pink patches in her cheeks growing steadily more red. "To just sit in your room all day, sulking on Daddy's dime."

"It's not Father's money." Holden burst out of his chair, his hands trembling.

"That makes it worse," Vivienne shouted back. "Burning through the money Mum left you."

"I'm not burning through anything," Holden was shaking now. "And why do you care? In a few years, you'll have yours, and then you can do whatever you want. You can stop being jealous of me."

"Jealous," Vivienne shrieked. "Of you?"

"You've always been jealous," Holden spat back. "Because I knew Mum better than you."

Vivienne stepped back as if she'd been slapped. Tears were now streaming from her eyes. "Well, I didn't have to know her to know that she'd be so disappointed in the way you're wasting your life." And with that, she spun and ran from the room.

Sophie turned mouth agape at Holden, who let out one shuddering sob, put his face in his hands, and strode from the room.

Mr. Morris and Sophie sat in awkward silence for what felt like an age. Mrs. Winthrop entered, deposited entree plates in front of Mr. Morris and Sophie, and walked silently from the room as if this was nothing out of the ordinary.

Finally, Mr. Morris spoke. "I'm so sorry for my children." He hung his head. "I should have given them better manners. I hope you won't think less of our family after this."

Sophie tried to think what to say. The fight had been horrible to watch, but the prospect of an awkward dinner with Mr. Morris seemed somehow worse. "It's ok," she tried to smile. "I'm from a big family. I'm surprised one of us hasn't killed each other yet."

Mr. Morris let out a weak chuckle. "Thank you for that. I sometimes forget that other families have problems too."

"It's normal," Sophie said. It was weird to try and comfort a man older than her father, but she felt like she should try, at least a little. "They've been through a lot." Then she added, "So have you. Those things can be hard to get over." As she said that, she thought about her mother and her missing sister, and vowed to cut her mother more slack the next time she was home. Maybe she'd even make an effort to write her more.

"Thank you," Mr. Morris said, bringing Sophie back from her thoughts. He gestured at the plates in from of them, "Should we continue with dinner? Mrs. Winthrop's lamb chops are the stuff of legend."

But Sophie was already pushing back her seat from the table. "I think I should go check on them, um Vivienne. But thank you, Henry," she said, emphasizing his name. "For everything, for letting me stay."

"My pleasure dear," he said, his voice filled with sadness, as he turned to face his plate in the soon-to-be empty dining room.

Sophie didn't have to think twice about which sibling needed her more. She would have an entire term to console Vivienne, to help her work through whatever it was she was feeling. If Vivienne even needed consoling at all. Her ability to bounce back quickly was one of her more impressive traits. But tomorrow, Holden would be alone once more, stuck in this massive manor with his loss and regrets.

She had a guess where she might find him, heading not for his room, but for the basement gallery with Sabrina's tapestries. She tapped lightly on the door and a few moments later was greeted by Holden's pale face, his hands still shaking as they gripped the edge of the door.

He said nothing, just returned to the bench, his head in his hands. He had taken off his suit jacket and unbuttoned his shirt sleeves.

Sophie sat down on the bench next to him and took his hands in hers.

"I'm sorry," he said to her before she had a chance to speak. "I promised you no more fighting. I'm surprised you even wanted to see me again."

"You were provoked," Sophie said softly. "You would have needed to be a saint to withstand all of that. Besides," she continued, "I've got an entire term to console Vivienne." He looked at her and attempted a weak smile.

"She's right, you know." He said, his voice full of sadness. "Mum would be so disappointed with how I've wasted my life."

"You haven't wasted your life—" Sophie started, but he cut her off.

"Well, then I've wasted my youth."

"Your youth was stolen from you." It was Sophie's turn to be angry. "No one should have to experience what you went through. Or Vivienne," she added pointedly. "It's a miracle either of you are as well adjusted as you are."

Holden couldn't help but let out a little laugh. "You're mental if you think we're well adjusted."

"You could be worse," Sophie was laughing now too. "All families fight. You should see me and my siblings. It's like I was telling your dad—"

"Oh shit," Holden cut her off again. "I'm so sorry, we just left you alone with Father. That must have been awkward."

"It wasn't great," Sophie conceded. "But I got out of there as quickly as I could. I do feel bad for leaving him alone."

Holden shrugged. "He's used to it."

"He's lonely," Sophie interjected. "And so are you. You really should make an effort to talk to him more. Otherwise, what are you going to do, just keep waiting around for your sister to bring home roommates for you to sleep with?"

"Hey, that's not what—" Holden stammered, but he looked up at Sophie and realized she was joking. "I take what I can get," he joked back.

Sophie punched him playfully on the arm, but he grabbed her wrist and pulled her into a fierce kiss. They began tugging at their clothes, Sophie pulling off his jacket and setting to work on his shirt buttons, Holden unzipping, as he called it "the ruffled monstrosity." Before Sophie could get to Holden's pants, he pulled her towards the nearest tapestry, a lush garden overflowing with tropical plants, and they settled into a soft patch of grass.

Afterward, Holden rolled onto his side to face Sophie, his head propped in one hand, the other slowly making its way down Sophie's cheek, her breast, her stomach, her inner thigh. "I've been thinking," he said, and Sophie wondered if they were headed towards round two, "that maybe I could come visit you at school this term. Or you could come visit me," he added quickly.

Sophie didn't say anything. Every day, she'd meant to give Holden the "no attachment" speech, and every day something stopped her. She enjoyed spending time with Holden, and it wasn't just about the sex, though that was good as well. But she certainly hadn't come home with Vivienne looking for a relationship, and the idea of dating her roommate's brother seemed complicated, even if she had to admit she'd spent most of last term hoping to start something with Jasper. She tried to come up with a response, but it was clear she'd paused too long, because Holden muttered, "Oh, I see," as he stood up and started fumbling for his pants.

"No," Sophie said quickly, reaching out towards him, but grabbing only air. "It's just that..." her voice trailed off lamely.

"It's just that what?" Holden stammered, moving from embarrassment to anger. "You just figured you could shag me all break and I wouldn't feel anything?"

Sophie flushed. She had been thinking that. Dammit. Why hadn't she been honest about their arrangement from the beginning?

"Or were you just using me to get to my mother's tapestries?"

That last bit stung, and Sophie flung herself off the ground. She looked around for her dress but then remembered it was still back in the gallery. "That's not fair," she said, turning to face him. "I haven't been sleeping with you just to get to the tapestries. I've been sleeping with you because—" She stammered, "I mean, you showed me the tapestries first."

"Yes," he stammered back. "Because I knew you would appreciate them. But you kissed me first. I was trying to be a gentleman."

"Oh," Sophie laughed hard. "A gentleman? So you wouldn't have even done anything if I hadn't made the first move? But suddenly you want some kind of relationship?"

The look on his face told her she had gone a step too far.

"Sorry for wanting to spend more time with you," he said, his face falling. "I can see now this never meant anything to you."

"Holden, wait," Sophie called out lamely, but he was already striding from the tapestry, leaving her standing naked and alone in the garden.

"You seem in a better mood this morning," Sophie commented to Vivienne, as the two of them made their way into the dining room for breakfast before setting off back to school. "I, uh, tried to check on you last night, but you must not have heard my knock."

This was a lie, but Sophie didn't want Vivienne to think she'd completely abandoned her. But after her fight with Holden, she'd been in no mood to deal with Vivienne.

"Oh, I wasn't in my room," Vivienne responded brightly. "I went for a swim and then decided to stop by the pub for a pint."

Sophie knew that "for a pint" was code for meeting up with that pretty girl, but it made her feel better to know her roommate hadn't been alone. "Well one of those things certainly seems to have cheered you up," Sophie teased her with a wink. Then noticing only two place settings at the table, Sophie added "I guess Holden isn't joining us."

"Who cares what that arse does?" Vivienne said, apparently not completely over the events of last night. "Though I thought maybe he would have at least had the decency to say goodbye to you."

Sophie didn't say anything, just helped herself to a plate of eggs. She tried to bring herself to go to Holden's room and apologize last night, but she couldn't think of any way to make the situation better. She had enjoyed spending time with him during break, but it didn't change the fact that she wasn't interested in starting the new term in a long-distance relationship with her roommate's brother. Especially when said roommate didn't have a clue what was going on, and would probably act like a pouty brat about the fact that Sophie and Holden had kept a secret from her for all of break. Not that Sophie had really meant to.

An hour later, Sophie and Vivienne were in the entryway with their bags when Mrs. Winthrop stopped them. "Vivienne, your father is in his study if you'd like to say goodbye."

Vivienne glanced at Sophie, who had no desire to spend any more awkward moments with Mr. Morris. "You go," Sophie told her. "I'll head back to school on my own. But please tell your father I said thanks again."

Sophie could sense Vivienne's hesitation, but she felt strongly that Vivienne should say goodbye to her father, and even more strongly that she didn't want to be there, so she simply grabbed her bag, thanked Mrs. Winthrop, and stepped out the front door.

"Where's Princess," Eryka asked, as Sophie emerged from the tapestry into their dorm room. "Was it so awful that you murdered her?"

"It was fine," Sophie shrugged, pushing some of Eryka's clothes aside to sit on the bed. "She's saying goodbye to her dad." And then, before Sophie could stop herself, she asked, "Did you know Vivienne had an older brother?"

Eryka raised an eyebrow at her. "Yes…" she said, a hint of curiosity in her voice. "You didn't know that?" She was now giving Sophie a searching look.

"I don't remember it ever coming up," Sophie said honestly. "You two must have discussed it without me."

"So I'm assuming that means you met him," Eryka continued, staring at Sophie as if trying to peer into her brain. "How was he?"

"Fine," Sophie tried to keep her voice light, but she could feel herself start to flush. It's not that she didn't want to tell Eryka, it's that she wasn't convinced Eryka would keep her secret from Vivienne. Or worse, Jasper.

"Uh, huh," said Eryka, turning back to her closet and cramming some clothes inside. "You look like he was better than fine."

Now Sophie was really blushing. "Look, just don't say…" She started, but her words fell away as Vivienne bounced through the tapestry and onto her bed.

"That was a quick goodbye," Sophie said, trying to cover up her abrupt change in conversation.

Vivienne ignored her, instead bounding over to Eryka to give her a big hug. "How was your break?" she asked.

"It wasn't bad," Eryka replied. "Jasper was a bit of a pill. But you know how brothers can be," she said with a smirk in Sophie's direction, while Sophie furiously shook her head at Eryka behind Vivienne's back.

Fortunately, Vivienne noticed nothing. "Don't even get me started," she said, turning to her closet to unpack.

Sophie turned to her own bed, where a stack of letters and postcards from Rush waited for her. She hadn't given him the Maxwell's address, but that hadn't stopped him from keeping up his regular correspondence. She felt a pang of guilt that she hadn't sent him a single letter over break.

Shoving the letters in her bag along with some paper, Sophie stood up. "I'm going to head to the library for a bit." She wasn't sure she wanted to leave Eryka alone with Vivienne, as she wasn't convinced Eryka would keep her secret, but she also didn't want to read Rush's letters in front of them. They weren't those kinds of letters, but Sophie was afraid any mention of Rush would lead to awkward conversations about sexual exploits they might have gotten up to over break.

"The library," Vivienne scoffed. "Didn't you get enough of that over break?" Eryka gave her a confused look, and Vivienne added, "She practically spent all of break in Mum's study."

Eryka opened her mouth to say something, and Sophie cut her off. "It was better than spending all day sitting on a boring beach."

Before anyone could say anything else, Sophie crossed the room, but as she closed the door, she heard Vivienne turn to Eryka. "Did you know she can't swim?"

Sophie sat in the library reading letter after letter detailing Rush's adventures over break, but all she could manage in return was a short letter stating vaguely how she went to the beach and hung out with Vivienne and her brother at the pub. She couldn't even bring herself to write Holden's name as if Rush would be able to infer something from this alone.

She and Rush rarely kept secrets from each other, and this omission felt close to a betrayal, though she couldn't figure out why. She'd had the "no attachment" conversation with Rush many times, and she wasn't sure he would even care about Holden. She wouldn't care if Rush was sleeping with someone else at college. She wanted that for him. But she still couldn't bring herself to tell the whole truth. It was as if spending time with girls was making her confused about her relationship with Rush.

What she did want to know, she realized suddenly, were more details on the tapestry Mrs. Rigo had found. Was it really a Sabrina Maxwell? Was it on display in the museum or still in storage?

She picked up her pen and continued the letter:

I was thinking a lot over break about the tapestry you showed me last summer. Did your mom learn any more about it? Is it on display in the museum yet? I wish I could have spent more time with it before leaving town.

Sophie paused again and looked back over what she'd just written. She didn't mention her suspicions that the tapestry might be a Sabrina Maxwell, or that she might have discovered a connected tapestry over break. She would share more later if it turned out that what she thought was true was true.

A shadow fell across her page and when she looked up, there was Jasper, looking as good as ever.

"You're in the library and term hasn't even started yet?" He questioned her with a smile, and she felt herself melt a little. It seemed her time with Holden hadn't gotten Jasper out of her system.

"So are you," she pointed out, standing up and shoving Rush's letters in her bag.

"Some of us have to get a jump start on the semester if we want to stay top of the class," he said, nodding towards the stack of books in his arms. "We can't all be prodigies like you. And here you are trying to get an unfair advantage. How's my sister supposed to compete?"

"If you must know," Sophie corrected him, sliding into her best attempt at playful banter, "I wasn't studying. I needed a break."

"A break? From what? You just got back."

"I spent the entire break at Vivienne's house," Sophie explained, though house seemed like too small a term.

"Right," Jasper said slowly. "Ryka mentioned that. Doesn't she live in a castle?"

"Something like that." Sophie went on. "But even with all that space, it was a bit…"

"Much?" Jasper volunteered.

"You could say that," Sophie laughed. "I just needed a moment to myself."

"I'm sorry to have disturbed you then," Jasper said, turning away.

"No, it's ok," Sophie said, perhaps a little too desperately. "I'm good now. Are you heading out?" Jasper nodded, and Sophie, figuring he had already sensed her desperation, asked "Can I join you?"

He nodded again and they set off from the library. "You know," he said after a moment's silence, "I was a little disappointed you didn't come to stay with Ryka over break."

"You were?" Sophie stopped walking, but then realized that was strange and forced herself to move forward.

"It would have been nice to get to know you a little better."

"It would?" Sophie cringed internally. Why couldn't she come up with better responses?

"Of course. But Ryka said that whatever Vivienne wants, Vivienne gets. And apparently, she asked you first." He turned to look at her for a moment. "Perhaps some other time."

They had reached the library doors, and as they stepped outside, Jasper gestured in the opposite direction of Sophie's dorm. "I'm this way," he said. "Have a good term." And he set off without so much of a backward glance in Sophie's direction.

His long, confident stride made quick work of the courtyard, and a feeling of disappointment settled in Sophie's stomach as she watched him disappear around a building. Was this why she wasn't willing to commit to anything more serious with Holden? Because she was holding out hope that something might happen with Jasper, even though he had never shown more than a friendly interest in her?

"Pub tonight?" Vivienne asked the moment Sophie stepped into the room. She had been so lost in her thoughts that she had barely noticed she was back in the dorm. "Eryka's already in."

It had been a complicated twenty-four hours, and Sophie was more than ready to put them to rest and start the term fresh. "Yes, please."

Chapter 11
East Lawn

Professor Rygge called Sophie to her office the next day. "I'm making a change to your work study," she told Sophie matter-of-factly when she sat down.

"Really?" Sophie smiled. "Thank you," she said, emphasizing the words. As part of her scholarship, she was required to spend ten hours a week working on campus. Last semester, she was stuck in the dining hall, scraping food off plates and shoving them into a massive dishwasher. The only way it could have been worse is if she'd had to wash them by hand.

"I talked to the dean, and you're being moved to tapestry repair."

"Oh," Sophie's face fell slightly. Sure, that was better than half-eaten sandwiches, but she had already done so much repair work in her life and her goal in coming to East Lawn was to distance herself from that work, not do more of it.

"I know repair work isn't what you want to be doing," Professor Rygge continued as if she was reading Sophie's mind, "but we're short-staffed, and I know you can handle it. You should feel honored," she said, giving Sophie a pointed look. "We usually don't give anyone that as a work-study job before their third year."

"Thank you," Sophie said, taking the info sheet Professor Rygge handed her.

"They're so busy you can probably pick up some extra shifts as well if you can fit them around your coursework. It might help you pay for France."

France. Sophie sighed. The first years had the option to go to France over their spring break, to see famous tapestries and visit a few of the more well-respected tapestry workshops. But the trip wasn't included in tuition, and Sophie wasn't sure yet how she could pay for it. She appreciated Professor Rygge making the suggestion.

"Thanks, Professor," Sophie said again. She shoved the info sheet into her bag and realized her half-finished letter to Rush was still there. Settling on a bench outside Professor Rygge's office, she scribbled a few extra lines about her new work-study assignment before stuffing it in an envelope and dropping it in the post box.

Their spring-term classes continued where they left off at the end of the fall term. That meant more of Professor Rygge's adulations for Sophie's weaving, more of Sophie's struggles with French, and more of Eryka's frustrations with Professor Ackerman's approach to tapestry history.

Eryka glowered, looking at the syllabus, which outlined their continued study of European tapestries, up to the present day. But Professor Ackerman was beaming as she pointed to Vivienne. "We'll be doing an entire segment on Vivienne's mother later in the term. It will be wonderful to get some first-hand information."

Vivienne flushed, and Sophie couldn't help but feel sorry for her. She knew Vivienne wouldn't have much, if anything, to contribute to the conversation.

"She's the worst," Vivienne burst out the second they had left the hall, Eryka nodding fervently alongside her in agreement. "What am I even supposed to say when we get there? I barely knew her." This statement might have come across painfully if someone else had spoken it, but Vivienne was matter of fact. "She might as well ask you," she said, turning to Sophie. "At this point, you probably know more than I do."

Sophie didn't know what to say. She didn't want to admit that Vivienne was right. All those hours in Sabrina's study, not to mention the tapestries Vivienne knew nothing about, the trip to Sabrina's workshop, and everything Holden told her, she was starting to become a bit of an expert on Sabrina Maxwell. Which was a nicer way of saying she was growing weirdly obsessed with her roommate's dead mother.

"Don't worry," Sophie tried to comfort Vivienne. "When the time comes, I'll slip you a few random tidbits I picked up in her journals. That should keep Ackerman happy."

"That's great," Eryka huffed, "but it doesn't change the fact that we aren't studying anything outside of Europe *again.*"

"But at least we've got France to look forward to," Vivienne said. Sophie's suggestion had done the trick and Vivienne was back to her usual perky self. "No mention of Mum there."

"Big deal," Eryka yawned. "I've been to France a million times."

Sophie wasn't sure how she'd even pay for the trip, and Eryka was talking about it like it was nothing. "Well, don't minimize it for the rest of us." Sophie burst out. "Especially those of us who may not be able to afford to go." Before Eryka could respond, Sophie stormed off in a huff.

"Truce," Eryka said, setting a beer in front of Sophie at the pub that night. Sophie hadn't said a word to either of her roommates the rest of the day, just nodded silently when they invited her to the pub that evening. She thought about saying no, but the idea of wallowing alone in their room was somehow worse.

Before Sophie could respond, Vivienne sat down next to her, flashing her a wide grin. "Eryka and I talked about it and we can loan you the money for France if it would help."

"What," Sophie sputtered, practically spitting out half her beer.

"That," said Eryka, giving Vivienne a pointed look, "was not how that was supposed to come out." Then she turned to Sophie. "But yes, we can give you the money."

"I'm not your charity case," Sophie spat back.

"It's not charity," Eryka said. "It's a loan. We expect you to pay us back—"

"With interest," Vivienne chimed in with a grin.

"You think this is funny?" Sophie snarled. She knew she was overreacting. They were just trying to help. But at that moment, all she could see was them flaunting the difference between their financial situation and hers. Before they could respond, she slammed the pint on the table and stormed from the pub.

Sophie feigned sleep when her roommates returned a few hours later, even though it was clear from the way they tiptoed into the room that they were hoping not to wake her. She was grateful that her first shift in the repair studio was early the next morning and snuck out before either of them was awake.

A petite woman, her mousy brown hair pulled back under a bandana, greeted Sophie at the door to East Lawn's repair shop. "You must be Sophie," she said, holding out her hand. "I'm Gloria. I run things around here."

Gloria shook her hand — it was exceptionally large and strong for a woman of her size — and Sophie tried to hide her surprise that someone that young would be in charge. Gloria looked to be no older than thirty. Her faded green coveralls were darned at the elbows and cuffed above the ankle, revealing knit wool socks and a pair of well-worn leather sandals.

Sophie had expected East Lawn's repair shop to be similar to her mother's cramped space, with tapestries in various states of repair practically stacked on top of each other. But this was a massive space, meticulously organized, where a dozen tapestries sat with room to work around each.

Gloria interrupted Sophie's thoughts. "Hannah tells me you've been working in your mother's repair shop for half your life."

"Who?"

"Sorry," Gloria laughed, "Professor Rygge."

"Oh, right," Sophie responded. She should have figured that out from context.

"We'll start you out with something simple, just a little patch job, so I can see your skill level. But I have a feeling we'll be moving you up to bigger projects in no time." Gloria kept her gaze on Sophie as she took in the various tapestries across the room, before continuing, "We take on a lot of projects. Stuff for the community, and of course, we're in charge of keeping the university's collection running smoothly, but we also get a lot of significant historical projects."

Sophie stopped in front of a tapestry featuring a riot of plants and animals, zigzagging across the surface in lurid color. She couldn't tell if it was supposed to be a tropical jungle or something closer to home. "That one," Gloria said, following her gaze, "is from the fifteenth-century. German. You won't be starting there," she added with a gruff laugh.

Instead, she led Sophie to a smaller tapestry at the end of the room, barely large enough for two people to step through at once. Sophie noticed a few spots where it had gone threadbare. "We'll put you to work on this one first. It's a favor to one of the professors here, but we've been too short-staffed to get around to it, and she's starting to get annoyed at how long we've had it. But that's not how favors work," Gloria added as an afterthought, more to herself than to Sophie. "Come on, I'll show you where we keep the supplies. I'm guessing you know how to color match."

Sophie nodded and followed Gloria to one end of the space with shelves upon shelves of wool thread in every conceivable color. While her mother's studio had a limited inventory, forcing them to dye colors to match, it seemed here that any necessary color could simply be plucked from the shelf as a perfect match. It must have cost a fortune. "I'll leave you to it," Gloria said, surprising Sophie with how much leeway she was giving her right from the start. Professor Rygge must have really talked her up, and it was starting to make her nervous.

But once she found the right yarns and settled in front of the tapestry, she realized she had nothing to worry about. It felt like home, and she was so ensconced in her work that she didn't even notice several other women enter the room until one of them called to Gloria, "Who's the new kid?"

Sophie couldn't believe her initial hesitation at being placed in the repair shop for her work-study. Even without the promise of extra money to help pay for her trip to France, Sophie found herself spending more and more time there.

It wasn't just the work, though that felt good too. Growing up, Sophie thought tapestry repair wasn't for her, but it turned out her frustrations were more from her mother's criticisms than from the work itself. Sophie soon found herself entrusted with even more complex projects, though as the low woman in rank, she was also given the most basic jobs.

But it was the women, more than anything, that made the repair shop what it was.

Sophie didn't realize how much she was lacking in close female friendships until she started working in the repair shop. Her sisters were much younger than her, and her only close friend growing up was Rush. She didn't interact much with her classmates now that she was in college, instead spending most of her time with her roommates. While she considered Vivienne and Eryka friends, she didn't think of them as confidantes, and her relationship with them had been tense since Sophie's blowup at the pub. And of course, there was her crush on Eryka's brother and her secret sexual exploits with Vivienne's.

The women in the repair studio were different. In some ways, they treated Sophie like a little sister, because she was the youngest and newest member of the staff. But mostly, they treated her like an equal.

There was Janice, the youngest in the group after Sophie. Like Sophie, she had started while on work-study at East Lawn, but her focus had been tapestry repair, and when Gloria asked her to stay on after graduation, Janice happily accepted. Janice seemed to be high more than she wasn't, but it didn't stop her from having an uncanny knack for recreating the most complex weave structures.

Janice also had an unexpected friendship with the shop's oldest employee. Rosemary was pushing sixty and as prim and proper as anyone Sophie had met in the four months since she'd moved to England. Sophie couldn't fathom how someone could sit so upright all of the time.

There was Innes, who had spent her 20s and 30s bouncing around various repair shops throughout Europe before landing at East Lawn. No one was sure whether this was just another temporary stop for Innes, but in the meantime, she regaled them with equally fascinating stories of the tapestries she worked on and the people she'd slept with.

Then there was Gloria. She rarely joined in with the other's laughter, outwardly maintaining her tough demeanor. But more than once, Sophie thought she caught her stifling a smile as she ducked into her office, shouting at them to get back to work. And despite her gruff exterior, she was quick to praise the women for their work, pointing out anytime someone managed to pull off a tricky repair.

Before long, Sophie found herself opening up to these women. She told them about the tensions with her mother, her friendship with Rush, and the awkwardness of sleeping with one of her roommate's brothers while crushing on the other's.

She expected Janice, Innes, and Gloria to be supportive of her tryst with Holden, but she was surprised when Rosemary voiced her approval. "You don't owe your roommate anything," she piped up. "Who you choose to sleep with is nobody's business but your own."

Sophie gave her a weak smile, thinking there must be a lot more to Rosemary than she let on when Innes stage whispered in her ear. "She would know. She gets up to some shiiiiiit."

Rosemary said nothing, just beamed, hummed softly, and turned back to the tapestry she was working on. Sophie turned to Janice for confirmation. "You don't know the half of it," she said to Sophie with a wink.

One morning a few weeks into term, Sophie arrived to find the women standing around a new tapestry. It wasn't technically Sophie's shift, but her morning color theory lecture had been canceled, and as was often the case, she opted to spend her free time in the repair shop. Sophie took one glance at the tapestry, with its swirling sky, and let out a little gasp of recognition.

"Is that a Sabrina Maxwell?" she asked.

"Very good," Gloria replied, turning to look at her. "How did you know that?" It occurred to Sophie that she hadn't mentioned Vivienne or Holden's last names.

"I'm a bit of a fan," Sophie said, and before she could get any further, Janice chimed in.

"Gloria used to work for Sabrina."

"You did?" Sophie said turning to look at her, her eyes wide. She tried to picture Sabrina's journals and thought maybe she'd seen some mention of a Gloria amongst the notes. She also did some quick mental math. "But you aren't old enough…"

"I'm older than I look," Gloria said smiling, and Sophie realized she must have misjudged her age on the first day they met. "But yes, I was young when I started working for Sabrina." There was a hardness in Gloria's voice that Sophie couldn't quite pin, but then Gloria continued, "I left when she was m— after she died." The hardness turned towards sadness.

"I'm sorry," Sophie said. "I had no idea."

"It's ok," Gloria said. "I don't like to talk about it much." But then she continued, "I worked as a weaver, but after Sabrina died, I was a mess. Did a lot of drugs, bounced around, tried to—" she stopped herself. "Let's just say it wasn't good."

The other women nodded slowly. It was clear they knew this story.

"But then someone reached out to me because they knew I used to work for her and asked if I could repair a tapestry they owned. I sort of fell into repair work, and that's how I ended up here." She finished, more brightly than when she started.

"Anyone who knows anything about Sabrina Maxwell knows that Gloria is the one you go to when you need repairs," Janice added with more than a hint of pride.

"Alright, that's enough gawking," Gloria's voice was harsh, but there was a mix of pride and embarrassment on her face. "Everybody get back to work. Rosemary, you can help me with this beast."

Sophie felt a pang of disappointment. As the newest member of the group, she shouldn't have expected to be assigned to the repair of such a valuable tapestry, but she had hoped all the same. She'd have to settle for sharing space with it, stealing a glance whenever she got a break from whatever boring, basic tapestry she was currently tasked with.

A few weeks before spring break, flush with cash from her extra repair shifts, Sophie stopped by the office to make her final payment for the trip to France.

"Your balance has already been paid," the receptionist said blandly when Sophie gave him her name.

"It's been what," Sophie stared at him, mouth agape. "By who?"

"No idea," he said in a vacant tone. "The note says they wish to remain anonymous."

Sophie huffed all the way back to the dorm and practically slammed the door to her room off its hinges as she hurtled inside. Eryka was sitting on her bed reading a book, and Vivienne was doing homework, scratching out what looked like a tapestry design on a sheet of paper.

"I thought I told you," Sophie was practically yelling, but neither of them seemed phased, "that I would figure out how to pay for France myself."

"You did," Eryka said mildly, not even looking up from her book.

"Then why did you pay for it anyway?"

"We didn't." It was Vivienne's turn to reply, and like Eryka, she didn't look up at Sophie.

"Bullshit," Sophie shouted.

Eryka turned towards her, "Why would we pay for someone who's barely spoken to us in weeks?"

Sophie wanted to continue arguing and opened her mouth, but couldn't think of anything to say, so she simply closed it again.

"She's got a point," Vivienne added. "You've been storming around here like we did something wrong." She looked pointedly at Sophie. "But if anyone's got a right to be mad, it's me."

"What?" Sophie stammered, momentarily confused.

"Holden," Vivienne said simply.

Sophie wheeled around to Eryka and hissed, "You told her?"

"She didn't tell me anything," Vivienne laughed. "You two are not as subtle as you think you are."

"You knew?"

"I figured it out," Vivienne said, clearly delighting in Sophie's shock. "That day on the beach you had your hand so far up his thigh I thought you two were about to start going at it on the sand."

"Oh." Sophie looked awkwardly at the floor. "Um, sorry."

"I don't care," Vivienne smiled broadly, "a girl's got needs. And I guess you could do worse than my brother.

Though it sounds like you did a number on him," Vivienne added, but she didn't seem too upset about it.

"I, um…" Sophie didn't know how to respond.

"He wrote me a letter," Vivienne continued, "asking about you while trying to seem like he wasn't asking about you. I told him to let it go, that you were being a bitch to everyone right now."

"She's not wrong," Eryka chimed in.

"I'm sorry," Sophie replied. "I don't know what's gotten into me."

"Holden," Eryka said with a laugh.

"And she hasn't even met him," Vivienne smirked. "But she's right. His perpetual bad mood is enough to drag anyone down."

Sophie wanted to defend Holden, but she still felt like she was on shaky ground with her roommates. "I'm sorry I've been such a jerk," she added lamely.

"It's fine," Eryka said, "just cut the shit moving forward, or we are not hanging with you in France."

"And you swear," Sophie said, the words tumbling from her mouth before she could stop, "that neither of you paid for me."

Vivienne sighed, exasperated. "You really did spend too much time with Holden — so paranoid." Then she smiled as if struck by a sudden idea. "Let's go to the pub, we need to find you a palette cleanser. It's time you had some happier D."

Even Sophie couldn't help but laugh.

"Unless you have to work," Eryka added.

"I don't have a scheduled shift today," Sophie said, happy to finally be on better terms with her roommates, and relieved that her secret about Holden was out in the open. "And since someone paid for France, I guess I don't need the extra hours." She turned to Vivienne and gave her a small salute, "Lead the way, ma'am."

Despite Vivienne's belief that Sophie needed a palette cleanser, there was only one guy she hoped to see at the pub.

Jasper was already at a table with a few of his architecture friends when they walked in. "Grab a table," Eryka told them, waving them on while she went to say hi.

Vivienne followed Sophie's gaze as the two of them sat down. "That," she said firmly, nodding her head towards Jasper, "is not what I meant by a palette cleanser." As Vivienne spoke, Sophie noticed her eyes flick towards Eryka.

Sophie sighed. "Maybe I'm not the only one who needs a palette cleanser."

It was Vivienne's turn to sigh and shake her head. "We really do make quite the pair."

"If it makes you feel any better," Sophie said, turning towards Vivienne. "I did feel bad not telling you about me and Holden."

"Oh, I know," said Vivienne, taking a swig of her beer. "I figured that's why you were being such a bitch. And for your punishment," she put down her glass and scanned the room, "you will now go talk to that guy." She pointed at an upperclassman Sophie vaguely recognized, sitting at the end of the bar by himself.

"He's by himself at a bar," Sophie said by way of an excuse. "Do you honestly think he'll be happier?"

"Anyone's happier than Holden," Vivienne said, practically shoving her out of her chair just as Eryka sat down at the table. "Now go."

The guy at the end of the bar, whose name was Patrick, was nice enough, but Sophie didn't find herself any more attracted to him after a couple of pints. She made sure to leave the pub at the same time he did, to keep Vivienne off her back, but said goodnight as soon as they turned the corner out of sight of the pub.

Once Patrick set off in the opposite direction, Sophie hesitated for a moment, thinking it would be weird if she went back to the room so quickly. She should at least be gone a little longer if Vivienne was going to think she had hooked up with Patrick.

She debated going to the library but at the last moment, changed course and headed to the repair studio. The lights were still on, and as she got closer, she could see Gloria alone in the room, working on Sabrina's tapestry. Gloria looked up when Sophie tapped softly on the window, and she got up to let her in the locked door.

"What are you doing here so late?" she asked Sophie.

"Killing time so my roommate thinks I fucked the guy I left the pub with." If this struck Gloria as odd, she didn't let on. "What are you doing here so late?"

"Just trying to make progress on this tapestry. I don't want the owner to think we're taking too long just to hike up the bill."

Something in Gloria's voice made it seem like that wasn't the whole story.

"It must be nice," Sophie said softly, moving to stand in front of the tapestry, "when you get to spend time with one of her works." She moved her eyes up, scanning the surface, which shimmered in the soft glow of the studio. "It's really incredible."

Sophie turned to look at Gloria, and for a moment she thought the corners of her eyes looked wet. But when Gloria spoke, her voice was gruff. "If you're going to hang around here gawking at tapestries, you might as well be useful. Grab a needle and get to work on that section over there." Gloria nodded her head toward a spot in the lower left corner that was becoming threadbare.

"Are you serious?" Sophie gasped.

"For Frigg's sake, it's just a tapestry." But Sophie thought she saw a hint of a smile. "Get to work."

Sophie could barely contain her excitement. Her mother always said the best way to learn a weaver's style was to get in there and do some repair work, and here she was with her fingers in Sabrina's tapestry.

Suddenly, Sophie was struck by a realization. "Gloria," she said tentatively, breaking the silence. "Did you weave this?"

Gloria gave a small smile. "I did."

"What was it like?" Sophie asked before she could stop herself. She'd heard the stories from Holden, but he had been a child. Here was a woman who had held Sophie's dream job. When Gloria didn't respond, Sophie continued quickly, "Working for Sabrina, I mean? Was it amazing?"

"I can see how you would think that," Gloria said, not looking up from the section of tapestry she was working on. "And in some ways it was. But Sabrina was incredibly exacting. Her standards were so high, and I was just getting out of school. There were so many days where I was in over my head.

"I'll never forget the day I had spent hours on a section of tapestry, when suddenly Sabrina stormed over, told me it was all wrong, and forced me to rip it out and start over."

This didn't sound like the Sabrina Holden described and Sophie's brain did somersaults trying to reconcile these two different memories.

"She made me stay late that night, to redo everything I'd ripped out. I was so furious, I wanted to quit. But Sabrina stayed late too, patiently showing me where I went wrong. That was when we—" Gloria paused, as if she'd said too much. "I mean, that's when I realized that you could be a tough boss and a caring boss at the same time. She really was both."

Gloria gave an uncomfortable cough, and Sophie looked away to give her a moment. Then Gloria continued, "Unfortunately for you, I never quite manage the caring part."

Sophie couldn't help but smile as she turned back towards the tapestry. But she also couldn't resist asking one more question. "Do you miss her?"

"Every damn day. Now get back to work."

Sophie made every attempt to be quiet when she crept back into her dorm room a few hours later, but Vivienne's head turned in her direction and her muffled voice whispered, "Feel better?"

"Yes," Sophie told her, falling into her own bed. It wasn't a lie.

Chapter 12
Paris

I f you had asked Sophie before she went to school what she was most excited about, the chance to go to France and see some of the world's greatest tapestries, and the places that made them, would have been high on her list. But now that she was firmly ensconced in the repair of one of Sabrina's tapestries, she was having a hard time tearing herself away. The repair job was moving at a decent pace, and Sophie feared it would be finished and sent away before she returned from her trip.

She tried to enlist her roommates to help rebuild her enthusiasm, but they were even more nonplussed than she was.

"What's your favorite tapestry in Paris?" Sophie asked Eryka one morning, a few days before the trip. Eryka grew up a stone's throw from France, so trips to Paris and beyond to look at and buy tapestries were commonplace.

Eryka shrugged, "Honestly, they all start to blur together after a while." And she added, with a long sigh, "Everything is so Euro-centric there."

Sophie doubted this was true. She imagined Paris had to be more multicultural than that, but she also didn't have Eryka's experience.

She tried Vivienne. "What's your favorite tapestry there?"

Vivienne wasn't quite as well traveled as Eryka when it came to France, but she'd made several trips there with her father and brother, and Sophie had to assume, Mrs. Winthrop, over the years. Now it was her turn to roll her eyes. "Who cares? The best tapestries in Paris are the ones that take you to the coast. And sadly, we're not going there."

Sophie was starting to get annoyed. "I thought you didn't do public tapestries?"

"I'll make an exception," Vivienne said, with a flick of her hair, "if they take me somewhere fabulous."

"You mean if they take you to the beach," Sophie corrected.

"Same thing."

"Is there anything you two are excited about for this trip?" Sophie asked, in a last-ditch effort to rebuild her enthusiasm.

"Clothes," Eryka's replied, at the same moment Vivienne chimed in with, "Girls."

Nothing they said made her more excited for the trip.

But Sophie's entire outlook changed the moment she stepped from the tapestry in the British Museum into the Musee d'Orsay in Paris.

She didn't know where to look first. Light from an arched glass ceiling flooded a massive interior that made the gallery at Weddlesmoore seem stumpy in comparison, and in every direction, signs pointed towards tapestries meant to take you to different parts of France, Europe, and beyond. Hulking statues stood in the vast passageway as if the travelers rushing by needed company on their journeys. Meanwhile, like Sophie, tourists gawked in awe — at the building, at the statues, but mostly, at the tapestries, some of which stood nearly two stories high and many more times as wide.

A little American girl, no older than three, squealed with delight. "Look at that one, Mommy," she cried, her voice piercing the indistinct jumble of French, and Sophie turned to watch her dart across the room, her haggard parents chasing after her. Sophie wondered for a moment what it would be like if her parents had taken her to a place like this when she was that young, but before she could register how different her life would be, Eryka and Vivienne pressed up behind her. "Come on," Vivienne said impatiently. "I want to get to the hotel."

"You mean you want to get to the bar next to the hotel," Eryka corrected her.

"Don't you?" Vivienne replied.

Sophie could have spent hours at the museum, but she also had no idea where she was going and reluctantly followed her classmates out into Paris.

"Why do we have to walk," Vivienne whined, a few blocks in. "Why couldn't we take a tapestry straight to the hotel?"

"I don't think it's that kind of hotel," Eryka replied dryly. Then she added, with a wink at Sophie, "I doubt they even have room service."

But Sophie was barely paying attention. The buildings in Paris were unlike anything she'd seen before. Everything looked like a miniature castle, and her eyes kept darting between ornate details and the shops along the walkway. Patisseries and boulangeries mingled with tapestry galleries and repair shops, plus so many boutiques that Eryka was almost as distracted as Sophie.

"You two are taking forever," Vivienne moaned, shoving them along.

The hotel, as Eryka had rightly guessed, was bare bones, but equally charming, as quintessentially French as Sophie imagined it would be. Professors Rygge and Ackerman stood in the lobby, distributing keys to Sophie's classmates. The hotel only had double rooms, so Eryka was paired with another girl from their class, and Sophie, to her disappointment, was paired with Vivienne.

"Don't worry," Vivienne whispered as they headed up the narrow staircase, clearly misreading the look on Sophie's face. "I won't bring any girls back to our room. I'd rather see their apartments anyway."

"What a relief," Sophie replied, feigning a weak smile.

They had the afternoon to explore Paris on their own before structured activities started the next day.

"I'm going shopping," Eryka announced, barging into Sophie and Vivienne's room as they were still unpacking. "You in?"

"I suppose," Vivienne replied, a look of longing on her face. "I guess I can't spend all day at the cafe."

"I mean, you could. It is Paris," Eryka replied. "But you'll have more fun with me."

Sophie saw an excited smile briefly cross Vivienne's face, but it quickly became impassive when she caught Sophie looking.

Eryka turned to Sophie. "What about you?"

Sophie hesitated. They were only staying in Paris for two days before moving on to other parts of France, and she wanted to see as many tapestries as possible in that time.

Before she could answer, Vivienne chimed in. "Let me guess," she said flatly. "More museums." Vivienne rolled her eyes at Eryka.

"Dude," Eryka chided Vivienne. "It's her thing." Then she turned to Sophie, "But promise you'll meet up with us later at the cafe down the street."

Sophie nodded, and Vivienne turned to Eryka with a broad grin. "Guess it's just you and me then." Vivienne's arm moved slightly as if to link arms with Eryka, but then she dropped it to her side, apparently thinking better of it.

Once they had left the room, Sophie checked the itinerary. She thought back to the works in her *Great Tapestries* book and tried to come up with a priority list. Now that she was here, she realized two days wasn't nearly enough time.

She also couldn't help thinking that Eryka had a point. Their itinerary was incredibly Euro-centric. They would spend all day tomorrow at the Louvre, and the next day, they'd spend the morning at the Musee d'Art Moderne de Paris, followed by the Centre Pompidou. Sophie knew this was also a modern museum — Professor Ackerman mentioned it in class — but she didn't know anything about the tapestries inside, because they weren't featured in any of her books. The Pompidou had barely been open for two months.

Sophie scanned the list again. Where was…

Professor Ackerman was in the lobby looking at papers when Sophie came down a few minutes later. "We aren't going to the Cluny?" Sophie blurted out, more forcefully than she intended.

"Miss O'Toole," Professor Ackerman said sternly, turning one eye on Sophie. "Do not think that just because we are in Paris you can let go of all propriety. Please address me properly."

"I'm sorry, Professor Ackerman," Sophie said, her cheeks turning red with shame and anger. Her relationship with Professor Ackerman remained as acrimonious as the first day of class. "I was just wondering why the Musee de Cluny wasn't on our itinerary. I mean," Sophie rushed on, unable to stop herself, "it houses one of the most famous series of tapestries in the world."

Professor Ackerman slowly turned her head towards Sophie, both eyes now boring into her, as if willing Sophie to question her judgment again. When Sophie said nothing, Professor Ackerman continued, "I would have thought that would have been obvious, Miss O'Toole." Still, Sophie said nothing, and Professor Ackerman gave an exasperated sigh.

"That tapestry is no longer used for transportation. If it ever was. Unicorns," she added, almost as an afterthought, followed by a small "harumph."

Sophie couldn't help herself. "But who cares if it isn't used for transportation? It's supposed to be one of the finest tapestries in the world."

Now Sophie had pressed her luck too far. Professor Ackerman stood up. "Miss O'Toole, I have been organizing this trip for over thirty years. Do you know how many students have been on this trip—" she was growing angrier now, slightly distracted, "even the great Sabrina Maxwell once—"

"Wha—" Sophie started, but one glance at Professor Ackerman told her not to push it. So that's why Professor Ackerman always brought up Sabrina. She had been her student.

"No student," Professor Ackerman continued, "has ever dared question my itinerary. If you don't like it, Miss O'Toole, you can just take a tapestry straight back to England and spend the rest of break alone in your dorm."

Now that she was here, Sophie didn't want to leave. "No, I'm sorry ma'am." She hung her head. "I won't question you again." *To your face*, Sophie thought to herself. She would go right on criticizing Professor Ackerman in her head, not to mention in private with Eryka.

Professor Ackerman turned back to her papers, shaking her head. "Of all the nerve," she muttered under her breath, before turning back to Sophie. "If the blasted tapestry means so much to you, go see the damn thing now. That's why we gave you a free afternoon."

Sophie nodded, and without saying another word, she headed from the lobby and out into the weak sunshine of early spring in Paris.

Once Sophie was out on the walkway, she realized she had no idea how to get to the Musee de Cluny. Her French was barely passable, despite being in a second term of French class, but she managed to flag down a couple and they pointed her in the right direction. It took a few more of these interactions and a few wrong turns before she found the imposing stone building.

Nearly every building in Paris looked like a castle to Sophie, but it turned out the Musee de Cluny really was — an elegant medieval mansion that had been converted into a museum. Sophie stood outside for a few minutes, marveling at the thick walls and high, turreted windows.

Sophie wandered the museum in search of the tapestries. Eventually she found a small doorway that led her through a darkened hall. Sophie stepped inside and let out a little gasp. Against dark walls, six tapestries hung in a square around the room, practically glowing in the low light. They were united by a lush red background, scattered with flowers and trees, and in the center of each was a young woman and a unicorn.

Just like in the history room at the V&A, low stanchions strung with ropes stood about two feet in front of the tapestries, to prevent anyone from trying to enter. Sophie stepped up the rope and leaned as far over as she could, aware of the guard eyeing her from the corner. The fineness of the weaving was unlike anything Sophie had seen before. Even Sabrina's tapestries couldn't match it, though they came closest. Sophie couldn't image how long it must have taken, even with a team of weavers, to construct such massive detailed scenes from such fine thread.

After moving slowly around the room, sucked into the detail of each tapestry, Sophie settled on a bench in the center to take in the full effect. The results were equally mesmerizing, and if Sophie didn't know they were woven, she would have sworn she was looking at an intricate, detailed mural. From a distance, different elements would catch her eye, and she would stand to get a closer look before returning to the bench to take in the full picture. She repeated this process for what must have been hours, until the guard gave a little cough to indicate the museum was closing, and she checked her watch and realized she was late meeting Vivienne and Eryka at the cafe.

Sophie walked from the museum in a daze. She itched to get back to a loom, to see if she could create anything close to those details herself.

Chapter 13
Paris

Sunlight flooded into the hotel room the next morning as Vivienne flung back the curtains.

"Shut those," Sophie moaned, pulling her covers over her eyes. Then, recognizing what was going on, she turned towards Vivienne, even as she used the covers to shield her face. "When did you get home?"

"Late," Vivienne said, bustling to Sophie's bag and throwing some clothes in her direction. "Or early," she flashed Sophie a smile, "depending on how you look at it."

"Good for you," Sophie muttered, turning her face back into her pillow.

True to her word, Vivienne had disappeared early the night before, with a young French woman she had spotted in the cafe. Sophie and Eryka had stayed, drinking bottle after bottle of wine that the waiter kept bringing, courtesy of this or that gentleman seated around the bar. Most of the men were far too old for them to be interested in — Sophie thought a few looked old enough to be her grandfather— but they weren't about to turn down free wine.

The thought of it now though made Sophie wretch, and she brought her hand to her throbbing head.

"Come on," Vivienne said impatiently, "we're due at the Louvre in an hour."

Sophie eyed her skeptically. "Since when have you been in a rush to get to a museum? Unless…"

"Unless what?" Vivienne turned away evasively.

"You're meeting that girl," Sophie blurted out, then immediately regretted it. The sound of her own voice hurt her head.

"Her name is Dominique," Vivienne corrected. "She's a student here in Paris, and when she heard we were stuck spending the day in the Louvre, she offered to join me and give me a private tour of her favorite tapestries."

"A private tour, huh? Something tells me," Sophie said, taking pains to keep her voice low, "that you aren't the only woman she's used that line on."

"Who cares," Vivienne shrugged. "It will be much more fun than whatever Professor Ackerman thinks we should see. Now come on," she said, grabbing Sophie's arm and dragging her out of bed. "We'll get you some coffee, that should help."

Eryka was already seated at a table outside the cafe, sipping an espresso, when they arrived. Compared to Sophie, who had taken one look at herself in the mirror and decided today was a lost cause, Eryka looked completely composed.

"How are you fine?" Sophie asked her, sitting down and placing her head in her hands. She heard the waiter come over and Vivienne ordered two coffees and a couple of croissants. Sophie was in no state to exercise her terrible French this morning.

Eryka seemed completely unfazed by Sophie's state and responded simply, "I'm part French, remember?"

"That's the trick?" Sophie eyed her as she gingerly took a sip of the coffee the waiter had just placed in front of her. "I'm part Italian, and I feel like I got bashed in the head with a rock."

"Yes, but did you grow up drinking wine with every meal?"

Sophie couldn't argue with that logic. Her parents weren't big drinkers, at least not around Sophie and her siblings. She and Rush would crash the occasional party in the woods, but that was usually to grab a beer or two before heading off to do their own thing. That kind of practice was fine for evenings at the pub, but nothing had prepared her for bottles upon bottles of French wine.

"Just be glad I was with you all night," Eryka said to Sophie, "or you would have ended up as some French guy's mistress."

"What?" Sophie and Vivienne said together, though in very different tones.

"You were giving serious do-me eyes to the guy at the end of the bar," Eryka teased her.

"The old guy?" Sophie questioned, her memory of events very fuzzy. "That's gross."

"He wasn't that bad," Eryka continued. "He looked rich. I know that's the way you like them," she said, nodding in Vivienne's direction.

"That's not true—" Sophie interjected, but Eryka cut her off.

"But I wasn't sure about your stance on married men, and when he mentioned his wife while the two of you were chatting, I figured it was time to get you to bed. So I told him you weren't feeling well."

"That did not happen," Sophie said, turning to look at Eryka.

"Your word against mine," Eryka replied, leaning back in her chair and finishing her last sip of espresso.

"Come on you two," Vivienne said, jumping up from her chair and draining her own coffee. "We're going to be late."

Eryka gave Sophie a questioning look. "She's meeting someone," Sophie said flatly, making one last attempt at her coffee between gags.

"Her name is Dominique," Vivienne said again firmly, "And we've got to go. I don't want her to think I've stood her up."

The entryway to the Louvre was filled with tourists, all chattering away excitedly as they waited to show their passports — many of the Louvre's tapestries went to international locations — and it was all Sophie could do to keep her head from exploding. Why hadn't she stopped drinking sooner last night? Why hadn't she drank more of her coffee this morning?

Professors Rygge and Ackerman stood at the front of a group of their classmates, passing out tickets and a typed list of the tapestries they were to see.

"We expect detailed notes on each one," Professor Ackerman said firmly, handing them copies. Sophie and Eryka exchanged glances, which Professor Ackerman accurately interpreted. "I've chosen them for a reason."

"The worst reason," Eryka muttered to Sophie as Professor Ackerman turned away.

Once their professor's back was turned, Vivienne whispered "Cover me" to Sophie and Eryka and slinked off in the direction of a young woman leaning against a column.

"Dominique," Eryka whispered dramatically, and Sophie couldn't help but giggle. "Come on," Eryka said, slightly louder now. "Let's go to the Middle Eastern wing."

Sophie studied the list Professor Ackerman had handed them. "There are no Middle Eastern tapestries on this list."

"I know," Eryka humphed, rolling her eyes. "But I can tell you whatever you need to know about the boring tapestries on this list. Plus," she added, giving Sophie, who looked more than a little disheveled, a once over, "there are always far less people in that section of the museum."

"Less people?" Sophie asked her, looking around at the crowds. "I'm in."

As Eryka had promised, the Middle Eastern wing was nearly devoid of people, at least compared to the main entry.

"Tourists are so predictable," Eryka said with an air of annoyance. "They all want to see the same old European shit they can visit anytime."

Sophie didn't want to admit that, had she not been hung over, she would have wanted to see those pieces as well. Instead, she wordlessly followed Eryka around the gallery.

"I can't focus on anything," she admitted after a few minutes of staring in vain at a tapestry.

"You need some fresh air," Eryka replied, grabbing her arm and dragging her toward a tapestry on the other side of the room. An intense light permeated mountains that folded their way down to the sparkling Mediterranean Sea.

Sophie eyed Eryka with suspicion. "Who are you, Vivienne?" Then, she added, "Besides, I can't swim."

"You don't have to go in the water," Eryka sighed. "But a little sea air and sunshine is just what your hangover needs."

Eryka was right. They stepped through the tapestry and the two of them walked along the beach. At first, the sun hurt Sophie's dry eyes, but after a few minutes in the salty air, Sophie's head started to clear. She plopped down on the sand and let the sunshine wash over her.

"Don't get too comfortable," Eryka laughed, but she dropped into the sand next to Sophie. "Professor Ackerman will be pissed if she finds out we're off at the beach instead of studying the tapestries on her pointless list."

Sophie thought of the professor's comment that the Lady and the Unicorn tapestries weren't good for anything because you couldn't go through them. "Please," Sophie said, rolling her eyes. "She probably went straight through a tapestry into some boring old European town the moment we were all out of sight." Sophie paused for a moment, trying to imagine what Professor Ackerman did for fun — she couldn't think of anything — then continued, "I'm guessing she just gave us the list to keep us occupied while she enjoys a free trip to France."

Eryka nodded, "Of course, she's only in it for herself. Why else would you let an entire class loose in a museum full of tapestries without any kind of guide? Still," she added, standing up and brushing sand from herself, "we'd better get back."

The museum was dark after the light of the beach, but Sophie had to admit she was feeling much better. She suggested grabbing a croissant at the museum cafe and then making a start on Professor Ackerman's list. She was ravenous, and now that her head was clearer, she remembered that it wasn't like her to completely bail on an assignment, even one from a professor she disliked.

"You go," Eryka told her, looking resolutely around the gallery they were in. "I've seen those tapestries a hundred times. I could write about them in my sleep."

Now that she was feeling more herself, Sophie had to admit that it was incredible to be spending the day in the Louvre. These tapestries may not have been Eryka's thing, but for Sophie, who didn't have access to these kinds of masterworks growing up, it was like a banquet after years of subsisting on bread and water.

On her way out of the museum, she stopped in the gift shop to buy a few postcards. Facing the wall with a small stack in her hands, she felt someone uncomfortably close behind her.

"I hope at least one of those is for me," a familiar voice said in her ear.

Sophie turned on the spot, barely registering the dark curls before she was enveloped in a massive hug. She leaned into it for a moment before pushing Rush away.

"What are you doing here?" she shouted, shoving Rush again. A few people looked around in concern, and someone grumbled "stupide americains" under their breath.

Rush looked at the ground, suddenly sheepish. "I convinced a few of my roommates to bum around Europe with me for spring break." He gestured over his shoulder, where a couple of guys stood, looking bored and awkward.

Sophie gave Rush a look. Bumming was hardly a word anyone would use to describe Rush.

"Besides," he continued. "I wanted to make sure you were enjoying my present."

Confusion crossed Sophie's face. "What present?" She looked around, expecting Rush to pull a package out from behind his back. "Did I miss something?"

Rush pulled a big smile. "This trip." He leaned in conspiratorially and whispered, "You know, your anonymous donor."

"That was you?" She stared at him. "How did you even know?"

"You mentioned it in one of your letters." He tried to sound matter-of-fact, but it was clear this wasn't the reaction he was expecting.

Sophie moved from confusion to anger. "What the fuck, asshole?"

"Woah, what?" Rush took a step back and put his hands up. "I thought you'd be thrilled."

"Thrilled? Thrilled?" Sophie was yelling and people were starting to stare, but she didn't care. "I got in a huge fight with my roommates because I thought they'd paid for me. We barely spoke for weeks."

Rush raised his hands in mock surrender. "Sorry, sorry," he said, giving her a grin. "I thought it would be more fun to surprise you."

For some reason, this just made her angrier. "So you just showed up here so you could lord your money over me? Did you pay for their trips, too?" She jerked a thumb at the two guys standing behind him, and they both averted their eyes. "Or did you come here for a booty call?"

Rush's face fell. "It's not about that Sophie." She knew she had touched a nerve. He never called her Sophie. "Where is this even coming from? You never cared that I had more money than you before. I just wanted to see my best friend. I wanted to do something nice for you because you're my friend. I miss you." He looked down, then corrected himself. "I missed you. You. Not whoever this—"

At that moment, a staff member hurried over to them, looking stern. "Mademoiselle et monsier, vous devez partir."

"Huh?" Sophie stared at her blankly.

"Partir," the woman said more firmly, pointing towards the exit.

They continued their argument out on the street, Rush's friends looking even more awkward than they had in the museum.

"Why are you so mad at me?"

"I didn't ask you for this," Sophie spat back. "I was handling it on my own."

"I know you didn't ask for it. I just wanted to do something nice for my friend." He emphasized the last few words.

But Sophie wasn't listening, "But then you just show up here, expecting, I don't know what, expecting—"

Rush cut her off. "I wasn't expecting anything. I came here because I missed my friend. And I thought it would be fun. You could meet my friends. I could meet yours. But," he shook his head sadly, "I don't even know who you are anymore."

Sophie just stared blankly, shaking with rage but unable to verbalize why.

Rush continued, "The old Slim didn't care if I paid for stuff. She didn't care that I had more money. She just wanted to hang out and have fun. That," he said, practically spitting out the word, "is who I came to Paris to see. Not whoever the fuck you are."

Before Sophie could say another word, he turned and stalked down the street, his friends following behind. It wasn't until they rounded a corner that Sophie realized she was still holding the postcards.

"You're late—" Eryka started as Sophie entered the cafe, but at the sight of Sophie's tear-stained face, she paused. "What happened to you?"

Eryka sat in a booth with what Sophie presumed were Vivienne and Dominique. They were so closely entwined that Sophie couldn't tell where one woman stopped and the other began. But hearing Eryka's question, Vivienne quickly extricated herself and Dominique politely disappeared towards the bar.

"You're a mess," Vivienne said in a tone that was more condescending than concerned.

Sophie told them about Rush surprising her in the gift shop, and the fight they'd had.

"Well I'd say you owe us an apology," Vivienne said when Sophie was done talking, crossing her arms and scowling. "You were mad at us, and here it was your fuck buddy all along." Eryka shot her a look that plainly said this wasn't the time, but Vivienne disregarded it. "Give me a break," she said to Eryka before turning back to Sophie. "I'm sick of it. It's not our fault we have more money than you."

"Your families have more money," Sophie pointed out, but Vivienne went on.

"Whatever. At this stage, it's all the same. But that really means it's not our fault. I don't know what fuck buddy's deal is, but I'm guessing it's the same."

"It just feels like you're flaunting it," Sophie said sulkily.

"Well we're not," Eryka said, getting fed up and chiming in. "You're our friend—"

"Speak for yourself," Vivienne interjected, but Eryka gave her another look.

"You're our friend," Eryka emphasized again, glowering at Vivienne, "and we want to spend time with you. It's just money."

"To you," Sophie was getting angry again. "It's not to me."

"It doesn't have to be such a big deal," Vivienne added.

"I don't want to be anyone's charity case." Sophie couldn't figure out how to make them understand.

"For fuck's sake Sophie," Eryka gave her a withering stare. "You're not a charity case. But you are a head case. You need to get over this shit, or you're going to end up with no friends."

"And no money," Vivienne added flippantly. Eryka looked like she wanted to strangle her.

"The point is," Eryka continued, "you need to work out whatever this shit is, or no one is going to want to be friends with you."

Sophie stood next to the table, taking big gulps of air and trying to work out everything Eryka had said.

"I'm sorry," she said finally, looking at them both.

Vivienne shrugged, "I'm over it," she said, getting up and moving towards where Dominque waited at the bar. "I've got better things to do in Paris than try to convince you to take money from your friends."

"She only means that a little," Eryka said with a smirk. Then she gave Sophie a serious look. "Just promise me this is the last time we have this argument."

"Promise," Sophie replied, sliding into the booth. "From now on, you can pay for me anytime."

"Great," Eryka replied. "Espressos and croissants are on me tomorrow morning."

"Croissants," Sophie repeated absentmindedly to herself, then, something shifted in her brain. "Shit, Rush," she burst out. Eryka and Vivienne weren't the only fences she needed to mend. She was kicking herself now. How could she have been so terrible to her best friend in the world? She sprang back up from the booth, "I have to find him," she told Eryka, her voice full of panic. "I messed up so bad."

"Do you even know where he's staying?"

"No idea," Sophie admitted. "But I've got to try."

"I'll come with you," Eryka said, standing up and throwing some francs on the table.

"You don't have to—" Sophie started, but Eryka gave her a warning look.

"Don't flatter yourself. I'm not doing this for you." She threw a glance in the direction of the bar. "A wild goose chase around Paris is better than third-wheeling Vivienne and Dominique for the rest of the night."

They set out, stopping at every hotel between there and the Louvre to ask if they had a Monsieur Rigo registered, but every request came up empty. Sophie was grateful for Eryka's company, not least because the search would have taken twice as long with Sophie's miserable French.

It was getting late when Eryka suggested they call it. "You don't even know if he's still in Paris," she pointed out.

"You go back," Sophie suggested. Eryka looked as exhausted as she felt. "I just want to check a few more places."

"You sure?"

"Yeah," Sophie replied. "Thanks for the help. I'll see you in the morning."

Sophie watched Eryka head in the direction of their hotel, before turning and practically sprinting to the Musee d'Orsay.

She wasn't sure what she had expected, that Rush would be waiting for her apology with open arms, but the shock of not finding him there hit her harder than she expected. She watched as, even at this late hour, excited tourists stepped out from tapestries, their faces filled with the same awe she had experienced yesterday morning.

Yesterday morning. That felt so long ago. She watched people coming and going, trying to think about where in Europe Rush might have set off to next, willing herself to think of his next destination.

This is silly, she thought, settling down on a bench. She couldn't go chasing him all over Europe. Then she put her head in her hands and wept. All around her, tapestries shimmered with possibility, but for the first time in her life, Sophie didn't care to look at any of them.

—#—

It was almost dawn when Sophie crept back into her hotel room, but thankfully, Vivienne's bed was also empty. Sophie was glad to avoid awkward questions. Instead, she sat at the desk, pulled out the hotel stationery, and wrote a long letter of apology to Rush. It was the best she could do.

"You look even worse than yesterday," Eryka commented when Sophie joined her at the cafe a few hours later.

"What's your hangover cure for being an asshole to your best friend?" Sophie asked her, putting her head on the table.

"I'm guessing you didn't find him."

Sophie shook her head in her arms. "I wrote him a letter," she said into the table. "I just hope he doesn't burn it when he sees it's from me."

"It will be fine," Eryka said. "I'm sure you've had fights before."

Sophie thought hard, then shook her head.

"I find it hard to believe," Vivienne said, flouncing towards them with Dominique in tow, "that there's a single person you've never fought with."

Sophie wasn't sure if Vivienne had meant it as a joke, but it only made her feel worse. She had a feeling Eryka was glowering at Vivienne on her behalf.

"Come on," Vivienne said, pouting, "we're going to be late again."

"Let me guess," Eryka said, standing up and putting a comforting hand on Sophie's shoulder. "Dominique is going to show you her favorite tapestries today too."

"But of course," Dominique replied in her silky French accent.

"You two go," Eryka said, increasing her pressure on Sophie's shoulder slightly, "we'll catch up."

Once they had walked away, Eryka sat down again and pulled Sophie's head up from the table.

"Do you want to go back to the hotel?" Eryka asked, her voice full of concern, and Sophie knew she must look like shit. "I can tell Professor Rygge you aren't feeling well."

"It wouldn't be a lie," Sophie muttered. "But that's ok, I'll go," she said, getting slowly to her feet. "I'm sure Professor Ackerman will make me do the assignment no matter what. And if I'm there, it will be less obvious when you let me copy your work," she added with a weak smile.

"That's the spirit," Eryka said, pumping her fist and setting off for the museum, Sophie trailing miserably behind.

Everything about the rest of the trip felt wrong. As they traveled further south into France, Sophie knew she should have been enjoying the warming weather and the chance to visit some of the best weaving studios in the world. But all she could think about was Rush. How his money had paid for part of the trip and how awful she had been to him.

To Sophie's horror, the tour of the Aubusson tapestry studio was conducted entirely in French. This would have been a challenge on her best day, but she was still so distraught over her fight with Rush that she would have had a hard time focusing even if it was in English. But French? What a disaster. She had no idea how she'd complete Professor Rygge's assignment.

"What's she saying?" She hissed at Eryka in a whisper as they clustered at the back of the group.

Vivienne shushed her — since when did she care about this stuff — but Eryka gave a withering stare and began to translate for Sophie under her breath.

"She says we're here on a good day. We're about to see something special. La tombée du métier"

"Le tom du what?"

Eryka sighed in frustration. "It means the fall of the loom. The work is done and it's time to cut the tapestry loose."

Sophie watched as several women armed with scissors climbed stools to release the massive tapestry from its wooden cage. Like a well-practiced dance, several more women caught it and carried it gently to a large work table, where they took care to make sure the edges were square as they laid it into place.

"Now they just have to bind the edges," Eryka said, continuing the translation.

The team worked quickly, whipstitching in unison. A sense of anticipation permeated the room, as everyone tried to move through this phase as quickly but exactingly as possible to get to the most important part: hanging the tapestry on the wall to test if it worked.

The women with the scissors had repositioned their step stools against a blank patch of wall. The room watched with bated breath as they attached clips to the top edge. Two more women worked ropes from the floor while those on stools guided the tapestry into place, their fingers barely skimming the surface.

At last, the tapestry reached its full, impressive height, and the director paused her rapid French commentary, took a deep breath, and stepped through the tapestry with a flourish. Sophie couldn't help but burst into applause alongside everyone else, and a few of the women even took a tiny bow.

"You can tell they aren't really French," Vivienne remarked snidely. "No Frenchwoman would act that way."

It hadn't occurred to Sophie that Aubusson hired non-French weavers, but of course, the best in the world meant just that, the whole world. She surveyed the room for a moment, imagining herself working here one day. Then she realized she had no idea what the director was saying and vowed to redouble her efforts at French once she returned to school.

Sophie could have spent several more hours just wandering the studio, taking in all the details, but the director seemed to be winding down, and it was clear they were not to be left alone in the workspaces. Instead, she dumped them unceremoniously in the workshop's vast galleries, to explore an encyclopedic collection of the studio's work over the years.

"Finally," Vivienne hissed the moment they were free.

"What," Eryka chided her, rolling her eyes at Sophie. "Have you had Dominique stashed in your pocket this whole time?"

"No," Vivienne's pink cheeks turned scarlet. "But she has, um, a detailed knowledge of the tapestries in the collection here. We've arranged to meet in one." And with that, she turned on her heel and made a beeline for the agreed-upon tapestry.

"She really does have needs," Eryka laughed. Sophie didn't mind. She could barely stand herself right now. She certainly didn't have the patience for Vivienne.

Sophie sat on a bench in the middle of the gallery for a moment, massaging her tired eyes, before pulling her notebook from her bag. "Can you fill me in on the parts I didn't understand?" She asked Eryka helplessly.

"I thought you understood everything about weaving," she teased, settling on the bench next to Sophie.

"I do when it's in English."

"Fine," Eryka agreed, "but after this, we're going to find a tapestry and have some fun."

Chapter 14
East Lawn

There were no letters from Rush when Sophie returned to East Lawn. She tried to console herself with the thought that he was only just now returning to school to see her apology, but she was fairly certain her apologies weren't enough. Why couldn't she just accept Rush's gift without complaint? All those years of buying her treats at the bakery, why did this feel so different?

Classes the next day did little to lighten Sophie's mood, especially when Professor Ackerman handed back their assignments from Paris.

"How did she have time to grade these that fast?" Sophie hissed at Eryka and Vivienne after Professor Ackerman walked away.

"Maybe you don't need sleep when you're this evil," Eryka hissed back. Then she turned to Sophie, "How'd you do?"

Sophie released the breath she was holding and flipped her papers over. Decent marks on her assessments from the Louvre, but she'd done dismally on the assignments from the Musee Moderne and the Pompidou. She flashed the pages at Eryka.

"Sorry about that," Eryka mumbled, showing Sophie her own equally poor marks. "I should have known Professor Ackerman wouldn't like my take on anything."

Sophie shrugged. "No changing it now, I'll just have to make sure I don't mess up the rest of the term." She could already feel her stomach churning at the thought of what a bad grade would do for her scholarship. But it wasn't Eryka's fault she had done the assignment poorly. If only she hadn't had that stupid fight.

She turned to look at Vivienne, who was seated on her other side, and was surprised to see full marks on everything. "How did you do that?" Sophie whispered, snatching the papers and showing them to Eryka. Vivienne usually did fine in Professor Ackerman's class, but this was next-level.

A sly smile spread across Vivienne's face. "Dominique," she said smugly.

"What?" Sophie said, not comprehending. "I thought —"

"You thought I was just fooling around." Vivienne laughed. "Don't get me wrong, there was plenty of that," she said with a shake of her hair. "But Dominique's getting her Doctorate in Tapestry History from the Sorbonne." She looked at Sophie and Eryka, both of whom were staring, mouths open. "I guess I just learn better when I'm satisfied."

Sophie couldn't believe what she was hearing. While she was getting in fights and having a miserable time, Vivienne was getting laid and getting the grades Sophie normally did. She turned to look at Eryka, who rolled her eyes and folded her arms across her chest as Professor Ackerman began today's lecture.

"I hope you all absorbed as much as possible at the Pompidou," she began, giving them all an infuriating smile, "because today we turn our attention to modern tapestries. And no discussion of modern tapestry would be complete," she was grinning now, as if leading towards a big reveal, "without a discussion of Sabrina Maxwell."

At those last words, every head in the room turned towards Vivienne. All the pink drained from Vivienne's cheeks and her smile slipped away. Professor Ackerman stared at her as if expecting Vivienne to take up the lecture.

When, after several painful moments, Vivienne said nothing, Professor Ackerman turned and addressed the room at large. "There's no need to be modest, my dear. Everyone knows your mother was England's greatest tapestry designer of the modern age. It must have been so wonderful to grow up under her tutelage."

In an instant, Sophie went from feeling angry with Vivienne to feeling angry on her behalf. Professor Ackerman could not be this much of an idiot. She must know how young Vivienne was when her mother died. Or was she so blinded by Vivienne's connection to celebrity that she hadn't bothered to work out the math?

Tears were welling at the corners of Vivienne's eyes, and Sophie thought back to the fight she had witnessed between Vivienne and Holden. To Sophie's other side, she could see Eryka's fists clenched in rage.

"Of course, my dear," Professor Ackerman went on. "I know how young you were when she was," she paused, then mouthed the word *murdered* dramatically, "but I'm sure you must remember something."

All eyes turned again towards Vivienne, as the tears now started to stream down her face. Sophie couldn't stand it.

"Are you serious?" Sophie sprang from her seat, shouting at Professor Ackerman. "What is wrong with you? Can't you see that this is upsetting her?" She gestured towards Vivienne. "Why can't you just teach Sabrina Maxwell like you usually would? Why do you have to make this into a whole thing?"

"Miss O'Toole," Professor Ackerman's voice rose with anger. "I will not be spoken to like that in my own classroom."

"Well, Vivienne shouldn't have to be spoken to like that ever." Sophie couldn't believe she was yelling at a professor like this, but now that she started, she couldn't seem to stop. "She doesn't remember anything about her mother's work. Stop making her a spectacle."

Everyone's heads turned towards Sophie, but they snapped to the front as Professor Ackerman's voice rang through the silence following the outburst.

"Get out of my classroom," she said, a growl in her voice Sophie had never heard before, even when she'd pushed her luck their first day in Paris.

Sophie didn't have to be asked twice. She scooped up her things and stormed towards the door in the front of the room. Before she walked out, Professor Ackerman gave one final blow, "I shall be speaking to Professor Rygge about whether it's appropriate for you to continue in this program."

Out in the hall, Sophie's breath came in short bursts as she squatted to the floor. What had she done? A few minutes ago, she was worried about a bad grade. Now she had shouted at a professor. This might be the end.

She barely had a chance to collect herself when Vivienne and Eryka burst out of the room, followed by at least half the class.

"That was incredible," Eryka said, giving her a wide grin and reaching to help Sophie up so she could slap her on the back.

"What's going on?" Sophie asked, eyeing the rest of her classmates.

"Solidarity," Eryka said. "We all knew Professor Ackerman crossed a line, you were just the only one with the guts to do something about it."

"She said she's going to get me suspe—" Sophie couldn't get the word out.

"Not on our watch," Vivienne said, speaking for the first time. "Daddy will make a call."

Sophie let out a sigh of relief. If anyone had the clout to get her out of this mess, it was Mr. Morris.

"Thanks," she said to Vivienne. "I owe you."

"No," Vivienne said. "Thank you. For standing up for me. I owe you."

"Let's call it even," Sophie said with a smile. "Just promise me one thing."

"Anything," Vivienne replied eagerly.

"The next time you hook up with a brilliant tapestry scholar, will you let me know so I can copy your notes instead of Eryka's?"

Vivienne gave her a weak smile.

Professor Rygge called Sophie to her office the next morning. "You know you can't speak to a professor like that, correct?"

Sophie wanted to argue with Professor Rygge, to say it was Professor Ackerman who shouldn't talk to Vivienne like that, but there was too much on the line. And Sophie respected Professor Rygge much more.

"I know," Sophie bowed her head.

"And you know," Professor Rygge continued, "that she would be well within her right to suspend you from her class and fail you for the semester?"

Sophie looked up across the desk, her mouth agape.

To her surprise, Professor Rygge shifted into a small smile. "But it seems Professor Ackerman has recognized that she was also in the wrong." Sophie still couldn't believe what she was hearing, but perhaps Mr. Morris's call had not been to Professor Rygge, but rather directly to Professor Ackerman. "She has agreed to take you back."

Sophie let out a sigh of relief.

"Not so fast," Professor Rygge wasn't ready to let her off the hook so quickly. "Your actions must have some consequences."

"What consequences?" Sophie asked. Surely anything would be better than failing and losing her scholarship, but she wouldn't put it past Professor Ackerman to come up with something awful.

"Well Professor Ackerman wanted you to sweep the history department from top to bottom, but I thought that punishment didn't fit the crime. In the end, we agreed that you would write an extra five-page paper on Sabrina Maxwell that you will present to the class before the end of term."

"Seriously?"

Sophie couldn't believe her luck, and it must have shown on her face because Professor Rygge added, "Just don't let Professor Ackerman know you're happy about it when she gives you the assignment, or she'll change it to something much worse."

As it turned out, the worst part about Sophie's visit to Professor Rygge's office was that it made her late for her shift at the repair studio. Sophie hadn't been in since the trip to France, and she was eager to see if Sabrina's tapestry was still there and get the other women's advice on her fight with Rush, who still hadn't replied to Sophie's apology letter.

She was in such a hurry, and so lost in thought about how she would approach the paper on Sabrina, that she didn't notice someone coming directly towards her until she nearly bumped into them.

"I heard you made quite a splash in class yesterday."

It was Jasper. Sophie felt herself flush, but couldn't think of anything to say.

"Sore subject," Jasper said, misreading her silence.

"Oh, um, no," Sophie said. "It's fine." Now, she thought to herself.

"It sounded pretty epic. Ryka can't stand Ackerman. It's one of the reasons she's thinking about leaving."

"She's what?"

Now it was Jasper's turn to flush. "Oh, I guess she hasn't told you yet. She's thinking about leaving East Lawn next term. Says she doesn't want to spend four years studying under Ackerman's regime."

This made sense to Sophie, but she was surprised Eryka hadn't mentioned it. But then again, Eryka kept things pretty close to the vest.

"Don't tell her I told you, ok?" Jasper gave Sophie an imploring look, and she felt her knees go weak. "I'm sure she's got her reasons for not telling you yet."

Sophie just nodded.

"Thanks," Jasper said, giving her a wide smile. "I owe you one."

It was like staring into the sun, and to give herself a reason to look away, Sophie checked her watch.

"I'm sorry," Jasper said. "I've made you late."

"It's ok," Sophie said, daring to glance in his direction. "I was late before I bumped into you."

"Class?" he asked, his voice full of concern.

"Work," Sophie replied, then added, by way of explanation, "The tapestry repair shop. It's less of a big deal. I'll make the time up later."

"I'm headed in that direction, too. Can I walk with you?"

Had Sophie been less flustered, she would have wondered where on earth Jasper was possibly headed that was also in the direction of the tapestry repair studio. All the architecture buildings were in the opposite direction. But she was too pleased to be walking with Jasper to be thinking that clearly.

"How was France?" He asked as they started walking side by side. "I couldn't get a read on Ryka."

Sophie said nothing. All she could focus on from the trip was her fight with Rush.

"Another sore subject?" Jasper asked, correctly interpreting her silence this time.

"Yeah, I just—" Sophie tried to think fast. She didn't want to tell him about her fight with Rush. "The tapestries were beautiful," she said finally. "But it seems I don't have a tolerance for French wine."

"You didn't try and keep up with Ryka, did you?" He looked slightly concerned and slightly amused. "I swear Maman put Châteauneuf-du-Pape in our baby bottles."

Sophie didn't want to let on that she didn't know what that was, so she just laughed. "It was a little rough. Oh, and Vivienne met a girl, which made her a bit insufferable."

"At least that should stop her from pining over Ryka."

Sophie stopped walking and stared at him. "You knew?" she asked him.

"Please," he said smiling, and Sophie started to melt again. She turned away and started walking. "Give me a little credit. It's super obvious."

Sophie squirmed. Was it obvious that she was pining for him? She tried to play it cool. "Well at least now she seems to have realized it will never happen." Unlike me, Sophie thought to herself.

"And maybe it means Vivienne will dart off to Paris more and you won't have to deal with her as often."

Sophie smiled at him. "A girl can dream."

—#—

The first thing Sophie noticed when she stepped into the repair studio was that Sabrina's tapestry was gone. She had a feeling this would happen, but it didn't change her disappointment that she would never see it again.

The next thing she noticed was that Innes was sitting at the desk in Gloria's cramped office.

"Where's Gloria?" She asked Janice, dropping her bag to the ground.

"Gone."

"What do you mean gone?" A note of panic rose in Sophie's voice.

"Calm down, it's nothing like that." Innes had come out of the office. "We came in Friday and she had left a letter of resignation on her desk."

"Of course, it took us a few hours to find it," Rosemary chimed in. "You know how her desk is."

"A letter of resignation?" Sophie couldn't believe what she was hearing. "What did it say?"

"Just that she was ready to move on." Innes shrugged, then looked at Sophie, softening. "Rosemary, will you get Sophie a cup of tea so she can calm down?"

Rosemary nodded, then looked at Sophie's shaking hands. "With whiskey," She added to herself.

"Look, it happens all the time," Innes said. "We're an itinerant bunch. Honestly, the only thing I'm surprised about is that I made it here longer than she did."

Janice and Rosemary both chuckled.

"But has anyone talked to her?" Sophie couldn't explain what was happening. Innes's explanation seemed plausible enough, but it still felt wrong.

"No. We figured if she wanted to talk, she would have said goodbye in person."

"So no one's even seen her. Has anyone been to her house?" Why were they all being so casual about this?

"For frigg's sake, Sophie" Innes cried, clearly exasperated. "I don't know why you're making such a big deal about this."

Sophie didn't know why they weren't making a bigger deal out of it. But at that moment, Rosemary came over with a cup and guided Sophie onto a stool. Sophie took a sip and sputtered. "That's a lot of whiskey," she said to Rosemary.

"Best cure for a panic attack I know."

Sophie took another sip, aware they were all staring at her, and cast around her mind for another topic. "What day did Sabrina's tapestry get picked up?"

"Thursday afternoon."

This time Sophie did spit out her whiskey.

Innes gave her a look. "What?"

Sophie tried to choose her words carefully. "Don't you think it's weird that Sabrina's tapestry left on Thursday and you came in on Friday to Gloria's letter?"

"So," Janice said, turning back to her work.

Sophie scowled. Why weren't they getting it? "It just seems... fishy, that's all."

"Fishy?" Innes raised an eyebrow. "Fishy how?"

"It was Gloria's tapestry too." Sophie went on, trying to put the pieces together herself. "She was the head weaver when she worked for Sabrina. It just seems like too big of a coincidence."

"Maybe you're right," Innes conceded. "But I don't think it's the conspiracy you're making it out to be. If anything, seeing her old weaving work made her realize repairs wasn't where she was meant to be."

"I'm sure you can understand that," Janice added.

"But," Sophie paused, something still didn't add up. "But, so you're saying she just decided to get a new job. Why not at least say goodbye in person?"

"I've done an Irish goodbye on every job I left," Innes said as if this was perfectly normal. "And it's not like Gloria was the touchy-feely type." Innes gave Sophie a piercing look. "You can't tell me you've never left someone without saying goodbye."

Sophie thought of the day last summer when she left Rush in the tapestry, in what she was now certain was one of Sabrina's tapestries, and she felt terrible again, thinking of their fight in Paris.

Innes read the look on her face. "Look, it happens. And I don't have time to sit here moaning about it, I've got work to do." She looked pointedly at Sophie. "And so do you. You're already half an hour late."

Sophie opened her mouth to explain her lateness, but Innes took it for continuing the argument and shook her head. "If it will shut you up, we can go to Gloria's cottage over my lunch break just to check in."

"I have class this afternoon," Sophie responded, though she wanted nothing more than to check in on Gloria.

"Fine." Innes let out an exasperated sigh. "After work then. Meet me back here when your last class is over." And with that she turned and marched back towards Gloria's office, grumbling about the mess of paperwork she had to deal with.

Sophie sat down at the tapestry she was supposed to be repairing and let out a sigh. There was no way she could focus until she knew everything was all right with Gloria. But it wasn't just that. The fight with Rush hung heavy as well.

Rosemary walked by, presumably on her way to get yarn, but stopped to take a peak into Sophie's cup. "That's expensive whiskey," she said, sliding it towards Sophie. "If you don't finish it, I will."

Sophie made a great show of taking a sip from her cup.

"I'm sensing," Rosemary went on, putting her hand on Sophie's shoulder, "that there's more going on than just Gloria."

Sophie burst into tears. Between shaking breaths, she told Rosemary and Janice, who had stopped her own work the second Sophie started crying, about her fight with Rush.

"We've never fought before, and I was so awful to him, and now I'm afraid he'll never speak to me again." Sophie finished, tears still streaming down her face.

Janice moved over to pat her shoulder and Rosemary got up and came back with the whiskey bottle, which she tipped into Sophie's cup before taking a swig directly herself.

"Give it time," Rosemary said. "I've fought with plenty of lovers, they almost always come back."

Sophie looked at Rosemary. "He's not my lover, he's my best friend."

"That you sometimes fuck," Janice pointed out.

"But that doesn't make him my lover."

"Either way," Rosemary said, "give it time. I'm sure he'll come around."

But Sophie didn't want to give it time. Every day that Rush didn't return her letters felt like another sign that she had damaged their friendship beyond repair.

Innes poked her head out of Gloria's office. "Sophie, I appreciate you're having a bad week, but can someone please do some fucking work this morning."

"Are we sure Gloria is gone?" Janice whispered as Innes slammed the office door. "Or has she just taken over Innes's body?"

The three of them dissolved into laughter before reluctantly turning back to their work.

Chapter 15
East Lawn

Sophie could barely concentrate through her afternoon classes. All she could think about was confronting Gloria, and finding out why she had left so suddenly.

"Pub later?" Eryka asked after Sophie said she was skipping dinner to go back to work.

"Sure," she replied. "I'll meet you there."

Sophie practically sprinted to the repair studio, but Innes didn't seem in any hurry to leave.

"Gloria had better hope she's not home when we get there," Innes grumbled, still battling a mountain of paperwork. "Or I'm going to wring her neck for leaving me with this mess. It's enough to make me want to resign too."

"Don't even joke," Sophie said, referring partly to Gloria not being home and partly to Innes threatening to leave.

"You've got to understand," Innes said, dropping a pile of papers on her desk with an air of resigned finality, "most jobs have an expiration date. People don't stick around forever."

"My mom's been running her repair shop in the same place in the same town since before I was born."

"That's not normal."

Sophie gave her a look. It was perfectly normal in her world. And sure, Mrs. Rigo had only come to work at the Honyeoke Falls when Sophie was eight, but she'd now been there for over ten years. People in her world didn't just leave.

Except she'd left. So why was she having such a hard time understanding why Gloria had?

"I just meant," Innes continued, "it's different when you work for someone else. And as much as this is one of the best places I've ever worked, we're still at the whims of the college. My guess is Gloria just got sick of it." Innes gestured to the mess of paperwork on the desk. "And after trying to do her job for one day, I can't say I blame her."

Sophie sighed. "Can we at least go see Gloria before you put in your letter too?"

"Fine," Innes said, putting up her hands in defeat. "You win, let's go."

As they set off from the tapestry studio, Sophie realized she had no idea where Gloria lived. They walked in silence, gravel crunching below their feet, as they wound their way towards the woods that stood past the far edge of campus.

"Gloria lives out here by herself?" Sophie asked as they set off through the trees.

"You know Gloria, she's a private person. I only learned where she lived because she was sick once and made me bring her work to do. Even then, she wouldn't let me past the front porch."

Sophie pictured Gloria alone in a house in the woods. What had she been doing since she left the repair shop? Would she be upset that they were intruding on her privacy?

Something of her thoughts must have shown on her face, because Innes said, "It's not too late to turn back."

"No," Sophie said firmly. "I want to know why she left."

Innes gave a sigh of irritation but continued on. They walked for a few more minutes before Innes gestured in front of them.

A small cabin stood in a clearing, its weathered wood exterior barely discernible against the trees. A stone chimney jutted out from one side and on the front porch, a pair of empty rocking chairs set expectantly on either side of a faded wood door.

Innes stepped onto the porch and gave a small knock, but there was no answer. Sophie followed her, and after a few silent moments, she pounded on the door, shouting "Gloria."

Innes grabbed her hand mid-knock. "Are you trying to break the door down?"

"I just wanted to make sure she could hear us," Sophie said, wrenching her hand from Innes's grip and turning to peer through one of the windows.

"It's not that big of a cabin," Innes said, now peaking through the other window. "It doesn't look like she's home."

"Should we wait?" Sophie asked, turning to look at one of the rocking chairs.

Waiting seemed like the last thing Innes wanted to do, but she settled into the other rocking chair. "Fine, but if she's not back in half an hour, I'm leaving." She reached into her pocket, pulled out a joint, and lit it. She took a long drag and then another before offering it to Sophie.

Sophie hesitated for a moment. Technically, Innes was her boss now.

Innes read the indecision on Sophie's face. "I'm not going to fire you," she said, exasperated, stretching her hand closer to Sophie. "And besides, you're off the clock." The tone in her voice implied that it didn't matter anyway, so Sophie accepted it and took a small puff before handing it back to Innes.

Innes took another long drag, leaned back into the chair, and closed her eyes. Sophie realized how stressed Innes must be since Gloria resigned. She watched as Innes's breathing slowed. Worried that Innes would drop the joint and light the cabin on fire, she took it from her hand, took a slightly longer pull, and then put it out.

Sophie stared around at the front porch and the neatly kept garden. Things were just starting to come into bloom. She could see daffodils peaking up to the side of the porch.

After a few minutes, Sophie heard Innes let out a small snore and decided it was safe to look around. She practically leaped from the porch and walked to the side of the house, peeking in every window as she went.

Inside, the cottage looked as weathered but well cared for as the outside. There was a little kitchen with a tea kettle on the stove and a small wooden table with a pair of chairs. Beyond that, Sophie could see a tiny living room with an overstuffed love seat and bookshelves full to bursting.

She continued around the back of the cabin until she found a window into the bedroom. A few clothes were draped over the end of the bend and a few more crept haphazardly out of drawers, but nothing seemed out of sorts. Sophie didn't know what she had been expecting. Signs of a struggle?

The shadows were getting longer as Sophie returned to the porch and Innes woke with a start just as Sophie settled back into her rocking chair. Innes checked her watch. "It's been over half an hour," she chastised Sophie. "Why didn't you wake me?"

Sophie shrugged. "You looked like you needed a nap."

"What I need," Innes said, getting up from the rocker, "is to catch up on work. Let's get out of here."

"I'm going to wait a little longer," Sophie said, settling into her chair.

"Suit yourself," Innes said. "See you at work tomorrow."

"I'm not scheduled again until Thursday." Sophie reminded her.

"Thursday then," Innes replied, the tone of her voice making it clear that it didn't matter, and she turned and walked from the porch, relighting the joint as she walked away.

Sophie waited until she was sure Innes was out of sight of the little cabin before she stood, pulling the pick out of her hair as she did. In a few moments, she had picked the simple lock and was standing inside the space between the kitchen and the living room. If the cabin hadn't been so small, she supposed it would have counted as an entryway.

The whole place smelled like Gloria. Something earthy with a trace of wool. The notion comforted her, but then it made her panic. What if Gloria was on her way back? Nothing she could see made it seem like she was gone for good. What would she say if she came home and found that Sophie had broken into her house?

Sophie turned towards the door but hesitated as her curiosity got the better of her. Now that she was in, it couldn't hurt to take a quick look around. Just in case — *just in case what?* Sophie thought to herself. Just in case something bad had happened.

But she had to admit, as she walked around the kitchen table, her hand trailing the worn surface of the counter, nothing seemed out of the ordinary. She opened the cabinets to a small selection of tea and honey. The refrigerator was mostly empty, but a few condiments stood waiting. Sophie even spotted some leftovers in a container. Nothing alluded to anything other than that Gloria had stepped out for a few hours. Certainly nothing, Sophie thought, now training her gaze towards the living room, made it seem like there was a struggle or that Gloria had left in a hurry.

Feeling that she was pressing her luck, Sophie wandered over to the bookcases. They were full mostly of novels — mysteries mixed with a smattering of erotica. Sophie pulled one from the shelf — the cover featured two women —

and felt a slight pang for this invasion of privacy. While Sophie knew that most of the tapestry books in Gloria's collection were in her office in the repair studio, there were a few books on tapestry technique shoved into a corner.

Ever the boffin, as Holden would say, Sophie pulled a couple from the shelf. She knew she was pressing her luck, but she wondered if any of them had come from Gloria's time in Sabrina's workshop. None of them were familiar to her, and none of them looked like repeats from Sabrina's extensive library. Before she could think, she settled into the couch to flip through them.

A crunching noise outside broke Sophie's trance. She jumped up, hastily shoving the books back into the shelf, when something tucked in the corner of the bookshelf caught her eye. Something that looked vaguely familiar.

She turned around, her heart racing, but there was no sign of Gloria, or anyone else for that matter. *It was probably just an animal,* she told herself, and after another long pause, she dumped the tapestry books back on the couch and fished her hand into the space at the back of the bookshelf, until her fingers made contact with the soft, leather-bound cover.

Sophie couldn't believe her eyes. It looked just like… With trembling fingers, she opened it slowly… It was. One of Sabrina's journals. Just like the ones she had spent hours with in Sabrina's study over winter break.

How had Gloria ended up with this? True, she had worked for Sabrina, but this was such a personal possession to have from your former boss. Sophie thumbed through the pages, back to the beginning, and studied the date on the first page with even more intensity. It was dated several months before Sabrina died. Not only was this Sabrina's journal, it was the journal that was missing from her library.

Sophie spun around in a circle, looking bewilderingly for other clues. "Why do you have this?" she muttered to the room. Was there something more to Gloria and Sabrina's relationship? And then, Sophie thought, with an even greater jolt, did Gloria know something about Sabrina's murder?

Sophie settled back into the couch, the journal in her hands. She didn't think it was a good idea to take the journal — what if Gloria looked for it when she got home? — but she had to know if there was anything important in there.

It only took a few minutes of perusing to realize the journal held no great secrets or conspiracy theories. She didn't know why she expected different. Both Vivienne and Mr. Morris had been clear that Sabrina's murder, while awful, was the simple case of a kidnapping gone wrong. But Holden? He couldn't shake the idea that something darker had happened. And his theories had seeped deep into Sophie's brain.

But here was the proof, or so it seemed, that Sabrina wasn't aware of anything nefarious happening around her. Mostly, the notebook was filled with sketches and notes for a new tapestry, one Sophie realized sadly, she wouldn't live to see made.

"Well that's it, Holden," Sophie shut the book softly, looking towards the ceiling. She closed her eyes for a moment, imagining what she would tell him when she went home with Vivienne over the summer holiday. *If he's even speaking to me,* she reminded herself. While their last encounter hadn't ended quite as dramatically as the fight with Rush in Paris, she hadn't heard anything from Holden since her last night at Weddlesmoore.

She opened her eyes again, furious with herself for all the messes she had made. But as she stared at the ceiling, something caught her eye. One of the ceiling boards was slightly askew as if someone had pushed it up and not put it back properly.

Sophie did some quick mental gymnastics. Standing on the couch wouldn't quite get her high enough to reach, but maybe if she stacked a kitchen chair on the little wooden coffee table.

It was precarious, standing on a wobbly chair on an even wobblier table, but it gave her just enough height that once she pushed the board away, followed by the one next to it, she could put her head through the ceiling.

Her head emerged into a dark crawlspace, covered — from what she made out in the dim light creeping in from a few small cracks where the roof met the walls — in dust and spiders. At first glance, the space looked empty, and she was about to go back down when she noticed the edge of what appeared to be a cardboard box tucked in a corner.

Sophie used all the strength she could muster to push herself into the crawlspace, unfortunately knocking the kitchen chair off the table in the process. It fell in a loud clatter and Sophie worried she had broken it. She couldn't even fathom a way to talk herself out of this mess if Gloria suddenly came home. She lay on the dirty floor for a moment, coughing up dust, before clambering over the ceiling joists.

While the rest of the crawlspace was covered in dust, the top of the cardboard box was remarkably clean. There was writing on it and she dragged it into the dim light to get a closer look. In beautiful, scrawling letters was the word "Middlebrook."

Sophie took a sharp inhale, then devolved into another coughing fit. Once it subsided, she stared at the handwriting on the top.

It was Sabrina's handwriting.

Middlebrook. Hadn't she just read that word?

The box itself wasn't heavy, just awkward in its width and flatness, and Sophie didn't want to try and open it up here amidst all the dust. She pushed it towards the opening in the ceiling, and then, with no other options, gingerly dropped the box onto the floor below. Then carefully, she climbed into the opening, hanging by her fingers until she felt the tips of her toes skim the coffee table. She let herself drop, but as her weight hit the coffee table, it shifted and she tumbled to the floor.

She surveyed the mess — the broken chair, the tipped-over coffee table, and the fine coat of dusk that now covered the living room couch — and tried to collect her thoughts. She knew she should probably clean up, but there was something about the way the box was hidden that made her think Gloria wasn't coming home anytime soon. Why else would she stash it there?

Sophie settled for cleaning herself up the best she could in the kitchen sink before returning to the box. Before she opened the lid, she grabbed the journal from the couch and flipped to one of the pages towards the back. There it was. *Middlebrook.*

Carefully, Sophie pulled the lid off the box to reveal a neatly folded — and what she could only assume was massive — sheet of paper. She peeled up a corner to reveal a subtle blend of color, and the reality of what she was seeing hit her. She let the corner fall back into the box and hastily shoved the coffee table and broken chair into the kitchen, trying to make as much space as possible on the floor.

The paper was so large that it spread across the floor and awkwardly onto the couch. But there was no mistaking what it was. The fully realized cartoon for Sabrina's last tapestry design.

"Why are you covered in dirt?" Vivienne demanded of Sophie when she came skidding into the pub an hour later.

She'd been so concerned with the cartoon that she hadn't bothered to look in a mirror.

After Sophie realized what she was looking at, she worked fast. She did the best she could to right the coffee table and brush the dust off the sofa. There was no fixing the kitchen chair, at least not without tools, so Sophie tucked it back under the kitchen table and hoped that Gloria noticed before she tried to sit on it. If Gloria was coming back at all. Then she had refolded the cartoon, tucked Sabrina's journal into her bag, and left, relocking the front door as she left.

She'd practically sprinted through the woods towards campus, the box tucked awkwardly under her arm, so she could stash the box in her room before Eryka and Vivienne were back from the pub.

Vivienne looked at her expectantly. Sophie wracked her brain. "I had to help clean out an old storage space at work," she said finally.

"And they don't have mirrors at work?" Eryka asked, coming back with a couple of pints.

"I was already running late, it didn't occur to me." At least they seemed to have bought her reason. "Fine, I get the hint." She said, responding to their stares.

Embarrassed she hadn't bothered to clean up, Sophie kept her head down on the way to the bathroom and ran straight into—

"We've got to stop meeting like this," Jasper said grinning.

Sophie looked up at him, even more flustered. They were standing so close together in the hallway that she could practically breathe him in.

"You've got some dirt on your face," he said, pulling out a handkerchief and brushing it gently across her cheek. Sophie thought she might pass out, and it took all her self-control not to fling herself at him.

They locked eyes for a moment and Sophie thought she saw a flicker of longing too, but then he tucked the handkerchief back in his pocket. "That's better," he said, turning away from her. "See you around."

In the bathroom, Sophie stared at herself in the mirror. Her face was still dusty, save the one spot Jasper had wiped away.

What was wrong with her? She was suddenly angry with not just herself, but Jasper. He was always so nice to her, but it never went further than that. Was he just a good guy, keeping an eye out on his sister's roommate, with no feelings for her at all?

She had half a mind to go out and tell him off right there at the pub, to tell him to stop being such a tease. Shit or get off the pot, right? But then she thought of Holden and Rush. She had already destroyed two relationships this year. Better to stay on friendly terms with Jasper than ruin another one. Though friendly terms were not what she wanted at all.

The rest of the term weighed heavy on Sophie. She hadn't heard from Rush, there was still no sign of Gloria, and she couldn't get her mind off of Sabrina's cartoon, stashed under her bed, or the journal she now carried in her bag.

She spent hours in the library, reading everything she could find on Sabrina Maxwell. Ostensibly, this was to complete Professor Ackerman's extra assignment, but in truth, she was trying to figure out if there was anything unique about the design for the Middlebrook tapestry.

Much had been written about Sabrina. Since her early death, she'd become an iconic figure, and besides the myriad books about the tapestries she created, there were several biographies, all, Sophie thought to herself bitterly, unauthorized.

Sophie didn't feel comfortable bringing so many books on Sabrina back to the dorm. She could bring one or two under the cover of Professor Ackerman's assignment, but she knew Vivianne wouldn't approve of her fixation with her mother. She could practically hear Vivienne's voice in her head. "You're just like Holden. There's no conspiracy, and even if there was, it wouldn't bring her back. Just drop it."

But Sophie couldn't drop it. With the cartoon stashed under her bed and Gloria still absent, she felt she owed it to — well she wasn't sure — but to someone to uncover the truth. Or maybe that was her way of justifying her growing obsession.

She spent longer and longer hours in the library, to the point where she no longer picked up extra shifts at the repair studio. This wasn't just about her learning more about Sabrina. Innes, Janice, and Rosemary still didn't think there was anything odd about Gloria's disappearance.

"We were there," Innes said a few days after they had gone to the cabin. "Everything seemed fine. She probably went on holiday."

Everything didn't seem fine to Sophie, and Gloria's absence left a massive hole every time she stepped into the repair studio. Despite her gruff exterior, she'd enjoyed spending time with Gloria.

And then there was her connection to Sabrina.

Sophie had found Gloria's name in a book that contained a list of the major weavers in Sabrina's studio. But there was no mention of Gloria in any of the biographies, nothing to hint at a deeper relationship that would lead to Gloria having the journal or the cartoon.

There was also no mention of Middlebrook.

Frustrated, Sophie turned to the library's collection of atlases. It took her a while to find any place called Middlebrook. She started her search near Weddlesmoore, then when that turned up nothing, she searched the area around East Lawn before turning her eyes towards London and the surrounding towns.

She had almost given up when she spotted it, a tiny mark partway between Manchester and Liverpool. But there was nothing she could glean from that little dot that told her why Sabrina had chosen that location for the design of her final tapestry.

Sophie turned back to Sabrina's journal. There were plenty of sketches and detailed instructions for the creation of the tapestry, but nothing that indicated if Sabrina had spent any time in Middlebrook or why that location might be special. Perhaps this was a commission for a client, but there was no indication of that either. The sketches and the cartoon itself were of little help. True, Sophie hadn't had time to inspect the cartoon to its fullest. She'd been in too much of a hurry at Gloria's cabin, and it wasn't safe to unfurl it in her dorm room. But from what she could tell it was unremarkable, save for Sabrina's signature swirling sky. Just a path leading through some trees, and a tiny building off in a clearing in the distance.

After combing every book in the library, not just on Sabrina, but anything that might slightly mention Middlebrook, Sophie had to conclude that maybe there was no mystery after all. While it pained her to think that Vivienne might be right, she resigned herself to finishing her paper for Professor Ackerman and letting the rest go.

But she couldn't bring herself to take the cartoon or the journal back to Gloria's still empty cottage.

Chapter 16
East Lawn

Sophie's first year at East Lawn was coming to a close. She finished with top marks in all her technical classes, which balanced her lackluster grades in French and Professor Ackerman's class, which Sophie had barely passed. Despite, Sophie thought with a huff, all the work she had put into the extra essay.

Sophie said her goodbyes to the women at the weaving studio, giving them each a hug and admonishing them to stick around.

"Promise me that none of the rest of you will leave while I'm away on summer break."

"I cannot make that promise," Innes told her as Sophie stepped in to hug her. Sophie knew her work hadn't gotten any easier in the month since Gloria had left, but she had hoped that the addition of a new tapestry repairer, who was slated to start over the summer, might alleviate some of Innes's frustration. Her voice softened as she returned Sophie's hug. "But I'll try my best."

Despite feeling like she was disappointing her family, Sophie had decided not to head straight home now that term had ended. Vivienne had bullied her into spending another week at Weddlesmoore, but Sophie was headed to Brussels with Eryka for a week beforehand.

Vivienne was of course pouty about this. "It would be so much easier if you just came home with me first."

"I'm sorry," Sophie teased her. "Am I keeping you from something important?" Sophie figured Vivienne was planning on spending as much of the summer in Paris with Dominique as possible.

"No, not really," she said, still looking frustrated. "It's just that I promised Daddy I'd spend a few weeks at home before I head off for the rest of the summer on a, um, study trip—" There it was, Sophie thought, smiling to herself as Vivienne continued, "And it will be so boring until you get there."

"I'm sure you'll find something to entertain yourself," Sophie said, thinking of the tapestry to the beach. "Besides, you could come to Eryka's with me," she added, while secretly hoping Vivienne hadn't changed her mind.

"You know I can't," Vivienne whined, stomping her foot a little. "Like I said, I promised Daddy I'd come home first. Plus, it's not like she," here she thrust her finger towards Eryka, who had just walked into the dorm room, "is coming to visit me."

"I told you, we're leaving for Egypt right after Sophie leaves. Maman and Mum planned it as a surprise. I didn't pick the dates."

"Well you could both just come home with me," Vivienne insisted, but this time Sophie cut her off.

"I've already been to your house. I want to see Eryka's before she goes away for the summer. You can have me after that, or not at all." Sophie felt torn by this threat. On one hand, she would be happy to be free of Vivienne for the whole summer. On the other hand, she couldn't shake the feeling of wanting to dive back into Sabrina's world, with all the new knowledge she'd obtained. If Holden let her.

Vivienne just stared at her in steely silence, and Sophie knew the choice was made. After a week in Brussels,

she'd return to Weddlesmoore before heading home to
Honyeoke Falls.

—#—

"Ready to go?" Jasper appeared brightly at their dorm room
the next morning, his bag slung over his shoulder. "I figured
Ryka would need help with all her luggage."

"All her luggage?" Sophie asked, confusion spreading
across her face. She'd arranged to leave some of her things at
East Lawn for the summer, jettisoning most of her meager
selection of clothing into storage to make room for Sabrina's
cartoon in her bag. She had decided, or at least mostly
decided, to show it to Holden once she got there.

Jasper gave Eryka a look. "You didn't tell her?"

"Tell me what?" Sophie demanded, looking pointedly
from one sibling to the other.

"I was going to wait until we were home," she said,
avoiding Sophie's eye, "but I guess there's no point in waiting
anymore." She gave her brother a nasty look. "I'm not coming
back to East Lawn next term."

"What?" With everything else going on, Sophie had
completely forgotten about her conversation with Jasper the
morning she'd learned Gloria had resigned. Now she stared at
Eryka in shock. "Does Vivienne know?" Vivienne had left
early that morning.

Eryka nodded. "I told her last night at the pub." That
explained why Vivienne's eyes had looked so puffy. Even with a
new woman in her life, the news that Eryka was leaving must
have hit her hard.

"What brought this on?" Sophie asked, even though
she already knew.

"Professor Ackerman," Eryka said with a sneer. "I
can't waste my time in a history department run by that," she

paused, looking for the right word, "that woman," she concluded finally.

So many questions flashed through Sophie's head as she fought off rising panic. Where was Eryka going? How would she cope with Vivienne without Eryka there as a buffer? But then she turned abruptly to Jasper, trying to keep her voice calm. "Are you leaving too?"

"Are you kidding me?" He let out a loud laugh. "I've only got one year to go. I'm not leaving now and losing half my credits."

Sophie felt her face flush with relief. "Don't worry," Eryka said reassuringly. "I've already asked him to keep an eye on you."

He put his arm around Sophie's shoulder with an air of brotherly protection. "I promised Ryka you could hang out with me anytime you need a break from Vivienne." For a moment, Sophie pondered what he meant by "hang out," sure his definition was very different from what she had in mind. She looked away from Eryka, afraid she could read what was streaming through her mind.

"I mean, it's not the same," she said, playfully throwing Jasper's arm off her shoulders as if it didn't faze her at all. "But I guess it will have to do."

Chapter 17
Brussels

The Adnan-Phillips house was a beautiful, narrow Art Deco building set in a small square and partially obscured by a riot of leafy trees. Sophie had expected the gallery to be attached, like her mother's repair shop, but Eryka explained that it was in a more commercial part of town.

"It's quieter that way," Simone continued Eryka's explanation as she greeted Sophie at the door, swooping in to give an air kiss on each cheek.

"And it forces someone," Claire gave a pointed look at her wife, before standing on her tiptoes to also extend air kisses to Sophie, "to leave work at work."

Simone flashed a wide grin, and it became clear where Jasper had gotten his smile from. "Guilty." Then she turned to Sophie. "Welcome to our home. We've heard so much about you from both our children." This bit of news threw Sophie for a loop. She expected Eryka to talk about her roommate, but what did Jasper have to say about her?

"Maman," Jasper scolded her, dragging his bag along with two of Eryka's in from the street. Then he looked at Sophie. "All I said is that you were much nicer than Ryka's other roommate."

Sophie tried to hide her disappointment. "That's a pretty low bar."

"Come on," Eryka said to Sophie, pushing past her brother into the living room. "I'll show you where to put your bag."

Eryka gestured towards a staircase that led to a second-floor landing, but Sophie paused for a moment to take in the space. There was barely an entryway. Instead, the front door opened into a narrow but light-filled living room, made bigger by the fact that it extended to the ceiling of the second story. On the side wall, before the stairs, hung a massive tapestry, filled with a warm glow that reminded Sophie of the one she and Eryka had taken to the beach in the Louvre.

Simone followed Sophie's gaze. "Home," she said softly.

Sophie turned surreptitiously towards Claire. "Mine's in the bedroom," she offered before Sophie could say anything. "Dreary English countryside can't hold a candle to vivid Mediterranean sun, as I'm sure you know by now."

Sophie thought of Sabrina's tapestries and the swirling sky she had come to recognize as her signature. It carried a power that even the warm Mediterranean sunlight she was staring at would struggle to compete with. But Sophie very much doubted Eryka's parents were keeping a Sabrina Maxwell in their bedroom. Surely Eryka would have mentioned that.

Before Sophie could say anything else, Jasper dropped Eryka's suitcases at her feet. "Make sure you take these with you," he grunted. "I'm done carrying them."

Visiting Eryka's house was very different from staying with Vivienne. While Vivienne showed little interest in spending time at home or with her family, it was clear that the Adnan-Phillips were incredibly close, and that Eryka was happy to be back in the city they called home. Every day, she took Sophie around Brussels, showing off her family's gallery and others that she loved, taking Sophie to museums, and showing her the history of the city.

Brussels had a cosmopolitan feel to it. Not like Paris, where romance seemed to seep from every corner, but rather the polar opposite, a city geared towards business, at least from the outside. But with business came money, which is why, Eryka explained, her mothers had chosen to open their gallery there. "Besides," Eryka added, "in a city less focused on pleasure, there's more need for escape. Which means more people looking to buy tapestries."

Evenings were spent around the dinner table. No matter how busy Simone and Claire seemed to be, they were always home from the gallery for dinner with Jasper and Eryka.

"We made a point of it when they were growing up," Simone explained.

"And now that they're both away at school, we know these days are numbered, so we're trying to make the most of them," Claire added.

The conversation was lively, different from the brooding affairs at Weddlesmoore, but not as overwhelming as dinners with Sophie's family. That was the difference between two kids and six. Simone and Claire could give their attention equally to Eryka and Jasper, which meant no one had to act out to get noticed. And while Jasper and Eryka teased each other, it was clear they also felt a deep sibling bond. As the week wore on, Sophie regretted that she had spent all of winter break at Vivienne's. True, there was the magic of Sabrina's tapestries, but she hadn't realized how on edge she'd felt cooped up in that drafty manor until she had the warmth of Eryka's home to compare it to. She began dreading the return to Vivienne's after this. But she tried to put it out of her mind. Eryka and her family were leaving for Egypt the following week, and there would be no invitation for a longer stay, at least not this summer.

The only thing that had marred her stay so far was Jasper. He was polite and friendly as ever, but this only tortured Sophie more. If only there was a way to show him how she felt, without making a fool of herself. If only there was a way to make him feel the same.

On her second to last morning in Brussels, Sophie was in the garden reading. Eryka was still in bed, but Sophie, who had wandered into the garden on her first morning there, had gotten up every morning since to enjoy the space. Surrounded by high stucco walls, the garden was a riot of leafy green calm, dotted by colorful flowers, and in the corner under the kitchen window, a vegetable garden that was Claire's pride and joy.

Sophie was so ensconced in her book and the peace of the garden that the clink of a coffee cup on the metal table next to her made her jump. She looked up, expecting Eryka, and was even more surprised to see Jasper, his own coffee cup in hand.

"Mind if I join you?" he asked, and Sophie was surprised to hear a slight nervousness in his voice.

"Of course," Sophie said, closing her book and reaching for the coffee. "Thanks for this," she added. "I didn't want to disturb anyone or make a mess of the kitchen, so I was waiting until Eryka was up."

"You might be waiting a while for that," he smiled slightly as he sat down, perching on the edge of the chair opposite Sophie and fidgeting with the handle of his cup. She looked at him expectantly. Why was he acting so strangely?

"What were you reading?" he asked her, though Sophie had a feeling he hadn't come out into the garden to ask about her book.

"A biography of Sabrina Maxwell," and then, before Jasper could say anything else, she added by way of explanation. "I know it's kind of weird, to read about your roommate's mother, but I, um, I just really love her tapestries, and I wanted to know a little more about her life." Strictly speaking, this wasn't a lie. Sophie did love Sabrina's work. But she was also reading the book in hopes of finding any mention of Middlebrook.

"Mmmhmm," Jasper nodded, still fidgeting in his chair. "Her tapestries are incredible."

"Are you ok?" She was used to the easygoing, self-assured Jasper, and the nervous ball of energy in front of her was making her self-conscious.

He let out a long sigh. "I was wondering," he said finally, "if you wanted to have dinner with me tonight."

Sophie's mouth fell open. "What?" she said, wondering if she had heard wrong.

"Oh," Jasper's face fell. "I mean, if you don't want to."

"What? No. Wait, I mean yes." Sophie said quickly. "I just didn't hear..." She paused, took a deep breath, and tried to contain the joy that was bubbling in her chest. "I just meant, I was surprised. Why haven't you asked me out before?" Then, before he could change his mind, she added, "I would love to have dinner with you tonight."

"You would," he said, letting out another deep breath and breaking into a grin.

"Yes," Sophie added firmly. "As long as the rest of your family doesn't mind that we won't be joining them."

"They won't mind," he said, letting his shoulders relax and sliding back into the chair. "And to answer your other question," he said, his smile widening, "I've wanted to ask you out since last term, but I didn't think it was appropriate to date my little sister's roommate."

"You have? You did?" Sophie stammered, and Jasper continued.

"And I wasn't sure if you were even interested in me. I didn't want to make things awkward."

Now it was Sophie's turn to smile. "You are really bad at reading signals," she laughed. "So, where are you taking me tonight?"

"It better be somewhere good." Eryka padded into the garden in her pajamas, carrying a cup of coffee.

Sophie looked at her. "Did you know he was going to ask me out?"

Eryka rolled her eyes. "He asked if it would be ok the minute I told him I wasn't coming back to East Lawn. I told him it was about time." She grabbed Sophie's hand and pulled her from the chair. "Now if you'll excuse us," she said to Jasper, "someone has a date to get ready for."

Sophie tried to protest — there were hours until dinner — but she could see Eryka already mentally sweeping through her closet, and decided it was best to go along. It didn't happen often, but when she had her moments, Eryka could be as stubborn as Vivienne.

At six o'clock that evening, Sophie stood in the living room, wearing one of Eryka's dresses and a pair of wedges, feeling unaccountably nervous and even more awkward. It was one thing to wait for someone to pick you up on a first date. It was another thing when you were staying in that person's house. Then again, maybe this was how all first dates felt. It occurred to Sophie now that she'd never had a proper first date, or technically, even a boyfriend. Just some guys she sometimes slept with.

She glanced around, wondering where Jasper was. She hadn't seen him all afternoon, though to be fair, she'd spent most of the day holed up in Eryka's room trying on clothes.

When she heard the doorbell ring, Sophie expected Eryka to get it, but Eryka was nowhere to be seen.

"Someone's at the door," Sophie called out awkwardly to the room. She knew Simone and Claire were already home from work, but neither one of them appeared.

The doorbell rang again and Sophie resigned herself to the fact that she was going to have to answer it. She couldn't imagine anything more awkward, but it rang again. Whoever it was was very persistent.

"Fine," she mumbled, cursing as she wobbled a little in the heels. Eryka had insisted she wear wedges "for the cobblestones, in case he takes you someplace in the center of the city." Sophie thought that was a reason to just wear flats, but she had been overruled.

She swung the door open, and there was Jasper, wearing a light blue suit, though his hair was as wild as ever, and holding a bouquet gathered from the garden. "Aren't you going to invite me in?" he said, flashing her a grin, and all of Sophie's nerves melted away.

"I mean, you live here," she replied, smiling, "but if you insist." She backed away from the door and he handed her the flowers, stopping to kiss her on the cheek as he passed.

"You look beautiful," he whispered in her ear.

She flushed. "I guess I should put these in water." Sophie looked around for a vase, then hesitated. She didn't want to start opening cabinets.

"I'll do it." Eryka had appeared on the landing. "Honestly, Jazz, you're ridiculous."

"It looks like your housekeeper has it handled," he said to Sophie with a straight face as he proffered his arm. "Shall we?"

Eryka gave him a shove as she walked past, and when she reached the flowers, she pulled off a handful of blooms and chucked them at Jasper's back. Sophie turned around to apologize, but Eryka mouthed "Good luck, have fun" and gave Sophie a wink.

—#—

Now that she knew Jasper was interested in her, Sophie found herself even more reluctant to depart Brussels. But with the Adnan-Phillips off to Egypt, there was no point. Where would she even stay?

On her final morning, Sophie thanked Simone and Claire for their hospitality. "Come back anytime, dear," Claire said, swooping in for a hug after Simone had kissed both her cheeks. "I know you're one of the things Eryka will miss most about East Lawn."

Sophie was hoping for a private goodbye with Jasper, but he had too much respect for his family, and her she supposed, to drag her away, despite what Sophie was picturing in her head. Instead, he leaned in and kissed her on the cheek, then whispered, "I'll be counting down the days until autumn." Sophie wanted to return the sentiment, but her voice caught in her throat, and she settled for kissing him on the cheek in return. Fall term seemed impossibly far away.

Then it was time to say goodbye to Eryka, and Sophie's eyes suddenly welled with tears.

"Stop that," Eryka said, trying to sound firm. "If you do, then I will."

But it was too late. Sophie did her best to inject a note of levity into her crying. "It's not you. I'm going to miss having access to your closet."

Now Eryka was laugh-crying too. "I thought you were upset that I won't be there to run interference between you and Vivienne anymore."

"That, and I won't have someone else to go to battle with me against Professor Ackerman."

Eryka stopped laughing. "That old bat," she said glowering, "is the reason I'm leaving. Promise me you'll torture her into quitting."

"If it makes you come back," she replied, enveloping Eryka in a watery hug. Then Sophie remembered that, as a weaving major, she only had to take one more history class, and she was going to do everything in her power to avoid taking it with Professor Ackerman.

"Speaking of coming back," Eryka added, pulling away from Sophie and wiping her eyes with the back of her hand, "you're coming here for winter break. I've already fixed it with Maman and Mum." Sophie opened her mouth to say something, but Eryka interjected, "I don't care what Vivienne says. She gets you all term. I get you for break."

"Ok, but you're going to be the one to break the news to Vivienne."

The five of them walked together to the Royal Museum, where Eryka, Jasper, Simone, and Claire hopped a tapestry to Egypt. Once they had gone, Sophie sat on a bench, taking in the scene around her. Commuters in suits mixed with families on their way to holiday. She knew she should get a move on, that Vivienne would be impatiently awaiting her arrival, but she was in no hurry.

Normally, she would have wandered the museum, taking in the other tapestries, but her thoughts turned to Jasper. The way he held her hand as they walked home from the restaurant. The feel of his lips when he gave her a goodnight kiss after their date. She would have liked more. Much more, if she was being honest. She would have slept with him on the spot. But he seemed to want to take things slow, and Sophie was trying to embrace the pleasure of courtship, even if it meant this summer would be its own form of torture.

Something bumped into Sophie's leg and she looked up to see a commuter stumbling, disentangling herself from Sophie's bag. "Keep your stuff out of the way," the woman called over her shoulder once she had regained her balance and carried on. Sophie wanted to shout at her that there was plenty of room and that she should be paying more attention, but there was no point. She watched as the woman disappeared a few tapestries later.

Sophie did her best to tuck her duffle under the bench, but the box with Sabrina's cartoon made it an awkward shape. She tried to imagine how, or even if, she would share her find with Holden. The two hadn't parted on great terms, and while she knew he would be excited to see it, she also had a feeling any reunion between them would be incredibly awkward, especially now that Sophie was seeing someone else.

Realizing she couldn't put it off anymore, Sophie stood, hoisted the bag over her shoulder, and set off for the tapestry to London.

Chapter 18
Weddlesmoore

Vivienne had offered to meet Sophie at East Lawn so they could take Vivienne's family tapestry to the manor, but Sophie insisted on taking public tapestries as far as she could go. Anything to buy her a few more Vivienne-free minutes.

She took a tapestry from London to the nearby village, but it was a significant walk to Weddlesmoore, and as her bag cut into her shoulder, Sophie began to question all of her life decisions.

Vivienne was waiting for her at the end of the lane, her arms crossed, tapping her foot. "What took you so long?" she whined. "I thought you'd be here this morning."

"I got distracted by a few tapestries on the way."

"What is wrong with you?" Vivienne moaned, turning towards the house and not bothering to ask Sophie if she needed help with her bag.

Mrs. Winthrop was waiting in the entryway. She said nothing to Sophie. Instead, addressing Vivienne, she said, "Tea is in your mother's study." Sophie hadn't realized how hungry she was until that moment, and as her stomach gave a low rumble, Mrs. Winthrop cast her a wary eye.

"It's been so boring here this week without you," Vivienne whined as Sophie sat down and helped herself to a few sandwiches.

"I figured you'd have spent the whole time at the beach," Sophie teased between mouthfuls.

Vivienne sighed. "Even that got old."

"What?" Sophie said in mock surprise.

Vivienne gave her a dirty look and continued. "And I had to stop going to the pub because I ran into that girl from winter break, and when I told her I was seeing someone else, she pitched a fit."

Imagine that, Sophie thought to herself. But then she added, out loud, "So you and Dominique are serious then? Isn't she French? And aren't you, well, you?"

"What's that supposed to mean?"

"Well, you know…" Sophie said.

"If you must know," Vivienne huffed, "we haven't talked about it. But I'm not fucking other girls, so that's that." Then she turned her eyes towards Sophie. "Speaking of…"

"I'm not planning on fucking your brother while I'm here," Sophie said, a little louder than she anticipated. Vivienne gave her a quizzical look, but Sophie was not about to confide in her about Jasper. Right now, it was a magical secret she wanted to keep for herself. "It's just less messy that way," Sophie said, trying to inject a note of finality in her voice.

"Fine by me. Fucking him messes with your head."

Sophie hated that Vivienne was probably right, and if it wasn't for Jasper, she would have made it a point to sleep with Holden out of spite. But it was moot now. Even though she and Jasper hadn't discussed it either, she had no intention of sleeping with anyone else. Sophie cast around for another subject before Vivienne had the chance to poke around in her sex life even more.

"What about Eryka leaving East Lawn?"

"I don't want to discuss it," Vivienne said, crossing her arms and legs and sinking into the chair. But after a moment's silence, she huffed. "This is all Professor Ackerman's fault."

Sophie couldn't argue with that, so she shoved a few more tiny sandwiches in her mouth.

"Aren't you done yet?" Vivienne asked, draining the last drops of her tea. "I want to go—"

"I know, I know," Sophie interrupted her. "To the beach. Fine. But after dinner, we're going to the pub." Vivienne looked like she wanted to protest, but Sophie added, "I'll run interference if that girl is there."

Sophie was glad she had the pub to look forward to. The beach was as boring as always, at least to Sophie, and dinner was awkward. Holden joined them for dinner at Vivienne's insistence, but he refused to make eye contact with Sophie, and hardly said more than three words to Vivienne.

"Would you grow up?" Vivienne spat at him finally, when he responded to Sophie's polite request to pass the pepper with a grunt. "I'm sure Sophie's not the first girl who realized she didn't want to sleep with you anymore."

With that, Holden shoved back his chair and stormed out of the room.

Sophie gave Vivienne a look. "What?" she said, handing Sophie the pepper. "He needs to get over it. You didn't do anything wrong. I mean, apart from lying to me about it."

But Sophie felt bad enough that when they got to the pub, she drained two beers before Vivienne was halfway through her first, and it was Vivienne who had to "shush" her as she stumbled drunkenly back through the tapestry a few hours later.

Once Sophie was sure Vivienne had gone to bed, and once some of her buzz had worn off, she padded down the hall to Holden's room.

"I'm still mad at you," he said, cracking the door open after several minutes of incessant knocking.

"I know," Sophie whispered, "but I think you're going to want to see this."

He pushed the door open further, and Sophie pushed passed him into the room, the box with Sabrina's cartoon slung under her arm, before he had a chance to change his mind.

She dropped the box on the bed and motioned for Holden to join her. "If you think I'm shagging you——" he started, but Sophie cut him off.

"Don't flatter yourself, I'm seeing someone." She wasn't exactly sure if it was true. She'd had one date with Jasper, one goodnight kiss. But she wanted it to be true, and she wasn't about to ruin her chances by fooling around with Holden again.

"Oh," he replied, his face falling for the slightest moment before he rearranged his features in something more neutral, and Sophie realized how harsh her words sounded. "Then what is it you want to show me?"

Sophie gestured to the box on the bed again, and Holden strode over, taking in the handwriting on the top.

"Middlebrook?" he said, his eyes wide. "That's where Father grew up."

It was Sophie's turn to be surprised. "What?" In all her research on Sabrina, she had never once seen mention of where her husband grew up. Sophie swallowed a wave of disappointment. Had she completely misread the situation? If this was where Mr. Morris had grown up, could it be that Sabrina was simply working on a gift for him?

But Holden was suddenly enthusiastic as if Sophie had presented him with treasure. "What's inside?" he asked eagerly. Then, not even waiting for Sophie to answer, he pulled the lid off with trembling hands.

Sophie reached for the cartoon, afraid Holden would tear it in excitement. "It's a design for a weaving. I think it's the last one she was working on before she—" Sophie couldn't let the final word fall from her mouth.

Holden looked wild-eyed between Sophie and the cartoon, which she spread out on the bed. He raked his hands through his blond hair before reaching out to trace the design before him. "Where did you find this?" he asked finally.

"It's a long story," Sophie replied. She didn't want to admit she'd stolen it.

"But it could be important," Holden said, then more to himself to Sophie. "Why wasn't it in Mum's studio?"

Sophie let out a long sigh. She couldn't think of a plausible explanation, so she decided on the truth. She told him about going to Gloria's, about noticing the crawl space and finding the box. "And I also found this," she added, pulling Sabrina's journal from her back pocket and laying it on top of the cartoon.

Holden picked it up and rifled through it. "This is from the last year of her—" he paused, then looked at Sophie. "How did Gloria get these?"

"No idea. And I haven't seen Gloria for months. I don't know if she's ever coming back." *Or if she's ok.* She couldn't bring herself to say that last part out loud.

Holden was still looking through the journal. "There's a lot about the Middlebrook tapestry in here."

Sophie nodded. "All her preparations. It was clear she was getting ready to start weaving on this one."

"And someone killed her because of it."

Sophie eyed him skeptically. "I think you're being a little dramatic." Now that she knew Mr. Morris was from Middlebrook, any conspiracy theories had flown from her head. "She was probably just making a present for your dad. And she asked Gloria to hang on to it so he wouldn't stumble on it in her workshop."

This all sounded perfectly plausible to Sophie, but it was clear Holden wasn't buying it. His suspicion of his father ran too deep.

"No," he said, shaking his head. "I think it might be a clue."

"A clue to what?"

"I don't know." He sighed. "But I need time to think it through." He turned to Sophie. "Can I keep it?"

Sophie didn't have to think twice about the cartoon. She was tired of carting around the awkward box. And while she was slightly concerned about what would happen if Gloria came back and discovered the box was missing, there was no way for her to know that Sophie was the one who had taken it. *If* Gloria ever came back.

She nodded. Holden picked up Sabrina's journal. "This too?"

This was harder for Sophie to part with. She liked having Sabrina's words with her. But she couldn't think of a good reason to keep it. After a long pause, she finally conceded. "You certainly have more right to it than I do."

With that, she crossed the room, leaving Holden deeply ensconced in the cartoon.

"You look rough." The words left Vivienne's mouth the moment Sophie sat down to breakfast.

"Gee, thanks," Sophie replied, reaching for a cup of tea, grateful she could blame the bags under her eyes on her hangover. After she'd delivered the cartoon and journal to Holden, she'd laid awake in the four-poster bed for hours, worried she had made the wrong choice.

"Beach this morning?" Vivienne asked hopefully. "Nothing like sun and sand to cure a hangover."

"Maybe for you," Sophie said, eyeing Vivienne blearily. As Vivienne's face fell, she added, "You go. I want to go back to bed for a few hours, but I'll join you later."

Vivienne looked down at her empty plate, then at Sophie for a moment, before springing out of her chair. "Ok, but if you're not up by tea time, I'm dragging you through the tapestry myself."

Sophie didn't doubt Vivienne would do it, and she knew at some point she would have to turn up at the beach. But for now, she attempted some tea before choking down a scone. Even with butter and jam, it felt dry in her throat.

She thought for a moment about really going back to bed. The four-poster was massive compared to the little bed in the shared bedroom that was waiting for her at home. But her curiosity was too strong. She headed to Sabrina's study, intent on working through her other journals for mentions of Middlebrook.

Sophie had barely made it halfway into the first journal when Holden appeared, looking even more tired than Sophie felt. His eyes were red and puffy, and Sophie wondered if it was the strain of looking at the cartoon all night, or if he had been crying.

"I've been thinking," he said, sitting across from her and putting his head in his hands. Sophie had a strong urge to reach out, to stroke his arm in comfort, but she resisted. She didn't want him to think it was some sort of invitation. "I've been thinking," he started again, "that we should weave the tapestry."

"Ok," Sophie said slowly. She wasn't fully comprehending.

"I mean you. I think you should weave the tapestry."

"What?" The word came out with the force of a laugh, but it was clear from Holden's face he was dead serious. "Holden, I can't weave an entire tapestry by myself. It would take forever. And where would I even weave it?" He had to know this was a ridiculous idea. "I'm sure there's a place you could send it to be woven. Maybe someone who used to work for your mom." She thought of Gloria, but that wasn't an option, even if she hadn't stolen the cartoon from her.

Holden shook his head. "I don't trust anyone else to do it. What if they said something to Father? He can't know what I'm doing."

"Surely enough money would keep someone quiet." Sophie couldn't believe the words were coming out of her mouth, but after almost a year of living with Vivienne, she understood what money could do.

"It's too big of a risk." It was clear Holden had thought this through. "But you could do it. I trust you. And I would pay you." He added quickly.

"Holden," Sophie was racking her brain for a way to talk him out of this ridiculous plan. "We don't even know if the tapestry is a clue. It could be anything. A gift. A commission. You're asking me to spend months, maybe longer, on something that might not mean anything."

There was something else too. Despite spending so much time with Sabrina's work, or maybe because she had, Sophie doubted her ability to pull off the tapestry. She had just finished her first year of school. People trained for years before they were good enough to work for Sabrina, and even then, they didn't start by weaving an entire tapestry themselves.

"It's possible," Sophie said slowly, "that my skills aren't even good enough. What if I spend all that time and the tapestry doesn't even work?"

Holden's eyes bored into her. "I seriously doubt that. From everything Viv says, you're the most skilled weaver I've ever met."

Sophie tried hard to keep from blushing, telling herself that this could easily be a lie. He was just trying to convince her to help him. But what if he was right? What if it was a clue? Maybe she could pull it off. And would she ever get another chance to weave one of Sabrina's designs? She opened her mouth, but he raised his hand and stood up. "Just think about it, ok," he said, striding from the room.

A few minutes later, Sophie found herself bursting through the tapestry into the blinding sun of the beach. She could see Vivienne bobbing out in the waves. Without giving herself time to think, she pulled off her jeans and waded out into the water in her t-shirt and panties.

"What are you doing?" Vivienne shouted, swimming back towards her as Sophie pushed her head under the water. She came back up, gasping for air. Vivienne reached her, questioning her again. "What are you doing? I thought you can't swim."

"I can't," Sophie laughed as she brushed the salt out of her eyes and shook the water out of her hair. She was careful to stay where she could stand, even with the swelling of the waves. "But you're right; this is exactly the cure for my hangover. And there's no better time to learn than right now." She was keen to put her obsession with Sabrina behind her, and even more keen to avoid Holden. She needed time to think. Maybe a part of her really did want to weave the tapestry. Maybe that's why she showed the design to Holden in the first place. But another part of her wondered if it was a pointless errand. Not to mention all the practicalities of executing a tapestry that big on the sly.

To Sophie's surprise, Vivienne was a more patient teacher than she expected, and after the first morning, Sophie was brave enough to doggy-paddle out further than she could touch. She doubted she would ever be the swimmer Vivienne was, but it was nice to no longer carry the shame of not knowing how to swim.

Sophie was amazed at how hungry she was after a day of swimming, and she and Vivienne ate greedily when Mrs. Winthrop deposited dinner in front of them that evening. Sophie was relieved when Holden didn't join them, but Vivienne put on her poutiest face when Mrs. Winthrop shared that Mr. Morris was too busy with work to grace them with his presence.

Once she'd helped herself to seconds of everything, Sophie headed off for an early bedtime, full and exhausted. Later that evening, she heard Holden knock softly at her door, but she just rolled over and pulled a pillow onto her head, determined to ignore him.

On the third morning of Sophie's stay, Mrs. Winthrop delivered breakfast to the dining room, and announced to Vivienne, "You'll have the house to yourself for a few days. Your father has gone to London for work and Mr. Holden is off as well." She spoke as if Sophie wasn't in the room.

"Where's Holden gone?" Sophie couldn't help asking. Did this have something to do with Sabrina's cartoon?

Mrs. Winthrop didn't answer Sophie. Instead, she looked at Vivienne and responded, "Who knows what your brother gets up to?"

With Holden gone, Sophie didn't feel the need to hide at the beach, but she couldn't figure out a way to tell Vivienne that her newfound enthusiasm for the ocean had waned the moment Holden left. After breakfast, they headed straight for the tapestry. Sophie had to admit that the beach was more fun now that she wasn't afraid of the water. Vivienne still ventured out further than Sophie dared, but bobbing alone in the water gave her time to work out a plan.

"Pub tonight?" she asked Vivienne once the pair of them had settled into dinner later that evening. She wanted to make sure Vivienne was good and asleep that night. But it seemed that, now that Vivienne was off the market, the pub had lost its appeal.

"Let's just stay in and play games tonight," Vivienne countered.

"All right, but if I'm playing games with you, I'm going to need some whiskey."

"Done."

Vivienne kept her promise, and when they settled into Sabrina's study later, arguably the coziest spot in the manor for gameplay, it was with a bottle of Mr. Morris's best whiskey. But to Sophie's chagrin, Vivienne seemed more interested in playing than drinking.

She also didn't seem ready for bed anytime soon. They played round after round, and no matter what Sophie tried — winning, losing — she couldn't get Vivienne to call it quits. It was well after midnight when, after what felt like the millionth yawn Sophie let slip, Vivienne agreed to call it a night. Sophie supposed she could have said she was tired earlier, but she needed to ensure Vivienne was asleep before she could put her plan into motion.

An hour after she said goodnight to Vivienne, Sophie padded back into the hallway. It was only then that she discovered the first flaw in her plan.

She had no idea where Mr. Morris's office was.

Vivienne had mentioned Mr. Morris slept on the opposite side of the house, so she set off, opening doors at random, hoping she wouldn't stumble on servants' quarters in the process. Surely they must be in another less impressive part of the manor.

She opened door after door but mostly found a string of empty bedrooms. How many people did this place sleep?

She indulged herself for a moment, imagining what she and her siblings would do with all this room. How lonely it must have been for Holden and Vivienne, growing up with so much vast space, especially once Sabrina was gone. No wonder their relationship was so strained.

After she had exhausted an entire hallway of bedrooms, Sophie decided that Mr. Morris's office must be downstairs. That was where Sabrina's study was, after all. She tried a few more doors, mostly finding empty parlors and sitting rooms. She could understand the purpose of so many bedrooms, but it was at this moment that she realized just how excessive the manor was.

Finally, she came to a locked door. It would make sense that Mr. Morris would keep his office locked, Sophie thought as she pulled the pick from her hair. It only took a few moments before she was pushing open the heavy wood door.

Mr. Morris's office was larger than Sabrina's study. Had this always been the case, or had he taken over a different space after his wife died? It also contained far fewer books. There was one shelf, mostly volumes about valuing historical tapestries. There was an elaborate wooden cabinet, also locked, that Sophie figured contained paperwork. She would try to open it after she had searched the expansive desk sitting in the center of the room. The walls were covered in ornate wood paneling, but on the wall behind the desk hung a large and impressive tapestry.

It was immediately clear that this wasn't one of Sabrina's. But if Mr. Morris didn't have his late wife's tapestries on display anywhere else, why would he hang one in his office? This one was much older. Late Medieval period, if Sophie had to guess, feeling incensed that she might have learned something in Professor Ackerman's class. The tapestry showed a forest, but not the kind of dappled, soothing affair you often saw in tapestries. This one was wild and dark.

Sophie walked up to it and ran her fingers across the surface. For a tapestry this old, it was well constructed, and for several minutes she inspected the way the threads made up the marled bark of the tree trunks and the way tiny highlights kept the leaves from dissolving into a giant dark mass. Then she came to her senses and remembered why she was there.

There was a massive leather chair at the desk, and Sophie sat down and skimmed the paperwork on the top. She was looking for any mention of Middlebrook, something that would indicate Sabrina's cartoon might mean something deeper. Or if she was being honest, she was hoping not to find any mentions of Middlebrook or any proof that Mr. Morris was engaged in anything shady. She was still looking for reasons not to weave the tapestry, mostly.

She opened drawer after drawer filled with legal documents concerning the family estate and notes on historical tapestries Mr. Morris had bought and sold. It seemed Mr. Morris used this office more for personal affairs than for work.

Once she had skimmed everything in the desk, being careful to put things back as she had found them, she turned her attention to the locked cabinet. Maybe there was something in there. She had just pulled the pick out of her hair again when she heard Mrs. Winthrop's voice in the hallway — "I didn't expect you back so soon" — followed by the sound of a key hitting the lock.

Sophie panicked. There was no way to explain why she had broken into the office and nowhere to hide, except— as quickly as she could, Sophie flung herself into the tapestry with such force she almost crashed into a tree on the other side. She stood, trying to calm her breathing, listening through the cloth at the muffled voices on the other side.

"Came back early — finished — needed to take care of — " followed by something Sophie couldn't make out.

"Would you like me to bring you a pot of tea, sir?" Mrs. Winthrop's sharp voice came through much clearer.

It sounded like Mr. Morris said yes, but before Mrs. Winthrop could retreat, Mr. Morris asked what sounded like a question. But all Sophie could make out was "Holden."

There was a stiffness in Mrs. Winthrop's voice, as if she didn't want to answer the question, but also couldn't lie to her boss. "Mr. Maxwell has gone to Middlebrook for a few days."

Sophie let out such a large gasp that she was worried they'd hear her inside the tapestry, but fortunately, at that moment, Mr. Morris exclaimed "Middlebrook?" with equal force. Then he muttered something Sophie couldn't hear, but it seemed that the fact that his son had gone to Middlebrook had evoked a slight panic in him.

"I'm not sure, sir. Who knows what Mr. Maxwell gets up to? Shall I go get that tea?" It was clear Mrs. Winthrop didn't want to carry on the conversation.

Mr. Morris must have said yes because there were several long minutes of silence while Sophie strained to hear what was happening in the office over the sounds of the forest. The dense foliage may have blocked most sounds, but Sophie could still hear animals moving around her. She shivered uncomfortably, wondering if it was safe.

"Your tea, sir." Mrs. Winthrop had returned. "Anything else I can get you, sir?"

Mr. Morris must have said that was all, to which Mrs. Winthrop said, "Thank you, sir. Good night."

There was silence in the office again, and Sophie strained to hear if Mr. Morris was moving around. She tried to listen for the scratch of a pen or the shuffling of papers, but it would be next to impossible to hear those sounds through a tapestry, even without the cacophony of animals around her.

Sophie shivered in the damp forest air. She badly wanted to leave, but she had no way of knowing if Mr. Morris was still in his office, or how long he might work. She slumped down against a tree and curled into a ball. Not only had she not found any evidence, but she was stuck here instead of cozy in the four-poster bed. She dozed off a few times, always waking in a panic. It was only when the first light of dawn began to break through the trees that Sophie felt brave enough to peek her head back through the tapestry.

Mr. Morris was gone. Sophie hesitated. She still hadn't explored the locked cabinet, but she had already pushed her luck too far. She slipped out of the office and moved towards her bedroom as quickly as she dared without running. Thankfully she met no one, and before she knew it, she was climbing into the four-poster bed. She was asleep the moment her head hit the pillow.

Sooner than Sophie would have liked, she was woken up by someone pounding on her bedroom door. Based on the light streaming through the windows, she figured it was Vivienne, here to chastise her for missing breakfast.

But it was Holden's face that appeared when she opened the door, looking tired and gaunt.

"I thought you were away," Sophie said, a note of surprise in her voice.

"I was, but I need to tell you what I've found."

Sophie hesitated for a moment, glancing down the hall to make sure Vivienne wasn't there, then opened the door to let him past. "This better be good," she mumbled.

His face shone with excitement. "I went to Middlebrook," he said the moment she had closed the door.

"I heard," Sophie murmured blearily. He gave her a quizzical look and she realized she wasn't supposed to know that. "You did what?" she forced herself into a loud exclamation.

Apparently, that did the trick. "I had to know," Holden said a little desperately. "I looked up old records and found the house Father grew up in. It didn't look anything like this. No place I could find connected to Father looked anything like this."

So much for the present theory.

Holden continued. "Then I started showing people the sketch and asking if they knew where it was."

"You did what?" This time Sophie was shocked. "You claim you can't trust anyone else to weave the tapestry and yet you're out there showing your mother's journal to random strangers."

"I didn't," Holden explained quickly. "I redrew the sketch onto a postcard. Made it seem like I was researching a bit of old family history."

He pulled the postcard from his pocket and handed it to Sophie. It was a faithful recreation of Sabrina's sketch, incredibly well-drawn. Sophie felt amazement for a second, then remembered Holden's stories of spending time drawing in his mother's studio. Of course he could draw. If he hadn't been so busy brooding over Sabrina's murder, he could be carrying on her legacy as a designer.

"Ok," she said, handing the postcard back to him. "So what did you find?"

"Nothing. No one in Middlebrook knew where this place was. And I walked all of the town and the surrounding countryside. I couldn't find anything."

"So the thing you needed to tell me," Sophie began slowly, an eyebrow raised, "is that you found nothing?"

"Don't you see what this means?" Holden was bursting with an excitement Sophie couldn't comprehend.

"This place is so well hidden, such a secret, that you can only access it through the tapestry. It's got to be a clue." He grabbed Sophie's hand imploringly. "And that's why I need you to weave it."

Sophie remained unconvinced. Then she remembered the shock in Mr. Morris's voice when Mrs. Winthrop told him where Holden had gone. Was he hiding something there? Something he didn't want discovered? Something worth killing for?

"I don't know." Sophie thought hard. "Say you're right. Say your mother knew something, and she was planning on using the tapestry to reveal it. Someone found out and they killed her for it." She emphasized the last part of that sentence. "If anyone found out I was weaving the tapestry…" She couldn't bring herself to finish the thought out loud.

"I can protect you."

"How?"

"We'll find someplace safe for you to weave. No one will even know until we've finished. And once we figure out what the tapestry reveals, we go straight to the police."

"We still don't know if the tapestry reveals anything. I think…" Sophie said slowly, "I think I need more proof before I commit months of my life to weaving this thing."

"Fine," Holden said, "You want more proof. I'll find more proof." And he stood up and stormed from the room. Sophie climbed back into bed, doubting very much he would find anything that would convince her.

—#—

A few hours later, there was another knock on Sophie's door. "There's no way you could have found anything else this fast,"

Sophie grumbled to herself. She opened the door to find Vivienne, waving a scone in her face.

"You missed breakfast," she said with a half pout. "Come on, I want to get to the beach. And what were you just saying?"

"Nothing," Sophie said, grabbing the scone and taking a bite. "Must've been having a dream. Just give me a minute to change and we can go."

Sophie spent the rest of the day trying to put Sabrina's tapestry out of her mind. She was curious, it was true, especially after what she'd heard last night in Mr. Morris's office. And the chance to weave one of Sabrina's designs? Well, that was a once-in-a-lifetime opportunity. But was it worth the risk if she and Holden were the only ones who would ever know?

They left the beach only when Mrs. Winthrop called them in for afternoon tea. Once they'd dried off and settled into Sabrina's study, Mrs. Winthrop deposited a tray of cakes in front of them and turned to Vivienne, "Your father will be joining you for dinner tonight."

While Vivienne squealed in delight, Sophie could feel an idea forming.

"Back to the beach," Vivienne asked brightly once they had finished their tea and snacks.

"You go," Sophie said, feigning a yawn. "I want to take a nap."

"But you slept so late this morning," Vivienne replied with her signature pout.

"I didn't sleep well last night. And then when I finally did fall asleep, someone," she gave Vivienne a pointed look, "woke me up and dragged me to the beach."

"Fine. Take your nap. I'll see you tonight for dinner."

Sophie watched Vivienne head towards the tapestry hall, then headed upstairs. But she didn't go to her room, despite how badly she needed a nap. Instead, she knocked on Holden's door.

His eyes lit up as he opened the door. "Did you change your mind?"

"Did you find more proof?"

His face fell. "No." He stepped aside to let her in the room. "I was thinking of trying to look through Father's study."

"Don't bother, I don't think there's anything there." When he gave her a look, she confessed to breaking in the night before and going through his desk.

"So you are interested," Holden said, a note of hope in his voice.

"I was looking for reasons not to do it," Sophie admitted. "At least, I think that's what I was doing."

"Still, you're curious. I'll take that as a good sign."

"Well then you're really going to like my next suggestion," Sophie said, diving into her plan.

—#—

"Four places," Vivienne said with a note of surprise, as she and Sophie entered the dining room later. Once again, Vivienne had shoved Sophie into one of her ruffled dresses, making Sophie more uncomfortable than she already was.

"Your brother will be joining you as well," Mrs. Winthrop informed her. Vivienne made a face, and Sophie remembered the last time all four of them had dinner together. It had not gone well. And Sophie really needed this one to go well.

"Promise me," Sophie gave Vivienne a hard look, "that you won't fight with Holden tonight."

"I can try, but he always starts it." That wouldn't be a problem. Sophie had forced Holden to make the same promise earlier.

"Just try, ok."

At that moment, Holden entered the room, followed by Mr. Morris. The four of them sat down, and Mrs. Winthrop brought in the soup course. Sophie gave Holden a look.

"So, Father, how are things at work?" he asked without any preamble. Not how Sophie would have started.

Vivienne practically spit out her soup. It was clear that Holden never asked that question. Even Mr. Morris raised a skeptical eyebrow.

"It's fine," Mr. Morris said. "Plenty of new designs coming down the pipeline, plus there are always requests for the old favorites."

Sophie could see Holden's hackles start to rise. Old favorites meant Sabrina's designs, and Holden thought H. J. Morris's versions of Sabrina's tapestries were hack jobs. Before Holden could say anything, Sabrina chimed in.

"Mr. Morris, um, I mean Henry," she stammered. "I was wondering if you'd be willing to give me a tour of one of your workshops." Vivienne dropped her spoon into her bowl with a loud clatter, but Sophie ignored her. "As you know, my focus is weaving, and I think it would be so beneficial to see a production weaving studio in action." She said it with all the charm and flattery she could muster.

Mr. Morris eyed her cautiously for a moment, while Vivienne gaped at her in disbelief. Then Mr. Morris spoke. "Of course, dear. I'm happy to help an aspiring weaver. I can arrange a tour tomorrow if you'd like."

"That would be wonderful," Sophie said, her face beaming with feigned enthusiasm. If Mr. Morris's workshop was as slipshod as Holden had made it sound, Sophie had no interest in that kind of facility. But then again, Holden's opinion of his father wasn't always credible.

"Father," Holden chimed in. "If it's all right with you, I'd like to accompany Sophie on the tour."

Vivienne's mouth dropped open further, and even Mr. Morris looked surprised. Holden continued, "I know it's been a while since I've been to any of the facilities."

Mr. Morris looked over at Sophie, who smiled wide and said, "The more the merrier."

"Then I'm coming too," Vivienne blurted out.

"What?" It was Sophie's turn for shock. This was not part of the plan.

"Of course, my dear. You'll be taking over someday. It's good for everyone to see you on the floor from time to time."

Sophie gave Holden a look. This would certainly make things more challenging.

Chapter 19
Weddlesmoore

There was a room just off the entryway of Weddlesmoore that Sophie had never been in, and it turned out to have a few tapestries connecting to Mr. Morris's office and several of his weaving workshops.

"It must be nice," Sophie said, sidling up to Mr. Morris the moment they had stepped through the tapestry, "to have such a short commute."

Vivienne gave Sophie a disgusted look, but flattery was part of the plan. If she could keep Mr. Morris distracted, Holden could sneak off and search his office for clues.

Sophie's job was to ask as many questions as possible out on the studio floor. This turned out to be quite easy. She was, as Holden repeatedly told her, a boffin, and Mr. Morris's workshop was, to her surprise, more interesting than she'd initially thought. Even if it lacked the skill she imagined must have existed at Sabrina's workshop. The threads weren't as fine and the color gradation wasn't as subtle.

The weavers in the workshop, for their part, seemed happy. Sophie wondered how they felt, if they were grateful to have jobs, or if they resented working on lesser quality tapestries. But she didn't dare ask. Her job was to keep Mr. Morris engaged at all times. Vivienne trailed after them, looking bored. Sophie figured she regretted coming, that she wished she was back on the beach. *Serves her right for messing up the plan.*

When they were standing along a wall of dyed yarn, Sophie engaged Mr. Morris in a conversation about wool sourcing, and Holden murmured something about the loo and wandered off. Mr. Morris was all too eager to talk about his preferred wool and went on a long rant about how he'd had to let go of a few unreliable suppliers. Before he was finished, Holden slipped back to the group, his eyes wide.

They continued the tour, Sophie trying to keep her enthusiasm up, which was much more difficult now that she was eager to know what Holden had discovered. When Vivienne started whining that she was bored, Mr. Morris suggested they cut the tour short, and Sophie, acting disappointed, reluctantly agreed.

When the three of them returned to Weddlesmoore — Mr. Morris stayed behind to work — Sophie wracked her brain for an excuse to speak to Holden privately. But before she could come up with one, Sophie was dragging her towards the beach.

Neither Holden nor Mr. Morris joined them for dinner, and afterward, Sophie feigned tiredness and headed off to bed early, leaving a disappointed Vivienne still seated in the dining room.

Once upstairs, Sophie went straight to Holden's room. Sophie had barely touched the door when it swung open.

"Finally," he said, yanking her inside.

"You found something?" Her eyes were wide, but she was trying not to get too excited. If these were anything like the clues Holden had brought back from Middlebrook, she doubted it would be enough to convince her to work on the tapestry.

"More than something," he said, pulling her over to the desk. "First, there's this." He thrust a complicated legal document into her hand.

"What's this?"

"It's a deed to some land in Middlebrook."

"So?" Sophie gave him a skeptical look. "Maybe it's the deed to his childhood home."

"No. The address doesn't match. It doesn't match any of the places I visited there. And look at the map." He pulled out a detailed map of Middlebrook. "I can't find this address anywhere. It simply doesn't exist."

"Are you sure?"

"I've been scouring the map all afternoon. Nothing. What if," he lowered his voice, "what if this is the place in the tapestry?"

"What if it's just an empty plot of land?" Sophie countered back.

"Ok, fine. But then what about this." He handed Sophie a very short letter:

Searched the cabin, found nothing. No sign of G. Must have cleared out. Looks like a dead end.

Sophie ran her fingers through her hair, thinking fast. G? Could this be referring to Gloria? Had someone searched her cabin after Sophie had been there?

Holden looked at her expectantly. "Do you think this means..." she whispered, unable to finish the thought.

"I think it means one of my father's associates was looking for the thing you already found."

"But why now?" Sophie wondered aloud. It had been almost seventeen years since Sabrina's murder. Why were they only searching for the cartoon now? She turned the note over. There was no date. It could be referring to anything, and it could have been written at any time. But Gloria's sudden disappearance and Sophie's nabbing of the cartoon would speak to the letter being recent. She turned to Holden. "Where did you find this?"

"The letter was in a drawer on Father's desk." There was no way to know if it was recent. But if it was recent, then why now? Did it have something to do with Sabrina's tapestry that the studio recently repaired? Did Gloria let something slip? Is this the first time someone connected to Mr. Morris had realized where Gloria was? Holden went on, crashing into Sophie's swirling thoughts. "The land deed was much more hidden. Clearly something he didn't want found."

"Or maybe," Sophie said, still trying to poke holes in Holden's theory, "it was hidden because who really needs to look at a land deed that often?" But she couldn't shake the feeling that something was wrong. Had Gloria known she was in danger? Was that why she hid Sabrina's cartoon and left? Would Sophie and Holden be in danger if anyone found out they had it?

"This deed wasn't with other deeds. It was tucked away."

Sophie thought hard. So Mr. Morris was trying to hide something in Middlebrook, the same town Sabrina had designed a tapestry for, the same design that Gloria had hidden. Potentially the same thing that someone had gone to Gloria's cabin to find. All roads pointed to the tapestry meaning something.

She looked at Holden and sighed. "All right," she said. "I'll do it."

"You will?" Holden's eyes were wide and he jumped up, pulling Sophie with him, and spun in a circle around the room. He had a look like he wanted to kiss her, but Sophie wrenched her arms from his grasp and backed away. Holden ran his hand through his hair awkwardly. "I'll pay you. I'll buy all the supplies. You won't need anything."

"What I need," Sophie said, "is a safe place to work on the weaving." If someone was searching for this design, it was essential that no one knew that Sophie had it or where she was weaving it. "Not to mention," she went on, "a loom."

"Looms are easy enough to get," Holden replied. *Sure, if you have money*, Sophie thought. "Just let me know what you want. And you can weave here. I'm sure we can find you a room. Mrs. Winthrop—"

"I'm not weaving here," Sophie replied flatly, cutting him off. "I can't spend my whole summer here." Didn't want to, was more like it. "And I'm not sure we can trust Mrs. Winthrop."

"She's the one who showed me mum's tapestries. Helped me set up the secret gallery."

"But she also told your dad you had gone to Middlebrook. I'm worried she's playing both sides." Plus, it felt too risky. If Mr. Morris was involved, Sophie didn't want to weave the tapestry right under his nose.

"What about Mum's old workshop?"

Sophie indulged the idea for a moment, imagining the poetic nature of weaving Sabrina's final tapestry in her studio. But that would still require her to spend the summer here, and there was no way to know who might be checking up on that property. With all the windows, it would be easy to see when there was activity in the space, even without a key.

"No," Sophie said. "That feels too risky." Then she brightened. "Come with me, I have an idea."

—#—

Sophie led Holden to the gallery with Sabrina's tapestries, then once they were locked safely inside, to the far wall with the little village under the swirling sky.

Holden eyed the tapestry, then Sophie, with suspicion. "You think we're going to find a place in Mum's hometown?"

"No," Sophie said. "Just trust me. There's something I need to show you."

They stepped through the tapestry, and Sophie looked around, trying to get her bearings. They were looking at the town a little more straight on, Sophie thought, trying to remember that day last summer. To her left, she could see grazing ponies and fields of lavender.

"I think it's this way," she said, dragging Holden to the left.

"What's this way?"

"You'll see."

They came to the top of the rise. It looked like the right perspective, and Sophie began pawing at the air, moving forward and back, left and right.

"What are you doing?" Holden seemed genuinely concerned for her sanity.

"It's got to be here somewhere," Sophie muttered to herself, and when she reached out again, her hand felt, not misty air, but the edge of the fabric. "Found it!" she declared. She grabbed Holden by the arm and pulled him through.

Sophie had expected to step out into the bright light of the Honyeoke Falls museum, and the darkness confused her. The tapestry was still hanging, she realized after a moment, in the storage room. And there, sitting on a pile of boxes, was Rush, reading a book.

He stood up when he saw them. "Sophie? What are you doing here?"

She opened her mouth to reply, and then suddenly burst into tears. Before she could stop, she flung herself into his arms. "I'm so sorry," she wailed, her voice breaking between sobs. "I never should have treated you like that. You were just trying to— I'm sorry, I was such a bitch. And now you hate me."

He put his arms around her and began gently stroking her hair. "It's ok," he whispered. "I forgive you."

Sophie pulled back and looked at him, mid sob. "You do?"

"Of course. I should have seen it from your perspective. I should have known you could handle it on your own."

"Then why didn't you reply to any of my letters." Sophie tried to calm her breathing, but fat tears still poured down her cheeks. "I thought you hated me."

"I was embarrassed," Rush said, raking his fingers through his dark curls. "I was wrong too, and I didn't know how to admit that in writing. I'm sorry."

Sophie looked at the ground, then poked Rush's foot with hers.

"But seriously," Rush went on. "What are you doing here? Your mom told Ma you weren't going to be home for a few more days. And then you just burst through this tapestry with some random guy."

At that, Holden let out a small cough, pulled himself up to his fullest height, and strode towards Rush, hand outstretched. "Holden Maxwell," he said, in his most proper British accent.

"Rush Rigo," Rush replied, extending his hand but giving Sophie a look that clearly said, *this guy? Really?*

Holden shook his head in confusion. "Is Rush your real—"

"Slim gave it to me," Rush cut in, clearly wanting to emphasize his history with Sophie. "But that's what everyone calls me."

Holden gave Sophie a quizzical look in response to her nickname. For her part, Sophie was relieved to hear Rush slide into her familiar nickname, to know that he had well and truly forgiven her for how she behaved in Paris.

"So what should I call—" Holden started, but Sophie stepped in, eager to end the pissing contest.

"Look Rush, we're here because we need your help."

"I don't want to help your new boyfriend," Rush blurted out, at the exact moment Holden said, "We don't need help from him."

"He not my boyfriend," Sophie said, looking at Holden. "And neither is he." She said, looking at Rush, then back to Holden. "No one is my boyfriend." She thought of Jasper, of the feel of his lips on hers. But he wasn't technically her boyfriend either, and he wasn't part of this conversation. "But we do need help," she said again to Rush.

"Before you tell me what you need, can you please explain to me how you got here?" It seemed like Rush had a guess, but wanted to hear the words from Sophie.

"This tapestry," she said, gesturing towards the wall, "is a Sabrina Maxwell."

"I know that. Why do you think it's still hanging in here? Once Ma realized who designed it, and where it went, she couldn't have it on display. The museum's not authorized to have people galavanting off to England anytime they want. And adding passport control would cost a fortune."

"Wait," Sophie said, suddenly confused. "If your mom realized the museum can't keep it, why is it still here?"

"It's being auctioned off later this fall, hopefully for big money. Ma's using the time until then to study it."

Sophie felt a pang of disappointment. This masterpiece wouldn't be staying here, wouldn't become the jewel of her small town museum. But hopefully, Mrs. Rigo would be able to buy something else magnificent with the proceeds of the sale. And Sophie had bigger things to worry about now.

"Holden is Sabrina's son," Sophie told Rush, trying to get back to the point. "We think we found a clue to his mother's murder."

"And you came all the way here just to tell me about it?" Either Rush wasn't following or Sophie wasn't explaining very well. "And how exactly did you get here anyway?"

"Holden has a similar tapestry by Sabrina at his house," Sophie couldn't bring herself to tell Rush that Holden practically lived in a castle. "And when I saw it, I realized this one was also a Sabrina Maxwell. I figured I could use that one to get through this one."

"That's highly illegal," Rush told her. Sophie rolled her eyes. This from the guy who taught her how to pick locks? "So these tapestries are the clue?"

"No, the clue is a design for a different tapestry." Sophie went on. "And we, I mean, I need someplace to weave it. Someplace with a door and a lock. Someplace no one will come looking for it. And since I'm going to be here the rest of the summer, I thought maybe you could help me find someplace."

"You want me to help you find a space big enough to weave a tapestry for him?" He gave Holden a dirty look.

"I assure you," Holden said suddenly, his eyes on Rush, "you will be well compensated for your help."

Rush flashed. "I don't need your money, man." Then he turned to Sophie. "Is that why you're helping him? Because he's paying you?"

"No, I mean, yes, I mean—" Sophie stammered. She hadn't technically agreed to let Holden pay her, but she hadn't said no to it either. She had agreed to weave the tapestry because this was probably her only chance to weave one of Sabrina's designs. And despite how complicated their relationship had become, she wanted to help Holden find closure. It had nothing to do with money.

She fixed Rush with a hard gaze. "I want to help him, ok. It was my choice." Then she decided to lay on a little guilt. "Help me find a place to weave here, otherwise I'll have to weave it at Holden's and I'll be gone all summer." She was bluffing, having already established Holden's wasn't an option, but Rush didn't know that.

"Ok," he said, though Sophie could hear the hesitation in his voice, "but even if we find a space big enough, where are you going to get a loom?"

"I think I can help with that," said a voice from the other side of the room.

Frances O'Toole was standing in the doorway.

Chapter 20
Honyeoke Falls

"**M**om, what are you doing here?" Sophie replied, in utter disbelief. Her mother was here? And offering to help?!?

"You thought Carla wasn't going to tell me that my daughter showed up early through an unsanctioned tapestry, with a gentleman in tow?"

Mrs. Rigo was standing next to her mother. Sophie didn't realize Rush's mom knew they'd arrived, but they had been making an awful lot of noise. Mrs. Rigo likely came to investigate, saw Sophie, and went straight to Frances.

"Sorry, dear," Mrs. Rigo gave her a look. "It's a code amongst mothers."

But Sophie wasn't mad, just surprised. She looked at her mother. "What do you mean, you can help?"

Frances gave a smile, clearly relishing her secret. "I'll show you, but first you have to introduce me to your friend."

Holden didn't wait for Sophie's introduction, he just strode over to Frances, extending his hand. "Holden Maxwell, ma'am," he said, and Sophie saw her mom melt slightly under his British charm. "It's a pleasure to meet you."

"The pleasure is mine," she said. Then she turned stern. "And just what are your intentions with my daughter?"

Holden flushed slightly, but Sophie stepped in between them. "Mo—om. I'm helping Holden with a project. That's all." She wanted to shut that door before her mother asked any more questions. "Now, you said you can help us?

With a loom?" Sophie couldn't help feeling incredulous. Her mother had everything needed to repair a tapestry, but Sophie had never seen even a hint of a full-size loom anywhere in the O'Toole household.

Frances gave her sly smile again. "Come with me." She looked pointedly at Holden and Rush. "All of you."

They left the museum and trudged through the plaza. Sophie watched Holden take in the details of the small town, and suddenly realized, with horror, that her mother was leading them back towards their house. What would Holden think? She had never tried to hide the fact that her family wasn't rich, but you could fit the entirety of the O'Toole's house in the Maxwell's entryway.

Sophie trotted forward and whispered in her mother's ear, "Where are we going?"

Her mother just smiled that stupid smile. "It's nice to see you too dear."

Now Sophie was fuming. Her mother had been awful to her all last summer, and here she was acting like there was nothing wrong between them. Like they were just pals off on an adventure. And what was with her willingness to suddenly help Sophie? On a mystery project she knew nothing about?

They didn't go into the house. Instead, Frances led them into the repair shop. No one else was there, but several tapestries, in various states of restoration, were scattered around the room. Sophie was suddenly aware of how shabby everything looked — the threadbare carpet, the tools scattered everywhere, yarn shoved into boxes along the wall.

But Holden took everything in with a look of great interest. He leaned in to examine a patch Frances was working on, then turned to her. "You have a keen eye," he said, and Frances beamed at him. "I can see where Sophie gets it."

Frances turned to her. "Your friend is quite charming." Behind Frances and Holden's backs, Rush feigned like he was going to wretch.

"Mom," Sophie gave her a look. "We're kind of in a hurry." She wasn't exactly sure what time it was, but they needed to get back to Weddlesmoore at some point before Vivienne woke up and they had a lot of explaining to do. "What are you going to show us?"

"Fine," Frances said, clearly disappointed she couldn't keep up her game or let Holden flatter her some more. She led them through a door at the back of the repair studio, a door that Sophie had never been through. She never saw her mother go inside, so she'd always assumed it was some sort of overflow storage closet, so boring she had never bothered to look.

But to Sophie's surprise, it was another room. Smaller than the repair studio, but larger, by far, than any of the bedrooms in the house. Pictures of famous tapestries hung on one of the walls, and light flooded in through a few high windows. And there, in the center of the room, stood a loom.

It was undressed but in perfect condition.

"Where did this come from?" Sophie asked in amazement. In all her life, her mother had never mentioned anything about owning a loom like this.

Frances turned to the boys. "Would you give us a minute? Maybe Rush can give Holden a tour of the town."

Sophie couldn't imagine a worse idea, not least because one of them might end up throttling the other. "Mom, Holden's not supposed to be here."

"Oh, it will be fine," Frances said, flashing them her weird grin.

As soon as they had left the room, Sophie turned to her mother. "Where did you get this?" she blurted out, at the same moment that Frances said, "What's going on?" She wasn't smiling anymore.

"What do you mean?" Sophie asked, feigning ignorance.

"Don't give me that shit," her mother responded. This was even stranger than the fake hospitality. Frances never swore. "You show up here early through an unsanctioned tapestry with some guy, and now you need a loom."

"Which you somehow have." Sophie's head was spinning, but her mother shot her a look, and it was clear she would not be answering any of Sophie's questions until Sophie answered hers.

"I'm helping him with a project." Frances eyed her skeptically. "His mother is Sabrina Maxwell, and he found a design for one of her tapestries that was never woven." She hesitated for a moment because that part was a lie. She had found the design, not Holden. But she pushed passed it, straight into another lie. "He thought it would be a nice tribute to her to weave it, and it seemed like too good an opportunity to pass up." That last part was true.

"A nice tribute?" It was clear Frances wasn't buying it. "And why exactly did you need to sneak into America looking for a loom to make this nice tribute?"

"Well…" Sophie paused, looking for the right approach. "Since I'm going to be home all summer, and we were, um, eager to get started, it just made more sense to look for a place here."

"And that was so important you had to come in the middle of the night?" Dammit. Sophie was hoping her mother wouldn't have clocked that fact. "What's really going on, Sophie?"

"Fine," Sophie said with a sigh. She knew she had been beaten, and if she wanted her mother's help, the only option was the truth. "Holden thinks this tapestry has some connection to his mother's murder. He asked me to help weave it because he thinks it's a clue. I said yes, because..." She trailed off. Would any of her reasons even make sense to her mother?

"...because you're you." Her mother finished the sentence for her softly. And then, just as quietly, "The loom belonged to your Aunt Sofia."

"What?" This was harder for Sophie to process than the fact that her mother had the loom. Frances never mentioned her vanished sister but had a secret space with her loom like some sort of shrine?

"Your grandfather built it for Sofia when she started school." And now her mother was talking about her own father, whom Sophie had never met. Sophie was so dizzy she thought she might fall over. "After Sofia—" her mother hesitated, "after we realized she was missing, I was afraid he would destroy it. When I moved out, I asked your father to help me take it."

"You stole it?"

"You don't understand. Your grandparents would have destroyed it, along with every other memory of Sofia, when they thought she was gone for good. I couldn't let that happen."

"Because you wanted to preserve her memory?"

Frances laughed. A cold, hard laugh. "I thought she would come back for it. She was my big sister. It took me a long time to give up hope."

Those last words hung in the air, and Sophie didn't have the heart to ask her mother when that day finally came. After a long silence, she asked, "Have you had the loom in here the whole time?"

Sophie asked the question with a hint of accusation in her voice. She expected her mother to say yes, and she was prepared to yell, that all this time she could have been practicing and learning at home.

But Frances had one more surprise up her sleeve. "No. I asked your father to set it up after you left for school, as a surprise for when you got home. I thought you should have it."

Chapter 21

Weddlesmoore

It was almost morning when Sophie and Holden returned to Weddlesmoore with a plan in place. Sophie would weave Sabrina's tapestry on the loom her mother had kept hidden. Her Aunt Sofia's loom.

"Do you mind if I stay here alone for a little bit?" Sophie asked, gesturing around the gallery with Sabrina's tapestries. "I need to spend some time studying your mother's work."

"Now?" Holden gave her an incredulous look. "Aren't you exhausted?"

Sophie couldn't argue with that. It had been a long night. But her brain was working overtime, and she doubted she'd sleep anyway. "I just want a few minutes," she told Holden. "Besides, if we bump into Vivienne together at this time—"

"She'll think we spent the night together." Holden finished. Sophie nodded. She did not need Vivienne thinking she and Holden were a thing again.

Holden handed her the key. "Just slip it under my door when you're done."

He left and Sophie sat on the bench, rubbing her eyes hard. She was exhausted. But she needed a moment to process everything. She spared half a thought for Rush. They'd made up, which after everything that happened the last few months, was like a weight had lifted. But it was the conversation with her mother that lingered in her brain.

It wasn't just the secret loom or the fact that her mother wanted her to have it. It was the way, once Sophie finally told the truth, that Frances had accepted the plan without any more questions. As if solving Sabrina's murder, if that's really what they were trying to do, would bring Sofia back too.

—#—

Sophie was not looking forward to trekking through the five tapestries it would take to get home, not now that she knew she could get to Honyeoke Falls in one, at least for the time being. But she and Holden had decided it was best not to draw attention to the connected tapestries, and an American girl wandering through the fields of a small town carrying an overstuffed duffle was sure to raise a few eyebrows.

This also meant, to Holden's dismay but Sophie's relief, that he wouldn't be popping in to check on the progress of the tapestry.

"People in the village will notice if you start coming through all the time." She didn't clarify if she meant the village in the tapestry or hers, but either way, it seemed too risky. "I'll send you weekly letters and update you on the progress."

"And that won't seem strange?" Holden asked. It was well past midnight on Sophie's last night in Weddlesmoore, and they were in Holden's room, finalizing plans for the weaving. "A letter from you every week? Someone will think we're dating."

Sophie laughed at this idea, as if letters were somehow more conspicuous than regular visits to a town on the other side of an ocean. "Who's going to see them? Vivienne's absconding to France and I'm certain your father doesn't check the mail. Mrs. Winthrop?" Sophie paused for a moment. "I guess the biggest risk there is that she would see it's from me and throw it away instead of giving it to you."

She tried to laugh it off, but she could see that happening. Mrs. Winthrop always treated her with disdain, if she acknowledged her presence at all. "I'll just put a different name on the return address."

Holden opened his mouth to argue, but Sophie gave him a firm look and asked, "Have you placed the order for the yarn yet?"

"It went out in this morning's post. I expect you'll have it a few days after you arrive home."

Sophie couldn't imagine what the order had cost. Sabrina's signature color shifts required a huge range of graduated colors and because she didn't have the time to dye each color by hand, she'd asked Holden to order wandering wool in every color she'd need. And the cost had fallen entirely on Holden, something that made Sophie a little uncomfortable. Even if she had gotten better about letting people spend money on her. And even if this was ultimately Holden's project and he *should* be the one footing the bill. At the same time, she was giddy with the prospect of it, all that wool, hers to work with.

"Thank you," she said, realizing she was grateful for the opportunity, even if she had been hesitant to agree at first.

He leaned his forehead against hers. "No. Thank you," he said, his voice earnest, his lips mere inches from hers. His breath was warm and comforting, and Sophie could feel his jaw tilting closer to hers.

For one brief second, she thought about leaning in, swept into the exhilaration of their secret plan, Holden's skin, his lips. Then she thought of Jasper, and she jumped back as if Holden had shocked her.

"You're welcome," she stammered. "It's late, I should get to—"

"I'm sorry," Holden said, standing up quickly. "I shouldn't have."

"It's ok," said Sophie. "But it really is late. And I've got a long day of travel tomorrow."

"Are you sure there isn't anything else we need to discuss?" His voice was hopeful.

"I think it's all worked out. Goodnight, Holden." In a different world, one just moments before, she would have kissed him on the cheek. But it felt too risky now. She walked to the door, and he followed after her, grabbing her hand in both of his. Her skin prickled.

"I really am grateful," he told her.

"I know," Sophie said, prying her hand free and pushing through the bedroom door. In the hallway, she leaned hard against the wall, willing her body to calm down, before finally heading off to bed.

—#—

Holden wasn't in the entry hall the next morning to see her off, which was a relief. Vivienne was there, and to Sophie's surprise, so was Mr. Morris.

"I have some work in London this morning, so if you don't mind, I thought I'd accompany you on the first leg of your journey," he said to Sophie. "We can take my private tapestry."

Sophie went suddenly mute. Did Mr. Morris suspect something? Was that why he wanted to join her? At least traveling by tapestry was quick. There was little time for small talk, or, Sophie gave an involuntary shudder, foul play.

"Are you ok, dear?" Mr. Morris asked, seeing Sophie flinch. "I hope my company isn't that onerous."

"Oh no," Sophie said, thinking quickly. "Just a little chill. Wet hair. I should have dried it better."

Looking to change the subject, Sophie stepped forward to hug Vivienne. "Tell Dominique I say hi," she whispered in Vivienne's ear.

Vivienne made a sound of mock outrage. "I'm going to study, thank you very much." Sophie was certain the only thing Vivienne meant to learn was every curve of Dominique's body, but since Dominique was studying tapestry history, maybe something would rub off.

"Thanks for letting me stay," she said brightly to Vivienne, letting her go.

Mrs. Winthrop arrived at that moment, carrying Mr. Morris's briefcase. As usual, she acted as if Sophie wasn't there.

"Goodbye, Mrs. Winthrop." Sophie tried to inject as much friendliness as she could muster in her voice without tripping into sarcasm. "Thanks for everything."

She thought she heard Mrs. Winthrop give a small "hrmph" before she turned on her heel and vanished from the entryway.

"I'll tell you what," Mr. Morris said, eyeing Sophie's clunky duffle. "I'll carry that if you carry this." He extended the briefcase towards her.

Now panic really set it. The corners of the box with the cartoon were bulging the fabric. Did Mr. Morris know what was in there? Was this his way of finally getting hands on it? She and Holden should have taken it to Honyeoke Falls last night, or the night before. Then it would have been safe.

"Oh that's all right," Sophie said, heaving the bag onto her shoulder in a way she hoped looked effortless. "It's not as heavy as it looks."

Mr. Morris gave her a funny look. "You're sure?"

"I'll manage," Sophie said, putting on a big smile.

Mr. Morris turned to his daughter and gave her a kiss on the cheek. "See you for dinner tonight, my love." Then he looked at Sophie. "We're having a special goodbye dinner before my little scholar heads off to France for the rest of the summer. It's a pity you couldn't stay and join us."

"I wouldn't want to intrude on your family time," Sophie said, resisting the urge to transfer the bag to her other shoulder. It was already heavy. "Shall we?" she said, gesturing towards the room off the hall with Mr. Morris's tapestries and hoping desperately it wasn't some kind of trap.

The trip to London was quick and in a moment, they were stepping out, not, as Sophie had expected, into a museum, but into a handsome, wood-paneled office, not unlike the one Sophie had broken into in Weddlesmoore.

"Where are we?" Sophie asked, trying to control her rising panic.

"I keep a small office in London," Mr. Morris explained. The room, like his office, had no windows, and he was standing between Sophie and the door. "This building belongs to my lawyers."

Sophie grasped the strap of her duffle a little more firmly and started to move around the office, keeping as wide a berth as she could from Mr. Morris in the small space. "I'd better be going," she said, trying to keep her voice calm.

"Are you sure you have to hurry off? Why don't you relax for a moment." He gestured towards a pair of armchairs in the corner. "Would you like a cup of tea?"

"No thank you," Sophie said, glancing around the room for an object she could use to defend herself — if it came to that. "I'm sure you've got plenty of work to do."

Sophie began to sweat. She was probably just being paranoid, but she couldn't shake the feeling that things were about to go very, very wrong. Was it just the cartoon he wanted? Maybe she could give it to him and walk out of the office unscathed. Or maybe, like Sabrina, she already knew too much.

Mr. Morris didn't appear menacing. If anything, his face showed a sense of concern for Sophie's odd behavior, but that didn't allay Sophie's concerns. She needed to get out of here, immediately. Was she strong enough to overtake him? She'd heard stories of people with super-human strength in times of crisis. Perhaps she could manage to push past him, through the door, and into — well, exactly what was waiting on the other side she didn't know.

"Are you sure you don't want —" Mr. Morris began, but at that moment, the door swung open, and a younger man entered.

The man looked between Sophie and Mr. Morris, then began stammering. "I'm so sorry, sir. I didn't realize you were already here. I didn't mean to interrupt."

Now was her chance. Sophie could make her polite exit. But her feet were rooted to the floor.

Mr. Morris looked at the young man. "It's not a problem, Frederick. This is Miss O'Toole. She's a friend of Vivienne's from school. On her way back to America, so I offered her my tapestry back to London."

Before the young man could say anything, Mr. Morris continued. "Sophie, this is Frederick Walker. He's clerking at the law firm for the summer. He went to school with Holden."

Sophie managed to unstick her feet and strode forward towards Frederick to shake his hand. This got her a little closer to the door, at any rate.

"Nice to meet you."

"Likewise," Frederick replied.

"I really must be going," she said, sliding around so that Frederick was now between her and Mr. Morris. "Thanks for everything," she said to Mr. Morris over Frederick's shoulder.

"I can walk you out," Frederick offered. "The building can be a little tricky to navigate."

Was this part of the trap? Was Frederick in on Mr. Morris's plan? But Sophie couldn't think of a valid reason to decline Frederick's help. She didn't know her way out of the building, and she certainly didn't want to stay here alone with Mr. Morris. Before Sophie could answer, however, Mr. Morris chimed in. "Thank you, Frederick. That's very kind of you." Then, to Sophie, "It's been a pleasure, my dear. I do hope we'll see you again over winter break."

Sophie nodded, though she knew she wouldn't return to Weddlesmoore anytime soon. She pushed through the door, Frederick trailing behind her, and it was everything she could do not to break into a run.

Once she was in the long hallway, however, she hesitated, not knowing which way to turn.

"You're in an awful hurry," Frederick said, striding in front of her to take the lead.

"It's a lot of tapestries back to America," Sophie offered, trying to sound casual. "And this bag weighs a ton."

"I can carry that for you if you'd like."

"No, thank you," Sophie said, a little too quickly. Frederick gave her a strange look. "It's my fault it's so heavy, too many clothes." She shifted the weight of the bag, trying to hide the square corners of the box inside. "No one else should suffer on my behalf."

Frederick shrugged. "Suit yourself," he said, before setting off along the hall and down a flight of stairs.

The silence was awkward, and Sophie, never good with silence, especially when her heart was still racing, cast around for a topic of conversation. "You went to school with Holden?"

Frederick gave a slight smile. "We were mates, for lack of a better word. Bit of an odd chap, so sulky all the time. I'm sure you learned that, visiting the family. But he helped me get this clerkship, so I'm grateful."

Sophie didn't know how to respond. Sulking was one way to describe Holden, but, given what he'd been through, she certainly didn't consider that odd.

"Is he still obsessed with his mother's murder?" Frederick went on. "It was kind of mental, the way he was always talking about it."

"It was a big thing that happened in his life," Sophie said, unable to conceal the annoyance in her voice. "But it seems like he's getting over it. I hardly heard him mention it at all when I was there." Sophie wasn't sure why she was lying to Frederick, but she certainly didn't want him to think she was aiding Holden in his obsession.

"That's a relief. It's time he moves on."

Sophie had said as much to Holden, but hearing the words from Frederick's mouth made her want to slap him. Who was he to tell Holden to move on? But before she could say anymore, Frederick had steered her into a small foyer, where, mercifully, light from the outside streamed through a little window set in a door. "Here we are," he announced.

"Thank you for helping me find my way," Sophie said, and before Frederick could say another word, she pushed outside. She was several buildings away, keen to put as much distance as possible between herself and Mr. Morris, when she realized she had no idea where in London she was.

The area was practically deserted, but she finally managed to flag down a woman who looked slightly irritated — she was probably late on her way to work — and ask for directions to the British Museum.

"You're a long way off," the woman replied, looking at her watch. "I wouldn't want to walk with that thing." She gestured towards the duffle. "There's a little museum just over there." She pointed to a slightly shabby wood building. "You can hop a tapestry to the British Museum inside."

The interior of the building was just as shabby as the exterior, a single room with three large, slightly faded tapestries. A security guard, as old and rundown as the building itself, sat on a stool by the door.

"The British Museum?" Sophie asked, slightly breathless.

The guard pointed a gnarled finger at the tapestry on the left wall and Sophie darted through it without another word.

Sophie didn't linger in the British Museum either, practically sprinting past tapestries until she found the one back to America. By the time she stepped out of the tapestry into the Guggenheim, she felt a sense of vertigo that was caused by much more than the museum's spiraling tower.

It was only when she reached the bottom — when she felt certain that her feet were on American soil — that she sat down on a bench and burst into tears.

Chapter 22

Honyeoke Falls

"**A**re you sure you weren't overreacting?" Rush asked when Sophie had finished telling him about what happened in Mr. Morris's office.

It was the next day, and Sophie had cajoled Rush into helping her warp the loom. They'd been at it for over an hour, and Sophie had spent the time filling Rush in on everything she knew about Sabrina, Holden, Mr. Morris, and the tapestry design she had found.

"I'm telling you, Rush," Sophie said with an exasperated sigh. "I think he knows something."

"I think spending time with Holden has made you paranoid."

Sophie let out a small noise of disagreement. That was exactly what Vivienne had said.

Rush continued. "Do you really think he killed his wife?"

"Of course he didn't actually kill her. But I think maybe he was involved."

"Because you found a few pieces of paper in his office. Maybe someone planted them there. Maybe he was also investigating her death." Rush was trying his best to poke holes in her theory, even as he went on helping her wind the warp.

Sophie didn't respond. She couldn't bring herself to admit that Rush might be right. It would mean weaving the tapestry was a waste of time. And she was in it now. She'd made up her mind.

Holden's shipment of yarn arrived the next day, just as Sophie was finishing the warp. She tore into the boxes like a woman possessed, and soon the floor was littered with balls of wool thread, rolling in every direction. It took every ounce of restraint not to throw herself into the pile. To hell with it, she decided, and dove in. This was her wool and no one else's. She may never have this much expensive thread all to herself again. She had a slight urge to take off all her clothes, to feel the wool against her skin. If only Jasper were there. She would pull him in, burrowing together in a nest of color.

Instead, she satisfied herself with arranging the wool across the floor, each color gliding and shifting into the next, waiting expectantly like school children lined up before a lesson.

The following day, a postcard arrived from Jasper. Delilah delivered it to Sophie where she sat at the loom, working on the first few tentative rows of the tapestry.

"You got a postcard from your boyfriend," Delilah teased, twirling it above Sophie's head. Sophie snatched it from her sister and gave it a quick scan, but there was nothing scandalous on the back. Not that she expected there to be. They'd only kissed, after all.

"He's not my boyfriend," Sophie told her in a huff, hoping that wasn't true. It was what she wanted, and she desperately wished they'd talked about it before she left Brussels.

"He says he can't wait to see you again," Delilah said, a slight note of derision in her voice.

Sophie's heart leaped as she skimmed for that line. Then she turned to Delilah with anger. "You read it?"

Delilah shrugged. "How else was I supposed to know who it was for? Besides, there's nothing else to do around here." She kicked the corner of the loom with her toe and eyed Sophie. "I could help you with this, you know."

"With the tapestry?" Sophie tried, but failed, to keep the skepticism out of her voice. "But you don't even know how to weave."

Angry patches appeared on Delilah's face. "I've been practicing. Ever since you left. And I've been helping mom in the repair shop. This is going to take you forever on your own."

Sophie shook her head. "I'm sorry, De. I don't think you're ready yet." It wasn't only that. She didn't want her younger sister mixed up in this. It was bad enough that she was working on this at home. What if someone found out and she put her mother or Rush or Mrs. Rigo in jeopardy? She couldn't risk her sister getting involved too.

Delilah gave a snort and a stamp of her foot, then stormed from the room.

Sophie turned back to the loom and had to admit her sister had a point. It was going to take her forever to weave this on her own.

It was late when Sophie finally came to bed. Her fingers ached from picking at impossibly fine fibers, but she felt a much greater pain knowing she had to undo most of the day's work. It would take her a while to get a hang of things before she could begin weaving in earnest.

Delilah was huddled under the quilt, but Sophie could tell by the way she was breathing that she wasn't asleep.

She thought about apologizing, but she didn't feel remotely sorry for shutting her sister out. Best to let it blow over. Delilah would surely lose interest in a few days anyway.

Besides, she had more pressing matters to worry about.

Sophie flicked on the small light on the desk in the corner of the room — Delilah jerked the covers over her head in protest — and examined Jasper's postcard. There was a building on the front. Sophie guessed it was made out of cement, but it looked more like fluffy rectangular marshmallows cantilevering out from one another. She turned the card over to read Jasper's note:

Dear Sophie,

So much magnificent architecture here in Egypt. I can imagine you creating tapestries for incredible buildings like this someday. Looking forward to seeing you soon so I can tell you all about the trip. Hope your summer has started well.

Yours,
Jasper

It felt oddly formal, but then again, it was a postcard. Anyone could read it. And what do you say to a person you've been on one date with and won't see again until the fall anyway?

She pulled out a piece of paper and tried to fashion a response. Her first attempt was pure smut, as she couldn't resist laying out all the things she wanted to do to him the next time they were together. "Well at least now that's out of the way," she murmured, crumbling it up and tossing it in the trash. Then she plucked it back out and tore it into tiny pieces. She didn't need Delilah or Penelope or worse, one of her brothers, getting their hands on that.

Her next attempt was too formal:

Dear Jasper,
   My summer is going well so far. Hope the rest of your trip
is great.
   Best, Sophie.

She balled that one up too, chucking it in the wastebasket.

Finally, she settled somewhere in the middle:

Dear Jasper,
   The week with Vivienne was painful, as usual. I can't
believe your sister won't be here next term to run interference. It
looks like you'll have to step in when I need a buffer. I'm happy
to be home now. Spending lots of time with my family.

She paused here. That was a lie. She'd been glued to the loom, and the rest of her summer would pass the same way. But she couldn't tell Jasper about the project, especially not in writing. She decided the best course of action was to bring the attention back to him:

Can't wait to hear about your trip.

Then, in a moment of boldness, she added:

Perhaps you can tell me about it over dinner when we're back on
campus.

   Best,
   Sophie

Her eyes were bleary as she surveyed the letter one last time. It was as good as she could manage for the time being. Exhausted, she flopped into bed, where she was overcome by a restless sleep, chased by dreams of tangled thread and Mr. Morris's face looming over her.

Three days into weaving, Sophie had made scant progress. She'd been too impatient to do more than a cursory test weave, and now she regretted that decision. She'd had to unpick the weft in more than a few places as she tried to get a sense of how Sabrina's weavers achieved such shimmering effects.

Sabrina's notebook wasn't much help. There were plenty of details about shading and color choice, but not much about the actual process of weaving. Whether this was because Sabrina trusted her staff to make decisions for her or she just couldn't be bothered to spell out the details of weaving, Sophie wasn't sure. But it was clear she was in over her head.

And the one person Sophie could have asked for help was still decidedly missing.

Once she'd decided to weave the tapestry for Holden, Sophie had sent a letter to Gloria's cabin. It had been brief. Sophie didn't want to let on what she was working on, in case anyone else was checking in on Gloria, but she had given Gloria her home address and asked her to get in touch. That had been almost a week ago, and there was still no answer. Even international mail didn't normally take that long.

Sophie's mother poked her head into the room. "Dinner's going to be at least another hour. The twins decided the roast your father had in the oven was their mid-afternoon snack."

"Huh," Sophie said, bleary-eyed. She'd been focusing so intently that she hadn't realized how late it was.

"Would you like some help?" Her mother asked, stepping into the room.

Sophie hesitated. "Don't you have work to do?"

"I'm done for the day." Frances regarded her daughter with a mix of amusement and concern. "You don't think your mom has the skills to help, do you?"

"No," Sophie said, a little too quickly. Then, trying to cover her tracks, "What makes you think that?"

"De told me you wouldn't let her help."

"That's different," Sophie replied, indignant. "She doesn't have the skills."

"A lot has changed while you were gone," her mother said, moving to join Sophie on the bench in front of the loom. "And you look like you could use some help."

Sophie couldn't argue that point. Tangles of thread lay scattered at the base of the loom, evidence of all the work Sophie had done and undone. Frances stepped deftly on a treadle, opening the space between warp threads, and passed a bobbin through. She worked in silence for a few minutes, and Sophie could only stare as she began to build a patch of color in Sabrina's swirling signature sky.

"How do you know how to do that?" Sophie asked, unable to keep the awe out of her voice.

Frances laughed. "You don't have to act so surprised. You think they didn't teach us how to weave in repair school."

"But that was a long time ago," Sophie said, and her mother shot her such a warning look that she fumbled, looking for another excuse. "I just meant, you don't really weave anymore."

Her mother stopped working, not even bothering to tuck the bobbins into the warp. Sophie watched them tumble a few inches before the strings became taught. "You think repairing isn't weaving?"

Sophie flushed. Of course she did. She had spent an entire semester in East Lawn's repair shop, and most of her childhood in her mother's. She knew repair took skill. But somehow, it felt different from weaving a design from scratch.

Frances was staring at Sophie, waiting for an answer, but when Sophie didn't come up with one, she sighed and returned to her weaving. Finally, Sophie spoke. "Can you show me how you're doing that?" Her voice was timid, like the first time she'd asked her mother if she could work on a repair.

"Here," Frances said, guiding Sophie's hands with hers. "In most tapestries, the colors meet and separate. But with this, you want to float the weft across the back in spots, so that you get these little dashes. That's how she gets so many colors in one space."

Dumfounded didn't even begin to describe it. Sophie had spent hours upon hours staring at Sabrina's tapestries. She'd even worked on one in East Lawn's repair shop. And somehow, she missed this part of the technique. But not her mother. Her mother had figured it out immediately.

Sophie returned to her section of the tapestry and tried the technique her mother demonstrated. The results were immediate and much closer to Sabrina's signature style than anything Sophie had done so far.

They worked in silence, side by side, a section of tapestry blooming beneath each of their hands. Finally, Sophie turned to her mother. "I'm sorry."

"For what?" Frances asked, taken aback.

"For doubting you."

"You're forgiven," her mother said, a little awkwardly, not taking her eyes off the loom.

Sophie waited. This seemed like the perfect moment for her mother to apologize for her behavior of the previous summer.

But Frances said nothing, and it occurred to Sophie that having her father set up the loom, that helping Sophie, was her mother's way of apologizing. Her generation just did things differently.

A few more moments passed before Sophie worked up the courage to ask her mother the question that had been on her mind since she first showed her the loom.

"Why are you helping with this?" she said into the silence.

Her mother paused, her hands suspended in the air, midway through placing a weft thread. "Because I know what it's like to lose someone too."

Chapter 23
Honyeoke Falls

L ate one afternoon, a week into weaving, Sophie was at the loom when Rush turned up. "You've got a visitor at the museum," he said dryly from the doorway.

"What?" Sophie's momentary confusion gave way to understanding. "Why didn't you bring him over?" she asked, slightly annoyed.

"I'm not his personal tour guide," Rush replied, a trace of irritation in his voice. "Besides, I don't know if it's a good idea for him to be popping into town anytime he wants through an unsanctioned tapestry."

Sophie agreed — she and Holden had talked about this, about his not drawing attention — but she was sure that wasn't why Rush didn't want him there.

"Fine," she said, dragging herself from the loom. "I'll go get him."

Sophie expected Rush to accompany her back to the museum, but as soon as they stepped outside the repair shop, he muttered something about running errands for his mother and hurried off.

She couldn't blame him. It was her mess to clean up, not his.

Holden was standing in the dimly lit storage room, his back to her, staring at the tapestry. Sophie was momentarily distracted by his broad shoulders, the way his hands were clasped together behind his back. Then she remembered why she was there.

"We talked about this. You can't just pop in anytime you want."

He turned to face her, a grin spreading across his face. "I just wanted to check in, that's all."

"I don't need checking up on." Sophie could feel her anger started to rise. "And it's not a good idea to use the tapestry like this."

Holden took a few steps closer to her, still smiling, but Sophie backed away as if he was a predator. "What's the worst that can happen? I own the one tapestry and this one was also produced by my mother's studio." He had the kind of nonchalance about it that comes from having money. As if to prove Sophie's thought, he added, "If it makes things easier, I could just offer to buy this tapestry as well. We could arrange to leave it here, or even move it to your house."

It probably would make things easier. But Sophie didn't want him showing up in town anytime he wanted, and certainly not directly to her house. Even though only Holden, Sophie, and Mrs. Winthrop knew about the gallery with Sabrina's tapestries, Sophie was still worried that someone — Mr. Morris if she was being honest — would find out Holden was going back and forth and that something was going on. She didn't want to put her family in danger.

And seeing him regularly would make it much harder to resist the feelings that had fluttered when she stepped into the storage room. But sleeping with him was no longer on the table, not now that Jasper was finally in the picture.

"I don't think that's an option," she started, trying to figure out a viable excuse. "The auction has already been scheduled for later this fall."

"Anything's an option for the right price," Holden said with a small wink.

"Look, I just don't think it's a good idea," Sophie said, trying to be firm. "And I think you should go."

"Now Sophie, don't be rude." Sophie's head whipped around to the woman standing in the doorway.

"Mom, what are you doing here?"

"I heard you and Rush talking and figured I'd come along to say hello to Holden as well."

Sophie eyed her mother suspiciously, but before she could say anything, Holden strode forward and kissed her mother on the cheek. "It's nice to see you again, Mrs. O'Toole."

Her mother was practically swooning. "Call me Frances. Why don't you stay for dinner, Holden? I'm sure Peter is working on quite the spread. If the twins haven't eaten half of it yet."

"That would be lovely," Holden replied, at the same moment that Sophie groaned, "Mo—om."

"Sophie," her mother said in her fake polite voice. "He's come all this way. We should at least feed him before he heads back."

"It's not 'all this way'," Sophie objected. "He took a tapestry *from his house*." She wanted to say "castle," but she could only imagine how her mother would act if she knew just how rich Holden was. They'd probably end up engaged before dinner was over.

Sophie shot Holden a look. "It's fine," he said to Frances. "I can head home, it's no trouble."

"And it's no trouble," Frances said, taking him by the arm and leading him from the storage room and out into the town plaza, "for you to join us for dinner."

Sophie lagged behind like an annoyed third wheel, wishing desperately that Rush hadn't abandoned her.

Frances deposited Holden at the door to the repair shop and turned to Sophie. "Why don't you show Holden the progress we've been making on the tapestry while I check in with your father and find out when dinner will be ready."

Sophie didn't argue. Instead, she unlocked the door and led Holden inside. She reached up, as always, to stop the bells, but Holden was in her way. His eyes trailed upward and he moved his arm up to stifle the tinkling.

They were standing inches from each other in the doorway. Sophie took a deep breath, inhaling his scent, then pushed past him into the room. "The loom is in the back," she said, giving her head a little shake to try and dislodge Holden from her brain.

"I remember," Holden said. But he didn't make a beeline for the back room. Instead, he stopped to examine a repair Frances had been working on. "Your mother does exquisite work," he said, his face bent close to the tapestry. He reached up and pushed his blonde hair from his eyes, but it flopped back into place.

"What are you doing?" The words burst from Sophie's lips before she could stop them.

"What do you mean?" Holden asked, his voice light, despite Sophie's tone.

"Dropping in here unannounced. Charming my mother."

"Your mother charmed me," he replied, and Sophie wanted to smack him across his handsome face.

"You can't just drop by anytime you like." Sophie tried to keep her voice calm, but she was practically shouting.

"You made that point perfectly clear," he replied in his droll English accent. "But it would have been rude to refuse your mother's dinner invitation."

Sophie gave a hard laugh. "Oh right, you couldn't refuse. Manners and breeding and all that shit." She ended the sentence with a kind of mock curtsey.

For the first time, Holden's face showed a hint of a frown. "I don't understand why you're mad at me."

Sophie didn't know how to explain that the only crime Holden committed was showing up unannounced looking handsome. And that the only reason this was a problem was that she was, in her mind at least, seeing someone else.

"It's just risky," she said finally. "I'm potentially putting my family in danger, and I don't need you showing up all the time drawing attention to it."

Sophie could see his mind working, but he didn't seem to have an argument. "Ok, I won't stop by unannounced anymore." Before she could say anything else, he added, "But it would be rude at this point to leave before dinner."

"Fine," Sophie said. "But this is the only time."

"Agreed," he replied. Then he smiled slightly. "Now can I see the tapestry?"

—#—

"Holden, what brings you into town?" Her father asked when they were all seated at dinner. Sophie gave Holden a look. She and her mother had agreed not to tell her father the specifics of what Sophie was working on. If he asked, she would just say it was a project for the next term.

Fortunately, Holden took the hint. "I'm spending a holiday in America," he said, reaching for the potatoes that Delilah had just passed him. Sophie's sisters had made it a point to sit on either side of Holden. "My little sister told me I should stop by and say hi to her roommate."

"How long will you be staying?" Peter asked.

Sophie shot Holden another panicked look. "Oh, no sir," Holden said, shaking his head. "I just popped in for the afternoon, I'll be heading out after supper."

Everyone at the table, except for Sophie, and it seemed, Sophie's mother, looked disappointed by this news.

Sophie was slightly nervous that rich, quiet Holden wouldn't fit in with her loud, messy family, but it was clear, as he was debating the merits of baseball versus cricket with Collin that he wasn't the least bit fazed.

"I pictured you as more of a polo player," Sophie joked, her earlier anger with Holden dissipating.

"I'm a man of many interests," Holden teased back, now helping himself to the cherry pie Penelope had just brought back to the table. For a moment, Sophie imagined a world where she and Holden were together, where he slotted in with her family. She imaged a world with unlimited money and even more unlimited access to Sabrina's legacy. But that could only be in a world where Jasper didn't exist, and that was a thought Sophie wasn't willing to entertain.

Late in the morning the day after Holden's visit, Rush showed up at the repair studio with a stack of brownies. "Hungry?" he asked.

"Famished," Sophie replied, shoving one in her mouth and grabbing a second. She had barely touched her dinner last night and had headed to the loom before breakfast, to avoid any awkward family conversations about Holden.

Halfway through the third brownie, she turned to Rush. "Are these from Annemarie's?"

He grinned. "I thought you could use a break."

She smacked him across the arm. "You ass." She wasn't sure if she was madder that he'd given her pot without telling her, or about the fact that he was right, she did need a break.

"Fine," she surrendered, standing up slowly. "Let's get out of here." She didn't want to admit that she was already too high to weave straight. "But you've got to distract my mom on the way out."

Rush made a big show of examining the repair Frances was working on, while Sophie crept out quietly behind them, trying not to trip on anything as she went. At one point, she too got distracted by a tapestry in progress, before Rush started wildly waving her on behind her mother's back.

Sophie thought they'd go somewhere in town, but instead Rush led her to her family's gallery, and into Sophie's favorite wooded tapestry. They walked in silence for a few minutes before Rush turned to her. "I'm seeing someone," he said with an exhale, as though he'd been wanting to say this since Sophie came home, but had been waiting for her to be in a good mood. "From school." He added.

"What's her name?" Sophie asked, a mix of curiosity and relief washing over her. She'd been worried that she'd have to rebuff Rush if he tried to fall into their usual pattern, but now she understood why he hadn't instigated anything.

"His name," Rush said, a little more quietly. "Is Paul." He waited a beat before continuing, "He's my roommate."

Sophie took the news in stride. "Is he nice to you?"

"Very."

"Is he good-looking?"

"Very," Rush said again, sounding relieved. "You could have met him in Paris if you weren't such a jerk."

"I deserve that," Sophie replied with a laugh. "What's he like?"

Rush launched into a clipped monologue that covered everything from where Paul had grown up to what classes Paul was taking to how Rush felt about his dimples. Sophie walked along next to him, taking it all in and relishing this new phase of their friendship. "Actually, the dimples were what did me in," Rush added, circling back around to that line of thought.

"We were sitting next to each other, studying, and suddenly, I just leaned over and kissed one of them. The next thing I knew, his tongue was in my mouth, and then——"

"Ok," Sophie said, putting up her hand to stop him, but still laughing. "I don't need all the details." She studied him for a moment. "I'm happy for you."

"Thanks," he replied, his relief palpable now.

"Did you tell your mom?"

"Yeah, she was happy for me too. Though I think there was a part of her that figured you and I would end up together."

"I always thought she thought that too," Sophie conceded. Then she took a big inhale. "I'm seeing someone too."

"Holden?" Rushed asked, raising his eyebrows to the sky.

"No," Sophie stammered. "I mean, ok, we did hook up when I stayed there over winter break, but that's over now." And she told him about her date with Jasper.

"What is it with you and your roommate's brothers?" Rush asked when she had finished the story.

Sophie gave him a look. "This from the guy who is literally fucking his roommate."

"Yeah," he said, giving her a grin. "Straight to the source. No messing around with a middleman. Or middle woman, in your case."

Sophie had to admit that would eliminate a lot of complications. "Now can we please go get something to eat for real?" She said, grabbing Rush's arm and dragging him back through the tapestry. "I wasn't kidding when I said I was famished."

—#—

A few days later, Rush showed up in the repair shop again. Most unusually, he had a bag slung over his shoulder. "I brought you a present," he said, shutting the door to the small room behind him.

"Oh really," Sophie said, looking up from the loom. "It better be good, to interrupt me." She was working through a particularly complicated spot and didn't appreciate the intrusion.

Rush reached into the bag and pulled out what looked like a long, thick wand. He pushed a button and it began to buzz.

Sophie eyed him incredulously. "A vibrator? Where'd you get that?"

He grinned. "Paul's given me a few ideas."

"Ew," Sophie burst out. "It's not," she paused, wrinkling her nose, "used?"

Rush burst out laughing. "What kind of a friend do you think I am? This one's brand new."

She gave him another look.

"I've been thinking about your fight with Holden, and I think I figured out your problem."

"Oh really," Sophie said, turning away from the tapestry. "What's that?"

"You need to get laid."

Sophie stared at him, her mouth agape, but he continued. "But you can't fuck Holden anymore. And I'm off the table. And you won't see Jasper again until fall term starts. Hence…" He wiggled the vibrator in her direction.

"Even if you were right," Sophie started, even though he was absolutely right, "I live in a tiny house with seven other people. Where am I supposed to use that?"

Rush looked around the room. "This door locks, doesn't it?"

Before Sophie could argue, he pulled a joint out of his pocket, lit it, took a drag, and then handed it to her. He placed the vibrator in her other hand. "I'll leave you to it," he said with a smile, closing the door behind him.

Sophie felt a little ridiculous as she locked the door and even more ridiculous for dragging the bench in front of it. But after a couple more drags on the joint she was starting to think maybe it wasn't such a bad idea after all. And as she nestled into a pile of yarn and slid the vibrator up through her cut-off shorts, she had to admit that Rush had a point.

By the time she unlocked the door and returned to her weaving an hour later, she was in a much better mood.

The rest of the summer passed in a blur of wool and color, though Rush made sure that Sophie took the occasional afternoon off.

Holden turned up two days before Sophie was scheduled to go back to East Lawn, escorted from the museum by an annoyed Rush.

"Nearly finished?" Holden asked as he strode into the room. His eyes fell on the final quarter of the cartoon, exposed behind the warp. "Oh," he said, his voice dripping with disappointment. "I guess not."

Sophie looked up from the loom, aggravated at the intrusion. "What did you expect? I'm only one person, your mother had a studio." She'd spent the entire summer at the loom, and this was the thanks she got. And while she had to admit she'd been learning a lot, and enjoying herself despite the occasional frustration, she still wasn't convinced the tapestry would even lead to any kind of clue.

She glanced over at Rush, who had such a smug smirk on his face that Sophie wanted to slap him. He had told her all summer she'd been wasting her time weaving the tapestry. "He's using you," he said, over burgers the day he'd gotten her high on Annemarie's brownies. Once he knew that she and Holden weren't a couple, he was ready to let her have it. "He's rich. He could hire someone to weave the tapestry for him. And instead, he's got you slaving away all summer."

"He doesn't trust anyone else to do it," Sophie tried to explain. "What if there's a reason the design was hidden?" But Sophie couldn't make Rush understand, and it was clear now, from the look on his face, that he thought Holden was nothing more than an ungrateful jerk who had manipulated Sophie out of her summer.

"So what are we going to do?" Holden surveyed the tapestry in detail, and Sophie thought she heard Rush exhale "We?" out of the corner of his mouth.

"Well I suppose it will have to wait until I'm home on winter break to finish it," Sophie said matter of factly. Then she added, "I'd be getting more done now if you weren't here bothering me."

Holden took a step back as if no one in his life had ever told him he'd have to wait so long for something. "But that won't work. And," he continued, casting around for a reason why, "the tapestry in the museum will be gone by then. You'll have to take the long way home."

"Don't you mean you'll have to take the long way?" Sophie said derisively. It was like having a conversation with Vivienne. "Besides, I thought you were going to buy it at auction."

"I can't now," he said, hanging his head, an air of sudden shame surrounding him. "Father cut me off."

Sophie just looked at him, her mouth open in surprise.

"I mean," Holden continued, "I'm still living in the manor, but he's cut off my allowance."

"I thought it was your mother's money," Sophie interjected.

"It is, but Father is executor until I turn twenty-seven. He says I need to stop wallowing about Mum and get an actual job."

That part was probably true, but there was something else wrong. "Do you think he suspects something?" she asked, her body starting to tremble like it had the day in Mr. Morris's office.

Rush must have sensed the change in Sophie because he hurried over and guided her back onto the bench. "Breathe," he murmured, slowly rubbing her back.

Holden shot him a dirty look but responded to Sophie's question. "That's why we need to finish as quickly as possible."

In her anger, Sophie regained some of her composure. "What do you expect me to do? I can't *not* go back to school."

"Of course not," Holden said matter of factly, "but you could come back and work on weekends."

"And how am I supposed to get here?" She couldn't afford to take five tapestries home and back to school every weekend.

"You can take Vivienne's tapestry back to the manor," he said, "and then take the tapestry to the museum here."

Sophie was even more skeptical about this plan than she had been about weaving the tapestry in the first place. And now she was having serious doubts about agreeing to do that. "How will I explain to Vivienne why I need her tapestry home every weekend? Plus, it's risky to keep using an unsanctioned tapestry."

"You can just tell Vivienne we're dating," Holden replied as if it was no big deal. Rush muttered "you wish" under his breath, but Holden carried on as if he hadn't heard him. "And no one will notice if you are in town. You live here."

"Except everyone knows I go to school in England." Sophie massaged her temples with two of her fingers. "Let's say I agree to come back and work on weekends—" She cut herself off. "—which I'm not agreeing to yet. What happens if we don't get it done by the time the other tapestry goes to auction? It might still need to wait until winter break anyway."

"I can help with that," said a voice from the doorway. Sophie turned, expecting to see her mother, but it was Delilah.

"What do you mean 'you can help'?" Sophie asked, slightly bewildered.

"I've been working on the tapestry all summer," Delilah admitted nonchalantly. "I saw you leaving that day with Rush. You looked pretty high, so I figured you wouldn't be back for a while."

Sophie looked at Rush. "Did she put you up to that?"

Delilah jumped in before Rush could answer. "No, he had nothing to do with it. I figured you'd notice what I did and yell at me. But you didn't. So I've been sneaking in all summer to work on it whenever you take a break."

It took Sophie a moment to process what she was hearing. True, there had been sections that she didn't remember working on. But she'd assumed her mother had done those.

"I told you not to help," Sophie spat at her sister, jumping up from the bench.

"Because you thought I couldn't do it," Delilah shot back, taking Sophie by surprise. She always thought of her sister as meek, perhaps a little cowering. But now she was standing toe to toe with Sophie. "Well I proved that wrong." Delilah crossed her arms across her chest as if she'd already won the argument.

"No," Sophie shouted. "I didn't want you to help because I didn't want to put you in danger."

Delilah took Sophie's proclamation of danger in stride. "I'm not a little kid. It's my choice to help. And it sounds like you could use it."

Nobody said anything for a moment. Then Sophie turned to Holden. "Fine. I'll come home on weekends to work. And Delilah can help in between. But this better be worth it."

Chapter 24
East Lawn

S ophie was relieved to see Vivienne's tapestry of Weddlesmoore already on the wall when she stepped into her new dorm room at East Lawn. She'd been worried Vivienne would put it away like last year, and she'd have to have an awkward conversation about why she needed access to it.

"I thought a girl had needs," Sophie said, gesturing to the tapestry after Vivienne gave her a hello hug. Even with only two of them, the room was larger than the previous year. In addition to two beds, wardrobes, and desks, a heavy-looking coffee table sat in the middle of the room, flanked by two chairs and a large, lumpy couch. There was also a door that led, much to Vivienne's delight, to an en suite bathroom.

"Exactly," Vivienne replied, giving Sophie a wink. "Why do you think it's there?"

Sophie gave her a confused look, and Vivienne sighed. "Dominique," she said, emphasizing every syllable. But Sophie still didn't get it. Vivienne went on, "I convinced Daddy to get a tapestry to Paris, to, you know, um, help with my studies." She gave a wicked grin. "But Mrs. Winthrop wouldn't let me take it to school." Now, she scowled. "So I've got to go home first." She gave Sophie a knowing look. "But I heard you'll be coming home with me."

"What?" Sophie said, momentarily confused. "Oh, yeah, right." Holden must have planted the seed.

"I told him," Vivienne said, in her bossiest voice, "he's not allowed to stop by unannounced. I don't need that under my roof."

Sophie wanted to argue that it was as much her roof, but there was no point. "That won't be happening. I promise." Then looking at Vivienne, she said sternly. "Can we keep me and Holden on the down low?"

"Are you ashamed of my brother?" Vivienne asked but then added with a laugh. "I would be."

"No, it's not that." Sophie tried to think of the best way to explain. "It's just that I sort of went on a date with Jasper while I was staying with Eryka. I don't want them to feel bad that things didn't work out."

"Understood," Vivienne replied. "A little discretion then." Sophie seriously doubted Vivienne was capable of discretion, but it was the best she could do.

"So," said Sophie, eager to change the subject. "How was your summer 'studying' in Paris?"

Vivienne began talking animatedly about everything, or almost everything, she had done with Dominique over the summer. While Vivienne talked, Sophie put away her clothes, being careful to stash Sabrina's journal deep into her closet, where Vivienne, or anyone else, was unlikely to find it.

Sophie wondered when she might see Jasper again, but he was waiting outside her dorm the next morning as she was leaving for class. Sophie hurried him along the path before Vivienne could spot them, but not before Jasper handed her a single rose and kissed her on the cheek. It was all Sophie could do to keep from smothering his mouth with hers.

"Dinner tonight?" he asked as they walked along, their fingertips brushing.

Sophie nodded. Words had suddenly failed her.

"Great, I'll pick you up at your dorm at seven."

"No," Sophie burst out. "I can meet you at your place." Jasper gave her a look and she thought fast. "I'll be coming from the repair studio. It doesn't make sense to go all the way back to my dorm."

"Seven at my place it is then," he said, kissing her again on the cheek and striding away.

Sophie could hardly concentrate in her classes all day, imagining how her date with Jasper might go. To her relief, now that she was in her second year, she didn't have to deal with Vivienne in class. She would be spending most of her time in business classes, while Sophie's classes were concentrated in the weaving studios.

At five of seven, she stood in front of Jasper's door, a greasy bag of fish and chips in her hand. She had no intention of going out this time. Vivienne had invited her to the pub, but Sophie had blown her off by saying she needed to work an evening shift at the repair studio.

"That's an awfully fancy dress for the repair studio," Vivienne said, as Sophie surveyed her floral print sundress and strappy sandals in the mirror.

"I'm not doing repair work tonight," Sophie lied quickly. "Innes asked me to give a tour to some VIPs." Sophie hoped Vivienne couldn't tell she wasn't wearing underwear underneath the dress.

Now, standing at Jasper's door, she wondered if she'd misread the situation. She knocked once and the door swung open. Jasper was standing there in gray slacks and a short-sleeve button-up shirt, dressed to go out.

Sophie glanced around his small studio apartment. Directly in front of them was an old couch, and beyond that, in the corner, a bed. To the right was a kitchenette, and on the table sat several aluminum take-out containers of what smelled like Italian.

Jasper pulled up the take-out bag in Sophie's hand. "I guess we had the same idea," he said sheepishly.

Before he could say anything else, Sophie dropped the bag on the floor and flung herself at Jasper. He caught her, his hands sliding up the dress to her bare ass. He let out a small "oh" in surprise and Sophie felt him get hard next to her thigh.

There was no time to waste. Sophie pushed him onto the couch, completely ignoring his shirt, she went straight to his pants. "A belt, too?" she teased him.

"I thought you might actually want to go out," he said, as he pulled off her dress and kissed her breasts.

"Not a chance," she said, climbing on top of him the moment she'd shoved his pants down. It seemed like she'd been waiting forever, more than just the summer, for this moment. And based on his eagerness, and how quickly they both finished, it was clear he felt the same.

"You don't have any tapestries on the walls?" Sophie asked. After seeing all the tapestries at his family home, the blank walls were a shock.

They were on the couch again, Jasper in boxers and Sophie wearing the shirt she'd extricated from him after their first round, the Italian take-out containers perched on their laps. At room temperature, the pasta was much more appetizing than the congealed fish and chips.

"Too much of a distraction," Jasper replied, setting down his empty container and taking a swig from a bottle of beer. "I know I go on about how much I'm into architecture, and I am, but I also have a hard time focusing. If I didn't remove all distractions, I'd never get my work done."

"What about me?" Sophie asked, setting down her own container and crawling across the couch towards him. "Won't I be a distraction too?"

He leaned his forehead against hers. "You are a distraction I'll gladly take," he said, before leaning in to kiss her.

They saw each other every night that week, staying in as if to make up for lost time. Sophie gave Vivienne excuses about having to work, but it was harder to hide her good mood. She had to remind herself to act cross with Vivienne just so she wouldn't suspect anything.

"Let me take you out to dinner this weekend." It was Thursday night, and Sophie was doing her best to leave Jasper's before it got too late. She didn't want to give Vivienne any more reasons to be suspicious. But it was hard to think about leaving, with Jasper's hand up her dress, working its magic.

"I can't," Sophie blurted out a little too suddenly. "It's just that—" she stammered, "I've got to go home this weekend."

"Home?" Jasper looked at her, but it wasn't accusation in his voice, just concern. "You've barely been on campus a week. Everything ok?"

"It's just a family thing." Sophie was trying to keep it vague. The concern in Jasper's voice hurt more than the lie. "But I can see you on Monday."

"Not Sunday," he said, kissing her neck and making her wish she'd never agreed to work on the stupid tapestry.

"It might be really late," she said. "I'm sorry."

He looked at her for a long while, and Sophie had to resist the urge to confess everything. But she didn't want to drag another person into the secret.

Finally, he said, "I guess I can wait until Monday. Unless you want to make it up to me now."

At that moment, there was nothing Sophie wanted to do more.

Sophie worried that traveling back to Weddlesmoore with Vivienne would be awkward, that she'd have to make up all kinds of excuses, but as soon as she'd said hello to Mrs. Winthrop, Vivienne practically sprinted towards the tapestry gallery.

It turned out Mrs. Winthrop was the one Sophie had to contend with. She gave Sophie a stern look, then said, in her driest voice, "You'll be staying here with Mister Holden, then?"

Sophie said nothing, but Holden stepped in. "She is my guest, I expect you to treat her with respect."

It was Mrs. Winthrop who was now silent, and the three of them stood awkwardly in the entryway until Holden spoke again. "That will be all."

"Yes, sir." Mrs. Winthrop turned stiffly and walked away, though Sophie was sure she was fuming on the inside.

Holden looked at her. "Do you think we need to take your bag upstairs so she doesn't suspect anything?" Sophie had brought not the giant duffle, but a small backpack with just the essentials.

"Hopefully, she won't notice. I just want to get home so I can get a few hours of work done yet today."

Holden seemed a little disappointed by this but led Sophie down to Sabrina's gallery. He paused in front of the tapestry that would take Sophie back to Honyeoke Falls. "Are you sure you don't want me to come with you?"

"I'll be fine. Just make sure you're back here in the gallery on Sunday afternoon so I can get back to school." Then she blurted out. "What will you do all weekend?" She meant to ask, how would he explain her absence to Mrs. Winthrop, but it came out wrong.

"I'll just stay in my room," he said. "Make Mrs. Winthrop leave all our meals beside the door. She'll just think we're otherwise engaged."

Sophie shuddered at the thought of Mrs. Winthrop imagining what she and Holden were up to all weekend, but there wasn't any way around that. "Ok," Sophie said firmly to Holden. "But I wouldn't eat the food she's meant for me. She'll probably try and poison it."

Sophie was examining the in-progress tapestry when Delilah entered the room, flinging her school bag on the floor. "Does it look okay?" she asked, her voice full of uncertainty. Panic filled Delilah's eyes as Sophie turned to her, and Delilah went on, "I can undo it if it's not right."

But Sophie burst into a wide grin and pulled her sister into a hug. "How did you manage so much?" she asked, as her sister squirmed out of her grasp. "Did you even go to school?"

Delilah's relief was palpable. "You're not the only fast weaver in the family," she said, sitting down at the loom. "Plus, it's the first week of school. Hardly any homework."

They worked all afternoon and into the evening, only pausing for dinner, which Sophie's father delivered to the small room, giving Sophie a welcome home kiss on the cheek as he deposited a pair of plates. They'd had to fill him in on what

they were doing, since the original story — that it was a project
Sophie was doing for school — didn't fly now that school had
started and the tapestry still wasn't finished. "Your sister's been
eating dinner in here every night this week," he informed
Sophie, chuckling as he exited the room.

"You haven't?" Sophie scolded her. "De, you need to
make sure you have a life too."

"I don't mind," she replied. "It's fun to have
something to focus on. There's so much drama at school
already. I thought high schoolers were supposed to be more
mature."

Sophie remembered that age all too well. She
wouldn't have survived freshman year if it wasn't for Rush.
"They'll get there eventually," Sophie started to laugh, but it
turned into a yawn.

Delilah studied her closely. "You look exhausted."

"Tapestry lag," Sophie said, trying to throw her off.
"My body thinks it's later than it is."

"No," Delilah said, still looking at her. Sophie turned
back to the loom to try and avoid her sister's scrutiny. "It's not
that. You look tired, but you also look..." she thought for a
minute, "happy."

Her sister had an uncanny knack for knowing what
was going on in Sophie's life. "Something's different about
you," Delilah had said when Sophie came home after the first
time she and Rush slept together.

Just like that time, Sophie said nothing. She focused
all her attention on the area she was weaving, but Delilah went
on. "It's the postcard guy, isn't it?"

Sophie was stunned out of silence. "How did you
know that?"

Delilah shrugged. "I could just tell. Does Rush
know?"

"Not all the details, but yes, Rush knows. Besides," Sophie said, turning to Delilah in excitement. "Rush has a boyfriend now."

"Good for him," Delilah replied. Then she continued, undeterred. "Did you tell Holden?"

Sophie sighed. "You mean, did I tell Holden that I'm sleeping with another guy while I'm fake dating him to cover up illegal international transport? I'm sure that would go over great."

"Well, does the postcard guy know about this?" Delilah gestured around the room. "Does he know you're fake dating Holden?"

Silence again, as Sophie turned back to the tapestry.

"You didn't tell him?" Delilah blurted out. "Where does he think you are now?"

"I told him I had to go home for a family situation."

Delilah was skeptical. "And he bought that?"

"He didn't have any reason not to."

"And you're going to use that same lie every weekend?" Sophie hadn't thought that far ahead. But she couldn't tell the guy that she was currently sleeping with that she was fake dating a guy she used to sleep with while working on a massive, potentially dangerous project for him.

When Sophie didn't reply, Delilah turned back to the loom. "You're playing with fire."

It was late when Sophie burst back through the tapestry into Weddlesmoore on Sunday night, and she was exhausted. She'd been up early every morning thanks to the time change but had forced herself to work late last night, Delilah by her side. The sooner they could finish the tapestry, the sooner they could, hopefully, solve the mystery behind it, and the sooner Sophie could get back to a normal life.

Holden was waiting for her in the gallery, pacing like a man waiting for news from the delivery room. "How's it going?" he asked her.

"It's fine," Sophie replied, sidestepping his attempt to kiss her on the cheek. "Delilah's been a big help. You owe her now, too."

Holden flushed at those words. He was clearly embarrassed by his new financial situation, but Sophie was too tired to care. "Where's Vivienne?" she asked.

"Already headed back to school," Holden replied, before turning to Sophie, a hint of desperation in his voice. "I promise I will make this up to you. Your whole family."

"You better," was all Sophie could think to reply.

—#—

"How was your family thing?" Jasper asked as he opened the door to his apartment on Monday night. Sophie had tried her best to cover the dark circles under her eyes, but she was sure something of her exhaustion showed on her face. "Everything okay?" Jasper asked, taking her hand and leading her towards the couch.

"It will be," Sophie said, "but I need to go home again this weekend." She hated lying to him, but better to get it out of the way now. She glanced into the kitchen behind him, but there were no takeout containers on the table tonight.

"I thought maybe we'd go out for dinner," Jasper said, following her gaze.

Sophie didn't want to run the risk of going out and bumping into Vivienne, but at the thought of coming up with another lie for Jasper, she burst into tears.

"Hey, hey," he said, pulling her into his chest and smoothing her hair. "It's okay," he whispered. Then, with a weak chuckle, he added, "We don't have to go out. I can cook."

Sophie looked up at him through eyelashes glistening with tears. His face was full of concern. "I don't want food," she said, trying to regain her composure. "I just want you." She leaned in and kissed him.

"Are you sure?" he asked, wiping away her tears. She nodded, kissing him again, and he scooped her up and carried her over to the bed.

Last week, Sophie had been in control, barely able to contain her intense desire. But now Jasper took the lead, moving slowly, checking in, focusing all his energy on her. The pleasure was so intense that she cried again, at the realization that things could be this good, and the knowledge of how close she was to screwing it all up.

"Where were you last night," Vivienne demanded as Sophie walked through the door to their room the next morning. Jasper had held her until she'd fallen asleep, and her exhaustion had carried her straight through until morning.

"I need to tell you something," Sophie said, ignoring Vivienne's question. "But you have to promise not to tell anyone. Not Eryka. Not your father. Not Mrs. Winthrop. Not even Holden."

"Are you cheating on my brother?" She wasn't accusing. If anything, there was a hint of glee in her voice, as if she'd like nothing more than to see Holden get hurt.

"I'm not dating your brother," Sophie said blandly. And then she launched into the full story — how she discovered the cartoon and Sabrina's journal in Gloria's cabin, how Holden had convinced her to help him weave the tapestry.

She hesitated here, not wanting to tell Vivienne about the gallery full of Sabrina's tapestries. She decided on a version of the truth. "Your brother has one of your mother's tapestries, and the museum in my hometown has another that goes to the same place. That's why Holden and I are pretending to date. So I can get home on the weekends to work on the tapestry."

"That bastard," Vivienne shouted. The last time she'd seen her this angry was the fight in the dining room over winter break. "I can't believe he roped you into this. He can't do this." She started to move toward the tapestry of Weddlesmoore, but Sophie grabbed her wrist.

"No," she shouted, pulling Vivienne back. "You can't tell him I told you. You can't tell anyone."

Sophie waited a moment for Vivienne to calm down, before continuing. "I was at Jasper's last night." Vivienne's face was blank as if she was expecting as much. "And you can't tell Holden about that either," Sophie added.

"If you're only pretending to date, why would Holden care if you're dating someone else?"

"I don't know," Sophie said. Delilah had asked the same thing. "It just feels messy, that's all." She wasn't interested in sleeping with Holden again, so why not just tell him? But every time she thought about it, the image of Holden the night last winter when she'd told him she didn't want to date him flashed into her mind.

"Does Jasper know about any of this?"

"No. And you can't tell him either," Sophie said firmly. "I just told him I've had to go home for a family situation."

"Are you sure that's a good idea?"

Sophie hated that Vivienne was trying to give her relationship advice, and she hated even more that Vivienne, like Delilah, was probably right. But she'd already set the lie in motion. There was no turning back now.

The upside of telling Vivienne the truth was that Sophie no longer had to hide her relationship with Jasper. They could walk through campus holding hands. They could sit in a booth in the pub, Sophie's leg thrown over Jasper's, his hand sliding up her thigh. She could spend the night at his place and not have to lie to Vivienne about where she was going or where she'd been.

All of this, at least, made Sophie's big lie to Jasper a little easier to manage.

Despite Jasper's admission that Sophie was a welcome distraction, they didn't see each other every night. The workload for Jasper's final year of architecture school was grueling, and Sophie had to cram all her schoolwork into the week, around classes and shifts at the repair studio.

Still, the times she was with Jasper were her happiest since she'd been on campus.

"You know," she said, twirling her finger along his chest, tracing little eddies in his dark hair, "if you didn't have such a strong sense of honor, we could have been doing this all last year." They were lying on his bed naked.

"I had roommates last year," he grinned, as her finger worked its way slowly down his stomach.

"You know what I mean," Sophie laughed, rolling closer to him. "Think of all that wasted time just because I was your sister's roommate."

"I don't know," he said, pulling Sophie on top of him. "I think you were worth the wait."

Chapter 25
East Lawn

It didn't take long for Sophie to realize that her workload was untenable. Classes, the repair studio, time with Jasper, and home every weekend to weave left her completely spent by the third week of classes.

At least, with the help of Delilah, and on occasion, her mother, the tapestry was coming along quicker than anticipated. If she could just hold it together for a few more weeks.

Late in the afternoon, on the first Sunday in October, Sophie, Delilah, and Frances stood at the loom, admiring their work. They'd reached the end.

"Now we just need to sew up the slits," Delilah said brightly. The way she maintained her enthusiasm throughout the project was impressive.

Sophie stifled a yawn and headed back to the loom, but her mother gave her a firm look. "I think you'd better call it a night and head back to school. Your sister and I can finish up this week and you can bring Holden back on Friday for the fall." Sophie was surprised to hear her mother use the French term for removing the tapestry from the loom.

But she didn't argue. Instead, she gave her mother and sister long hugs and headed back toward the museum.

"It will be ready on Friday," she told Holden the moment she stepped into the manor. "Mom and Delilah are putting the finishing touches on it this week."

She expected him to be overjoyed but not to pick her up and twirl her around the room. She'd never seen him look so happy. He set her down, gushing, "Thank you," and then leaned in. His face was barely an inch from hers.

Sophie jumped back. "I should head back to school," she said, turning to walk through the gallery. She wanted to share in Holden's joy, but all she could muster was relief that this whole mess would soon be over.

Unfortunately, her relief was short-lived. When she climbed out of the tapestry and into her room, Vivienne was sitting on the chair, opposite someone on the couch. It was Jasper.

"Hey," Sophie said as if it was totally normal to climb out of her roommate's tapestry. There was a bouquet on the coffee table.

He stared at her for a full minute, while Vivienne frantically mimed something behind his back that Sophie couldn't understand. When he finally spoke, it was with the air of someone trying to process but being stampeded by cattle. "I thought you said you had a family thing."

"I did." She walked over to kiss him, but he turned his head away.

"Then why were you coming from Vivienne's?"

She put on her broadest smile. "It's a bit of a shortcut. Vivienne's family has a tapestry that, believe it or not, is connected to one in my hometown. Much quicker than going through the museums."

Technically, it wasn't a lie, and for a moment it looked like Jasper would buy it. But then, with the worst possible timing, Holden burst through the tapestry, carrying Sophie's cardigan. It must have fallen from her bag when he twirled her around.

"You forgot—" he started, then stopped, looking from Jasper to the flowers with a mixture of confusion and hurt.

Vivienne tried to cover. "Thanks, bro," she said, popping up and grabbing the cardigan from Holden. Sophie couldn't remember a single time she'd heard Vivienne use the word "bro." "I'm going to want that this week."

"You're welcome," he said. He scratched his head, before turning to Jasper and extending his hand. "Holden," he said as if this was a perfectly normal situation.

Jasper extended his hand in return, but his gaze never left the cardigan. Panic rose in Sophie as she realized, a beat too late, that she had worn that same cardigan to Jasper's last week. "Isn't that your cardigan?" He asked.

Vivienne did her best to channel outrage. "You borrowed my jumper?" She accused Sophie.

But Jasper wasn't buying it. He looked at the three of them, shaking his head slowly, then said, "Why does it feel like the three of you know something that I don't?"

Vivienne shoved her brother towards the tapestry, then followed him through. "I think we better leave them to it."

"What's going on?" Jasper asked, his eyes narrowed.

Yet again, Sophie burst into tears. Through great heaving sobs, she told Jasper about finding the cartoon, about how Holden convinced her to weave it, about going home on the weekends when she didn't finish it over the summer.

"And are you sleeping with him too?"

"What?" How could he ask something like this? She was so obviously into him and only him. "No." But she couldn't bring herself to lie anymore. "I mean, we have, but that was last year, over winter break. Before you and I were even together."

Jasper stood up. "I don't believe this. I have to go."

"But I told you, I'm not sleeping with him." Sophie was getting desperate. She grabbed at Jasper's hand, but he pulled it away.

"You still lied to me. You told me you had a family thing when you were sneaking off every weekend to help your ex."

"He isn't my ex. We were never a couple." Tears streamed down her face. How could she make him understand? "I was helping him. And I couldn't tell you…" she trailed off, unsure how to explain. "I couldn't tell you," she started again, "because it wasn't my secret to tell."

He paced around the room for a moment, raking his hands through his hair. Sophie took a few deep breaths, and for a moment, she thought it would all be ok. Then he grabbed the flowers from the coffee table and stormed from the room, leaving petals in his wake.

Sophie was still curled on her bed, sobbing hysterically, when Vivienne crept back through the tapestry an hour later.

For the rest of the week, Sophie tried to muster enthusiasm for the finished tapestry. But all she could think about was how she'd ruined things with Jasper, how she'd screwed everything up, so close to the finish line. Twice, she stopped by his apartment and knocked on the door, hoping he'd hear her out. There was no answer, even though she was sure, on at least one occasion, that she could hear him moving inside.

Friday rolled around, and it was all Sophie could do to focus during her morning classes and her afternoon shift at the repair studio. She was so distracted that Innes gave in and let her go early.

Vivienne was waiting for her in their dorm room.

"I'm going with you," she announced, in that tone of voice that inferred she always got her way.

Vivienne was impossible to argue with when she was in this mood, but Sophie had to try. "I don't think that's a good idea. Holden doesn't know you know about the tapestry."

"I don't care if Holden knows or not. She was my mother too. I deserve to know what happened just as much as he does."

"Fine," Sophie conceded. She didn't have the energy to argue. "But you're telling Holden."

Holden was waiting for them in the lobby of Weddlesmoore. He gave Vivienne a quick kiss on the cheek, then stood waiting, assuming she would flounce off to the tapestry to Paris. Instead, she stood in front of him, arms crossed.

"I'm coming with you."

"You told her?" Holden questioned Sophie, his face somewhere between anger and betrayal.

Sophie just shrugged, but Vivienne jumped in. "This isn't just about you. I deserve to know, too. And Sophie's *my* roommate, and you roped her into this ridiculous project. Besides," she added, "you're both so paranoid. You need someone who can think straight."

Holden looked desperately between them, then realized he was beaten. "Fine," he said. "But I'm in charge. You both do exactly what I say, understood?"

Sophie nodded, but Vivienne muttered, "We'll see about that," under her breath.

All Sophie could think about was getting home and getting to the tapestry as quickly as possible. She was ready to put this whole mess behind her. But when Holden pushed open the door to his mother's gallery, Vivienne stopped short.

"What is this?" she said, moving slowly into the room.

Holden looked at Sophie. "You didn't tell her about this?"

"Tell me about what?" Vivienne rounded towards her brother. "That you've been hiding a room of Mum's tapestries from me? For who knows how long?"

Sophie stepped between them, facing Vivienne. "You have plenty of time to be mad at him about this later." Vivienne scrunched her face, and Sophie added. "And plenty of time to be mad at me, too. For now, can we just get on with it?"

To her credit, Vivienne kept quiet as they stepped through the tapestry and walked the now familiar path through the fields and about the village. She only cracked when they emerged into the storeroom in the museum of Honyeoke Falls. "Where are we?"

But Sophie didn't answer. "Rush!" She exclaimed. Rush was sitting on a box, reading a book. "What are you doing here?"

He smiled. "Your mom told Ma. Some kind of mother's code of honor, I suspect. And I didn't want to miss all the fun. I'm coming with you."

This was getting ridiculous. Now they were taking a posse into an unknown tapestry. But Holden stepped in before Sophie could say anything. "You most certainly are not."

"Look, mate," Rush said, emphasizing the word, which Sophie had never heard him use before. "Someone there needs to have Sophie's best interest at heart. And no offense, but I don't trust you as far as I could throw you."

"I don't need looking after," Sophie asserted. "But honestly, I could use help dealing with these two." She nodded her head between Holden and Vivienne before turning to Holden. "I did the work, and I say Rush comes."

"Fine," Holden grunted. "But I'm still in charge."

Behind him, Vivienne stifled a giggle.

—#—

"You must be Vivienne," Frances said, stepping forward and giving her a hug the moment the four of them entered the repair studio. "Sophie's told us so much about you."

That wasn't true, but Sophie wasn't going to argue.

"And you, Holden dear," Frances continued, turning towards him and letting him kiss her on the cheek. "Lovely to see you as always."

Rush turned to Sophie, muttering out of the corner of his mouth. "What does that make us?"

Sophie rolled her eyes. "Don't get me started. She's got some sort of weird Anglo-fetish."

"Where's Delilah?" Sophie asked when the greetings were done. "She's with your father. He's helping her hang the tapestry in the gallery. There wasn't a big enough wall in here."

The tapestry looked even more impressive hanging on the wall of her family's gallery than it had on the loom. They'd had to remove two others, which were rolled up against the wall on the far side of the room.

Sophie stepped forward, and inspected the details, like she always did. It took a moment to register that she was looking at her own weaving. Hers and her mother's and her sister's.

She turned to look at her mom and sister, tears welling in her eyes. "Thank you."

"Yes," Holden said, stepping towards them. "Thank you, ladies, for all your help. But we should get going."

Rush rolled his eyes behind Holden's back, and Sophie couldn't blame him. She'd never seen Holden step in and take over a moment before, but it was a side of him she didn't like. Even if he did have a point.

"I guess this is it," Sophie said firmly. And without waiting for the other three, she stepped through the tapestry.

As she did, Professor Berger's words from their first day of class popped into her head. "You can't design a tapestry for a place you've never seen before." But that meant...

Sabrina had been here. Presumably not long before her death. Instinctively, Sophie reached for Holden's hand, giving it a squeeze. He returned it, his fingers grasping Sophie's as if she was the only thing tethering him to reality.

Rush gave Sophie a look, and she wrestled her hand free from Holden's. "We should get going," Rush said, and the rest of the group nodded in agreement.

All they'd been able to see in the tapestry was a roofline set in a clearing in the trees, so that's where they headed. Every crunch of gravel or snap of a twig made Vivienne jump, and more than once Sophie grabbed desperately for Rush's arm. Holden was stoic, his jaw set, like someone about to complete a very grim task.

In her time working on the tapestry, Sophie guessed the building was a barn or perhaps a workshop. As the low-slung building emerged — revealing a sloping roof set atop rough stone walls with scant windows —Sophie's suspicions seemed confirmed. But as they drew closer, the setting looked more homey. A small door had been eked out from between the stones, and it opened onto a well-manicured garden. A pair of rocking chairs flanked the front door, and smoke rose gently from a chimney.

Holden strode forward towards the door, but Sophie grabbed his arm and pulled him around to the side of the house.

"We can't just go barging in," Sophie hissed at him. "We need to find out what we're up against." The place didn't seem dangerous, but they had no way of knowing what was inside.

They crept along the side of the building and Sophie peered into a small window. She'd barely had time to register a cozy living room when she recognized the woman sitting on the couch. It was Gloria.

"What the fuck?" Sophie whispered, dipping back below the window and shaking her head. "I don't understand." True, she'd taken the cartoon from Gloria's house. But how had Gloria gotten here? Had she woven another version of the tapestry?

"Let me see," Holden said, jostling Rush out of the way. He and Sophie carefully pulled themselves up, so just their foreheads and eyes were above the sill.

It was indeed Gloria, sitting on the couch. She turned expectedly as another woman entered the room, carrying two cups of tea. She set both down on the coffee table before kissing Gloria on the mouth.

Beside Sophie, Holden slumped to the ground, his face ashen.

Chapter 26
Middlebrook

Sophie didn't know what the normal reaction was to seeing a mother you thought was dead for the last seventeen years, but taking off in a mad sprint wasn't what she had in mind. Before she could register what was happening, Holden was halfway up the path they'd come down.

"I'll go," Rush said, jumping to his feet. "You stay and figure out... well, whatever the fuck is going on."

Sophie watched Rush dart out of sight, then turned to Vivienne who was now staring through the window. Like Holden, all the color had drained from her face.

"Come on," Sophie said, reaching out her hand to help Vivienne up. But Vivienne was frozen. "Come on," Sophie said again, more gently this time, and she took Vivienne by the shoulders and led her to the front door.

Disbelief was melting into anger, and it was all Sophie could do to keep from barging through the front door. Her thuds echoed in the trees around the house. A moment later, Gloria's face appeared in the door. "Soph—" she started, looking astonished, but Sophie pushed past her into the living room, followed closely by Vivienne.

Sabrina looked like Vivienne, only softened by age. Her blonde hair had mostly given way to gray, her breasts were lower, and her hips more supple. But there was no mistaking who it was. Her mouth made an "oh" of surprise as Vivienne stepped out from behind Sophie.

"Mum?" Vivienne asked, her voice barely above a whisper.

Sabrina was standing now, her arms extended towards Vivienne. "Baby girl," she said, tears welling at the corners of her eyes.

Vivienne crossed the room in two strides, then slapped her mother hard across the face. Sabrina crumpled under the force, or the shock, and suddenly Gloria was at her side. Sophie grabbed Vivienne's arm as it swung up again, and when that wasn't enough, she wrapped Vivienne in a bear hug, pinning both arms at her sides.

Sophie gave Gloria a look. "Could someone please tell me what the fuck is going on?"

For a moment, no one said anything and the silence was punctuated only by Sabrina's heavy breathing as she sprawled on the floor, trying to compose herself. Still trapped in Sophie's arms, Vivienne was shaking in silent rage, her eyes fixed on her mother in a kind of hard stare.

When it seemed like no one was going to volunteer any more information, Sophie deposited Vivienne in a chair and moved towards Gloria, still crouched on the floor next to Sabrina. "You owe us—" Sophie started loudly, "I mean, you owe her," she jabbed a finger towards Vivienne, "a very large explanation."

Gloria sighed, then replied, "Fine," in the exasperated voice Sophie knew so well. But recognizing this person that Sophie thought she knew — that she had been genuinely worried about for the last half year — only made Sophie angrier. How was Gloria part of, well, whatever this was?

Gloria helped Sabrina to her feet and guided her towards the couch, before heading to the kitchen and returning with a bottle of Scotch and four glasses. She set one in front of Sabrina, who sat on the couch with her head in her hands. "Tell them," Gloria said gently.

Sabrina looked around, unsure of where to start, then gave a deep sigh. "It was just too much."

"What was?" Sophie asked, pushing away the whiskey glass Gloria had just set in front of her.

"The pressure." Sabrina took a great swig of whiskey. "To be 'Sabrina Maxwell, Britain's greatest living tapestry designer.' To be a wife. To be," she looked apologetically at Vivienne, "a mum."

Vivienne didn't meet her eye. Sabrina took another swig of whiskey and went on. "I was miserable. I didn't feel like I had any place where I could be truly myself. It felt like everyone just wanted whatever part of me served their needs best. But I didn't know how miserable I was until Gloria came along. For once, it felt like someone saw me — loved me — for who I actually was. She made me realize how happy I could be. And it made my old life feel like a lie."

Sophie understood that feeling, but in reverse. She'd been happy, and then she'd ruined it. Still, she couldn't imagine running away from her entire life. "But why not just get a divorce? Abscond with Gloria to this cabin in the woods? Why did you—" the realization hit Sophie all at once "—fake your own death?"

Sabrina sighed. "Leaving would have changed one thing, but it wouldn't have fixed everything. It wasn't just that I didn't want to be married anymore. I didn't want to be Sabrina Maxwell anymore."

"Did you know," Sophie asked, giving Gloria a hard stare, "that she was alive this whole time?"

Gloria shook her head. "She didn't let me in on the plan. I thought she was gone, like everyone else."

"I'm sorry, my love," Sabrina said, kissing Gloria's hand. "It was too risky." Vivienne made a noise like she was going to interject, but when they turned to look at her, she just downed her glass of whiskey and poured herself another, keeping her eyes fixed on the glass as she filled it to the top.

Sabrina turned to address Sophie. "I left the cartoon and notebook hoping Gloria would figure it out. I'm guessing that's how you found us."

Sophie didn't owe either of these women an explanation, and she wasn't about to confess to breaking into Gloria's house. She would be the one to ask the questions. "How did you find her?"

The question was directed at Gloria, but Sabrina answered. "By the time I realized Gloria might not have understood my clue, she had fallen off the grid. I looked for years, and had pretty much given up hope when I learned she had resurfaced at East Lawn." Vivienne let out what sounded like a scoff and polished off another glass of whiskey.

"And you forgave her?" Sophie turned to Gloria again, incredulous.

"It took me a little while," Gloria admitted. "But I realized this was our second chance. I never stopped loving her. I never stopped wishing she was alive." She put her right hand on top of Sabrina's, which was already intertwined with her left.

How could they just sit there, looking so happy, while Vivienne, her eyes puffy, her cheeks flushed, tried to drown herself in whiskey? And Holden. Holden, who'd spent his whole life pining over his mother. Holden, who...

Sophie sprang from her chair with so much force that Gloria and Sabrina jumped. "I need to go find Holden. I need to make sure he's ok."

She took the whiskey bottle and the glass from Vivienne. She had half a mind to smash them both against the wall. Instead, she set them on the kitchen counter, before giving Gloria and Sabrina a stern look. "Don't let her drink anymore." They nodded. "And for frigg's sake," she added, "try not to make this situation any worse."

Before they could answer, Vivienne leaned over the arm of the chair and vomited all over the floor.

—#—

Sophie was halfway up the path when she spotted her mother and Delilah, sprinting toward her at full speed.

"What's going on," Delilah gasped, while Frances stood, her hands on her knees, trying to catch her breath. "Holden came sprinting out of the tapestry and took off, Rush on his heels. We thought something terrible had happened." Delilah looked around. "Where's Vivienne?"

Sophie pointed down the path. "She's back there, in the house, with Gloria," Sophie paused, struggling under the unbelievability of it all before she added, "And Sabrina." Both Delilah and Frances let out little gasps of surprise, though Sophie thought she saw another emotion flash across her mother's face. One she couldn't quite read.

"Her mother?" Delilah asked, her brow furrowed. "Isn't she supposed to be—"

"Dead, yeah. It's a long story." They both stared at her, expecting an explanation, but Sophie wasn't sure she could give one. "Look, I left Vivienne back there. She's, well, let's just say she's not doing so great. Can you go check on her? I need to find Holden." And before either of them could argue, she set off back up the path and through the tapestry into her family's gallery.

Sophie sprinted through Honyeoke Falls, not caring how this might look to anyone else, and before she knew it, she was flinging herself through the tapestry in the museum's storeroom. She found Rush, looking bewildered, in just about the same spot she'd left him the summer before.

"I lost him," he apologized to Sophie. "By the time I made it here, he'd already vanished. I didn't know—"

"It's okay," Sophie said, grabbing his arm and dragging him in the direction of the second tapestry. While they ran, she filled him in on the rough details of what had happened in the cabin.

"That's messed up," Rush said when Sophie finished telling him.

Sophie didn't answer. She'd felt the tapestry back to Weddlesmoore, and she dove through, pulling Rush along with her.

It took Sophie a moment to register what she was seeing.

Holden was still in the gallery, but it was Holden like she'd never seen him. Wild-eyed and totally out of control, he had a knife in his hand and was slashing at Sabrina's tapestries.

Sophie could only imagine the pain Holden felt at this moment, but every slash through the tapestries was like someone stabbing her. Whatever kind of person Sabrina had turned out to be, Sophie couldn't bear to see her masterpieces destroyed.

"Holden, no," she screamed, running at him. Before he could do anything else, Sophie was on him, grabbing at the arm with the knife. There was a scuffle, and sudden pain flashed through Sophie's right arm as she crumbled to the floor. Blood radiated from her bicep and dripped down her arm, where a massive gash exposed the muscle below.

It was Rush's turn to yell. "Sophie," he shouted, dashing across the room. There was a loud clatter as Holden dropped the knife and backed away from Sophie, his hands over his mouth as he shook his head in disbelief.

Rush pulled his shirt over his head and tore it in two, and by the time he reached Sophie, he had wound half into a tourniquet that he tied around her arm. He used the other piece to mop up the blood from Sophie's body. "Are you okay?" he asked, breathing heavily. He seemed to be suffering a greater shock than Sophie.

She looked at him, then at the tourniquet. "Is there anything you don't know how to do?"

"I'll take that as a yes," Rush replied, his face flooding with relief. "But we need to get you to a doctor."

"And you—" Rush's voice was full of malice as he turned to Holden. But at the sight of Holden standing against the wall, his whole body shaking, tears streaming down his face, Rush's demeanor changed. "You okay, man?" he said, approaching Holden slowly.

Holden dropped to the floor, his silent tears turning into a massive wail, like a wounded animal.

He looked at the tapestries, hanging in tatters, then at Sophie, her left hand pressed against her bloody bicep. "What have I done?" he cried, shaking his head.

Sophie scooted across the floor to him and leaned in close. "It's okay," she said. "I'll be okay." She locked eyes with him. "Are you?"

He shook his head again, "I just don't understand. How could she… why did she…" His voice trailed away.

"I don't know," Sophie said quietly. There would be time later — days and weeks and years — for Holden to uncover the truth behind what Sabrina had done. To try and come to terms with a different mother than the one he'd idolized all his life. But for the moment, he didn't need any more pain. And Sophie knew the truth would be harder for Holden to swallow than the fact that Sabrina was still alive.

Holden looked around at the tapestries hanging in tatters, then back at Sophie. "I'm sorry. I know how much they meant to—"

She cut him off. "You had every right." Like Holden, Sophie knew she'd have to reconcile the woman she'd idolized with the woman she just met. But any pain she felt looking at the devastated masterpieces — at the remnants of a career Sabrina had walked away from without a second thought — well, that was nothing compared to the pain Holden was experiencing. "Besides," she said, giving him a slight smile, "I know some people who can fix those." She paused, leveling her gaze on Holden's face. "When you're ready."

Chapter 27
New York City

On a gray day in the middle of November, Sophie woke early and hopped a tapestry from East Lawn to London, followed by one to New York City, where Sabrina's tapestry — the one Mrs. Rigo had discovered — would be auctioned off. Sophie had no plans, and certainly not the money, to bid, but she needed to know where this tapestry would end up.

Mrs. Rigo was there, resplendent — in what was surely a nod to the tapestry, which hung behind a low stage at the front of the room — in a lavender suit. She chatted with the auction organizers and prospective buyers but broke away when she saw Sophie.

"It's nice to see you," she said, giving Sophie a hug. "Rush wanted to come, but couldn't get out of a test."

"It's nice to see you too, Carla," Sophie said, forcing herself to use Mrs. Rigo's first name. "And thank you," she added quietly, giving Mrs. Rigo another hug.

"Whatever for, dear?"

Sophie gestured around. "For... everything." It occurred to her that Mrs. Rigo had known all along they were using the tapestry illegally, but she'd kept her mouth shut.

"Well, you're welcome." The auction director waved Carla over. "I should go, enjoy the auction." She winked at Sophie and walked off.

Tuxedo-clad servers circulated the room with glasses of champagne and Sophie felt conspicuously out of place in her floral dress topped with a denim jacket. But it didn't stop her from grabbing a glass as she made her way to the back of the room.

After a few minutes of prognostications, bidding began. Paddles went up here and there around the room, and every bid was immediately countered by a man in the front of the room. Sophie could just make out the dark strands in his graying hair. As bids climbed higher and higher, Carla stood at the front of the room, grinning widely. Sophie imagined the things she could do for the museum with this money.

The bids started to fade until only the man and an older woman a few rows ahead of Sophie were left. They battled it out for a few more moments until the man threw in a bid that drew a gasp from the crowd. The auctioneer looked towards the woman, who shook her head sadly. The gavel fell, and the man turned to give a wave to the crowd.

It was Mr. Morris.

He was signing paperwork when Sophie approached him. He ended with a flourish of the pen and turned to look at her.

"Sophie, my dear," he said, giving her a kiss on the cheek. "So lovely to see you." He gestured towards the desk. "I've just finished giving instructions to have the tapestry shipped to your mother."

"For repair?" she asked, unable to conceal her confusion.

"No," he smiled. "To have." Sophie stared at him, her mouth agape, and when she didn't say anything, he continued. "It's the least I can do after everything your family did for mine." Sophie still didn't say anything, so he leaned in closer and added, barely above a whisper, "for bringing Sabrina back."

"You want to thank me? For *that*?" Sophie asked, finding her voice again. This all seemed so improbable. "I figured you hated..." Sophie trailed off, unsure if she was referring to herself or Sabrina. If she had never shared the cartoon with Holden… If she had never agreed to weave the tapestry… She knew the only person who should feel any kind of remorse was Sabrina, but it didn't stop her from feeling guilty about her role in this situation. She'd wanted to help Holden, not cause him more pain.

And it wasn't just her guilt over finding Sabrina. Sophie had finally figured out the look on her mother's face when she'd told her and Delilah what had happened. It was jealousy. Jealousy for Vivienne and Holden, who, despite their pain, had gotten back someone they thought was gone forever. But instead of anger, this time Sophie felt only guilt. Guilt that she had solved the wrong mystery. That she had brought the wrong person back.

Mr. Morris looked at her with a sad smile. "For what she did to the children, I don't know if I can ever forgive her." Sophie knew how he felt. "But all those years that I thought she was gone, all I wanted was for her to be alive and happy. And there's no denying both of those things are true.

"Plus," he continued, gesturing to a woman who was walking over, "it's helped me realize that it was time to move on."

The woman walked over, shimmering in a cocktail dress made from a textured fabric with golden threads woven throughout, her shiny long hair cascading down her back. There was something strangely familiar about her. "Hello, Sophie," she said beaming, wrapping her arm around Mr. Morris's waist.

"Mrs. Winthrop?"

She smiled. "You can call me Jane."

Sophie had always assumed Mrs. Winthrop was much older, but seeing her here, without her work uniform and severe bun, Sophie realized she was probably the same age as

Mr. Morris. Sophie shook her head. This would take some getting used to.

Mrs. Winthrop beamed at her, and as if she could read Sophie's mind, she said, "It's taking us some time to get used to as well." She gave Mr. Morris a quick kiss. "I'm going to go say hi to a few people."

He watched her walk away, and for the first time since Sophie had met him, there was a lightness about him.

"And Holden?" she asked.

She hadn't seen Holden since the day they'd discovered Sabrina. When it became clear the bleeding in Sophie's arm wouldn't stop without stitches, she and Rush had returned to Honyeoke Falls to see a doctor. Holden, after finally regaining his composure, had gone to get his father, and the two of them had set out to find Vivienne and confront Sabrina. Vivienne's memories of the rest of the night were clouded in a fog of whiskey, but from what Frances and Delilah told Sophie, there had been much yelling and many more tears. Sophie hadn't spoken to Holden since, and when she was healed enough to go back to school a few days later, she had taken the long route, rather than going back through Weddlesmoore.

It had been Mr. Morris, rather than Holden, who delivered Sabrina's damaged tapestries to East Lawn for repair.

Mr. Morris shook his head slowly. "This is hardest on him. It's going to take some time. I'm trying to be gentle."

"Does that mean you've reinstated his allowance?" Sophie asked.

"For now," Mr. Morris replied, not returning Sophie's slight grin. "There's no parenting playbook for what Holden's been through. I'm just glad," he said, now managing a small smile, "that Vivienne has you to help her through this."

Sophie nodded. But Vivienne's pain was different from Holden's. She had no memories of Sabrina. Holden had thought she hung the moon.

For her part, Sophie was still angry with Sabrina for abandoning her children. But she was equally angry at her for abandoning her art. She was a once-in-a-generation talent, and she had thrown it all away. For what? To hide in a house in the woods?

Mr. Morris gave Sophie a long look, then sighed. "I do hope your family gets some enjoyment out of the tapestry," he said. "I've made arrangements for all the proper permits. And its partner is still at our home if you ever want to take, er, a quicker route back to school." He gave her a wink and a kiss on the cheek, then disappeared into the crowd.

Sophie's eyes found the tapestry, as magnificent as the first day she saw it. How many more works like this might exist if Sabrina hadn't done what she'd done? The forced scarcity of Sabrina's choice — what the rest of the world still thought was Sabrina's death — made this tapestry even more significant. It took Sophie a moment to catch up with what had just happened. The tapestry, this tapestry — one of Sabrina's masterworks — would be sent to her mother's house. To her family's house. It was theirs. It was hers.

Chapter 28
Brussels

Snow pressed against the windows of the bar. True to her word, and despite everything that had happened with Jasper, Sophie was spending winter break visiting Eryka in Brussels. Vivienne had also come for a few days before she would join Dominique's family in the south of France. The three women stood around a small table, catching up.

"After everything that happened, you didn't want to spend winter break with your family?" Eryka asked Vivienne. It wasn't clear whether Eryka was asking about Holden and Mr. Morris or Sabrina.

Vivienne shrugged. "Mum invited me to spend time with her and Gloria over break, but I'm not ready for that much quality time yet."

After much deliberation, Vivienne had decided that the Middlebrook tapestry should come back with them to East Lawn. For the first few weeks, it had sat rolled in the corner, until one day Vivienne asked Sophie to help her hang it on the wall.

"I need more answers," she'd told Sophie firmly. She'd made several trips since the first, and Sophie had the sense that Vivienne was in search of more than answers. But Vivienne had evaded Sophie's questions anytime she brought it up.

Vivienne took a swig of her beer, then continued. "Father and Holden are going to see her while I'm gone. Just a short visit."

Sophie looked at her in shock. "Really?" The last she had heard, Holden still wanted nothing to do with his mother.

"I think Father convinced him to go by saying he could be rude to her the whole time," Vivienne said with a small laugh. "Get some of his anger out."

Sophie let out a sigh of relief. She knew Holden had a long way to go to deal with everything that had happened, but at least he was making a start.

"And there was no way I was getting in the middle of that, Besides," Vivienne added, turning her attention to Eryka. "A girl's got needs. And you're on the way to France."

"I'm flattered," Eryka said dryly. "And speaking of needs," she went on, looking pointedly at Sophie and then gesturing towards the door. Jasper had just walked in.

This was the first time Sophie had seen him since arriving in Brussels, and she busied herself with her beer. Jasper pointedly avoided looking in their direction, choosing a spot at the far end of the bar.

"Well, I guess that's that," Sophie said, putting down her beer and bracing herself for a very awkward couple of weeks. She looked at Vivienne. "Any chance I can join you and Dominique in Nice?"

It was Eryka who answered. "I don't know," she said slowly. "I talked to him. I don't think he's mad anymore. If anything, he's embarrassed."

"Embarrassed?" Sophie asked. "About what? I lied to him."

"But you had a good reason." Eryka sighed. "And I think he figured that out pretty quickly. But then everything happened with," she looked at Vivienne, who just shrugged, "and you were hurt and he didn't come to check on you. And then it seemed like he missed his window. And now he's embarrassed that he waited so long."

Sophie snuck a look towards the end of the bar. Jasper was staring at his beer, looking as miserable as Sophie felt. Was there still a chance for them? But she looked at Eryka. "I don't know. I didn't give him any reason to forgive me for what I did."

"But you never did any of it to hurt him," Eryka argued. "He knows that now. He just figured it out a little late." She gave Sophie a pointed look. "Is it too late?"

Sophie didn't respond. Instead, she drained her beer and gestured towards the waiter for another round. "Enough of this nonsense," she said firmly, looking at Eryka, unwilling to hope that Jasper might actually forgive her. "We want to hear about how amazing it is to be at a university without Professor Ackerman."

Eryka grinned and took a swig of her beer. "You have no idea."

Sophie woke early the next morning, before Eryka and Vivienne. She padded downstairs, thinking vaguely of making coffee, but instead, she pulled on her coat and boots and headed into the garden. Last night's snow had stopped, but it coated the shrubs, making the branches bend. She crunched along the path and stood, watching a few birds forage through the bushes.

Footsteps crunched behind her, and she turned, expecting Eryka or Vivienne, but it was Jasper, moving towards her with two cups of steaming coffee.

He paused just in front of her as if he'd forgotten why he was there, before thrusting the coffee into her hand. She took a sip and they stood in awkward silence for a few minutes, staring at the birds and avoiding each other's gaze. Sophie felt goosebumps rising that had nothing to do with the cold.

"I'm sor—" Sophie started, but Jasper cut her off.

"I was wondering," he said, his face breaking into a cautious grin, "if you wanted to join me for dinner tonight."

About the Author

M. E. Auman is a writer, artist, and self-described textile nerd. When she isn't flitting off to museums in search of great art, you'll find her in a small town in Pennsylvania making jewelry, baking croissants, and surrounded by too many plants and even more books. *The Fall of the Loom* is her first novel.

Visit her website at meauman.com

www.ingramcontent.com/pod-product-compliance
Lightning Source LLC
Chambersburg PA
CBHW050020120726
47903CB00006B/1847